ADVENTURE AWAITS

VOL 2

EDITED BY

C. MARRY HULTMAN

First Edition
Published by
Breaking Rules Publishing Europe, 2021.

Adventure Awaits vol2
Cover Illsutration by
Amanda Jansdotter Bisssett
978-91-986841-5-5

"Until you step into the unknown, you don't know what you're made of."

— Roy T. Bennett

Adventures

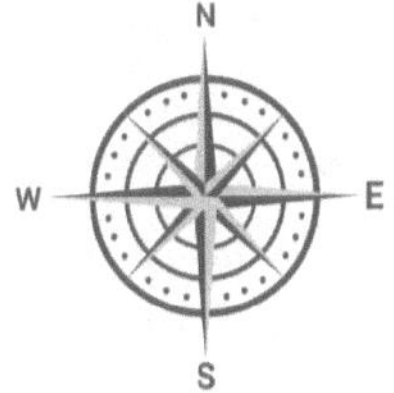

SWARLEY PAXMORE: LOVE'S GREAT ADVENTURER

GREGG CUNNINGHAM

Long Island 19th May 1912.

This has to be one of the toughest campaigns I have ever fought through. Indeed, I confess having had little in the way of sleep for several days now, since my Sergeant Major and most of my cavalry regiment appear to have been slaughtered on the battlefield fighting off those abhorrent, winged creatures invading New York from above. Those devils from another dimension spilling through the tear in the sky as a result of Tesla's failed experiment to master his electromagnetic obsession.

The last I saw of Sergeant Major Smithy was him rushing headlong into the swirling mists of battle with one hundred of my men by his side, their swords raised and their roar deafening. A fine sight to witness, but with so many men laying down their lives for King and Country, I wonder where the reinforcements will come from, as I have heard not a single order from our sovereign leader.

Even the President of the United States, Teddy Roosevelt and his rough riders have gone AWOL since that last aeronautic battle above Wardenclyffe.

So, with little choice, I have taken control of the ragtag survivors and ordered one final charge on the beasts to recapture Tesla's laboratory and return favour to our allied armed services.

And since that conjuror Tesla somehow made the Titanic disappear into thin air, albeit with him on board the vessel, I have no way of knowing what the hell he was trying to achieve with such a cunning and bold plan.

Even my beloved nurse Nancy has eased her affections towards me, having taken a rather fond liking to Corporal Carter, one of the younger conscripted soldiers from the Regiment. I confess to having let myself go over the course of our adventure. My moustache is indeed requiring some serious trimming and unless Wardenclyffe can be stormed and Tesla's wicked apparatus can be destroyed, I may never set eyes upon my beloved Nancy again.

This, I fear, shall be my last diary entry for a while, as I need to gather my battle plan for the early morning charge and our final push to victory in our attempt to capture Wardenclyffe.

I bid you adieu,
Captain Swarley T. Paxmore.

VOLUME 2

1.

"Good God Sergeant Major!" says I, watching as Smithy staggers blindly toward me from the battlefield fog, his regimental tunic bloodied and torn. The sound of heavy swords clang, rattling against the winged demons' scales as the bugle call to arms echoes.

"Steady on, old girl," I reassure Betsy, my mount, with a stroke to her neck, turning my attention to the Sergeant Major's fumbling.

"What the deuces are you up to?"

"Swarley!" Smithy cries out in blind surprise, wiping the blood from his brow as one of the creatures appear from the smog ahead and lurches forward towards us both, its foul stench permeating the air.

"They wiped us out Swarley."

"What… all of you?"

"Most of our Cavalry yes. Best we scarper like the rest and regroup, Sir."

Now I'm no coward on the battlefield and seldom yield to any foe baring down on me during a fight, but seeing that huge menace of a demon lumbering towards me from the wooded canopy, broken wings flapping like a ship's torn rigging caught up in a storm, my instincts tell me to skedaddle as far away from those snapping teeth as possible.

"Here, grab my hand," I yell back to my Sergeant Major, taking a hold of his firm grip, roughly guiding him up onto Betsy's saddle, my body aching with crippling age.

"Much obliged, Sir," says he, as I pull on Betsy's reigns and turn her thumping hooves around, taking us straight into the otherworldly green hue drifting over the prairie. "We're going back in, Sir?" Smithy queries my decision as we gallop back into the descending madness.

"Quite so, Smithy, we'll circle around and catch the bugger on a pincer attack," says I as the beast roars behind us. "Good to see you again, old boy. I thought you had copped it during the last attack."

"Take more than these buggers to take me out the game, Sir," he laughs, raising his sword again as we make a sweeping charge for the beast stumbling around behind us. "But I must confess I'm getting a bit long in the tooth for these bloody shenanigans Swarley."

"What of the others, Smithy?" I yell back, tugging on her reins and reaching for my sword as Betsy jumps over the fallen logs through into the dense tree line.

"I got separated from them in the fog Sir, we were losing too many men in the charge, so I had to split our attack and leave our wounded for the nurses to attend too.

My thoughts turned immediately to my beloved nurse Nancy and Smithy sensed my concern.

"She's a tough one is Nancy, Sir. I left her to lead the wounded towards Tesla's Laboratory with Corporal Carter. I'm sure she's fine."

Carter, that bloody lush! I knew that young buck would hang around my girl like a fart in a tin bath. The sooner I can get myself bathed and scrubbed up, the better. I had barely enough time to voice my objection at

Smithy's decision to leave her to fend for herself, when the deafening roar of the beast screeches above us, and a winged appendage swoops out, striking Smithy from our mount and sending us all into the ground as Betsy tumbles. Both myself and the Sergeant Major Smith are sent tumbling as the beast grabs Betsy by the throat and throws her against the bow of a large palm tree with little effort. Betsy, in her panic, breaks free from her saddle, stumbles to her feet while snorting off the attack and brays in defiance, before galloping into the wooded tree line away into the foggy madness.

"For Roosevelt and the Colonies," says I, sweeping the greying hair back over my balding sweating head and slicing my sabre in the air like a demented madman with his walking stick in the air. Smithy stumbles to his feet and readies himself for the flanking attack. We look like a pair of Chelsea pensioners making our way to the breakfast buffet bar in our retirement home as we get up from the ground.

"Sod that blighter Sir. Him and his cronies fled the battle before the fight even started."

"Really, how rude," says I, as the beast rears up and flexes its enormous wingspan. I fear it is actually going to spew fire breath upon me as I stand on, reluctant to yield my ground like Saint George against his mighty dragon, only I had no shield to protect my modest delicates. Regardless, I clutch the handle of my weapon tight, my arthritic fingers cracking as they tighten, then thrust my sabre into the air and slash at the creature's belly as Smithy attacks the beast from the rear.

"For King and Country then Smithy."

"Quite Sir," he retorts, charging the beast and slashing his own sword.

The beast lets out an almighty roar as I thrust and parry my way through my routine for several minutes with all the skill and dexterity of a mummified Japanese Samurai, stumbling over fallen trees and watching on while Smithy clambers onto the back of the creature like a ferret up a drain pipe. I only take my eye off the fight for a second hoping Smithy would deal the fatal blow, but that's enough for our winged foe to swat me to the ground and stamp down between the shattered tree stumps, shaking Smithy free from around its neck. I scurry away like a field mouse evading the clutches of a hawk, dodging the talons on all fours as they tear through the wooden splinters and blood-soaked foliage, the ghastly abomination rearing up and sending Smithy flying once more.

The confounded demon had us beat for sure until I hear from out of the woods the familiar sound of Enfield rifles quickly reloading, echoing under the canopy. Both riders fire off several more shots that crack violently in the air, causing me to turn to see Corporal Carter astride his horse. The brute of a young man with his flowing golden locks swept back over those muscular shoulders of his, clutching his rifle to his eye and taking aim again. Riding alongside is my beloved nurse Nancy astride Betsy, riding bareback, like she was a reincarnation of Calamity Jane, pounding over the prairie with her perfumed red hair flowing behind her and her magnificent bosoms jiggling like two adorable puppies fighting inside a sailor's duffle bag. I watch on in awe as she takes aim down her barrel once more, striking my ghastly attacker without mercy. The dragon topples to the ground with a torturous screech like a giant redwood being felled, thrashing and kicking out as both Smithy and I scramble to our feet.

"Good god woman, great shooting, I must say."

"Beggin' yer pardon my darlin, but we aint's got time for pillow talk," she smiles, pulling up on the reins. "There's more of 'em bloody thingy's behind us," she winks and reaches down her gloved hand for me.

"Betsy!" I muse, stroking her bloody mane, "well done girl."

Nancy looks like an Amazonian warrior goddess sat there astride Betsy above me as the setting sun faded over the horizon, disappearing into the fog, her red hair cascading down onto her torn tunic, exposing her milky white shoulder and ample curves. She gives me another saucy wink as she hoists me behind her, and I feel that stirring once more.

"God, it's good to see you again, my darling Nancy." I lean in for a kiss, but she flinches away.

"Now is not the time my sweetness-" she feigns my advances, "Howie… rather Corporal Carter says we needs to make for Tesla's lab, there's too many of them creatures to fight off and that thing up there don't seem to get any smaller."

Damn that blighter, Carter!

We all look skyward to see that damn beastly, eerie tear lingering around the moon is indeed still lingering high above the clouds, although no winged demons seemed to spill from the electrical scarring.

"Corporal Carter at your service, sir." Carter salutes, as Smithy clambers up behind him. "We should go now, Sir, before these buggers regroup, I mean."

I sneer at the handsome young buck with all the distaste I can muster. Damn his golden hair and damn his perfect teeth, "then what the devil are we waiting for man?" I guffaw, leaning into my warrior woman's perfumed red hair once more as we ride off for the sanctuary of Wardenclyffe. The sky is indeed still rumbling with the threat of another storm and I confess this worries me.

As our mounts pound towards Wardenclyffe and I clutch my arms around my warrior princess, I wonder just what madness is waiting for us inside that god-awful place. What contraptions of menace shall we find awaiting to be unleashed on our unguarded world?

"Hold on Swarley, we're nearly there."

"Open the damn door," says I, as we dismount and pound on the heavy wooden barrier obstructing our access to bricked sanctuary. I'm not sure if it's our knees cracking as we dismount, or the shingle crunching beneath our feet. Corporal Carter insists he and nurse Nancy cover our flank as both Smithy and I search for a way into the sinister looking building under the looming gaze of the huge metal structure towering above us. The lifeless bodies of the winged beasts hang limp on the criss-crossing girders that hold up that bulbous lightning catching contraption of Tesla's. This immense structure reaches high into the evening sky like a lighthouse shining its beacon of terror for all to see for miles. I suddenly feel icy shudders down my spine, flashbacks to the fighting we endured beneath the Blackpool tower… where we lost so many men to these beasts.

Out on the open grassland, I count at least another hundred or so vermin, stampeding towards us through the dust clouds like a hoard of charging buffalo, snapping, roaring beasts intent on only one thing.

Feeding.

"It's locked, Sir," Smithy coughs, informing me as I shake the bars of the window like a demented baboon at the local zoo.

"Damit Smithy, there must be another way inside." I pause, staring at my courageous sweating mount with an idea. "Grab her reins." I back Betsy towards the door and slap her rump. "Go on girl."

Smithy holds on tight as Betsy's powerful hind legs kick out, her hooves smashing against the door before she rears up again.

"And again, old girl!" I slap her rear again as the wooden panelling splintered and split, shattering the door frame in an almighty crash. The heavy doors swing open and I run inside sabre held high ready for another surprise confrontation.

The room is quiet.

"Quickly Smithy, inside," my orders echo in the vast chamber as I search the hall for something to barricade the entrance.

"And the horses Sir?"

"Damn right Smithy!"

Corporal Carter escorts Nancy inside, protecting

her from the beasts as they stumble over the remains of the door, while Smithy and I frantically search for something large enough to fill the gaping hole. Outside, I see the pack of creatures looming as Carter turns back and takes a knee, firing off another volley.

"Over there," says I, pointing to the large bookshelf stood against the far wall. "We can use that."

But no sooner have I barked my orders of salvation when a thundering beast crashes through the skylight above and lands in a heap of crunching glass on the mosaic black and white tile work decorating the hallway. Nancy takes aim with her Enfield as both horses in Smithy's keep break free from their reins in panic, trying to flee back through the doorway whence they came. Smithy curses, taking refuge by the large alcove as the winged serpent screeches, swatting out talons and spreading its broken appendages, pinning Smithy against the wall.

This time I feared there is no escape for Smithy or poor Betsy.

I watch on as it snatched Betsy into the air, her back broken in two as the foul beast's teeth tear into her. Smithy sees his chance and bolts from his cover.

"BETSY." I cry out in horror.

"DAMN YOU BACK TO BLIGHTY!"

I ready my charge as more vile beasts' roar outside the building, while Carter raises his discharged weapon and rifle butts another creature as it pokes its lumbering head inside the gaping doorway.

"There's too many of the buggers Sir!" Carter yells out as I watch Smithy spring to his aid, slashing

16

his sword and bounding into the melee without thought of his own safety or wellbeing. Several beasts are now converging at the entrance, slicing and swooping claws through the doorway like wide eyed cats playing with frightened mice.

"Use your fists if you have to sonny, just don't let the bastards break through." Smithy orders.

"I'll use my teeth if I have to Sergeant, they won't get past me!" Carter winks as the dust swirls around us.

Damn the cocky swine.

"Good lad, you know what to do sonny."

"It's just like Egypt all over again, Sergeant." Carter retorts as one of the foul intruders rakes his sharp talons over Smithy's chest, tearing a deep gash in his tunic.

Smithy slumps with a clatter of his sword as Carter turns, shielding his Company Sergeant Major on the floor.

"Swarley, over 'ere," Nancy shouts over, grabbing my arm and pulling me from my impending doom. "We can hide down there." she points to the open doorway by the grand staircase marked BASEMENT.

I nod, following her lead as Betsy thrashes a last beat of her hooves against her attacker.

"On me chaps," I yell above the commotion, following Nancy as she scurries towards the stairwell down into the darkness, stopping to hold the door ajar for me. "Move it, Corporal, this isn't a Sunday picnic on Wimbledon Common," says I, clutching the metal door awaiting the others by the stairwell.

Carter grabs Smithy by the torn lapel and I watch the young fellow dragging his groaning leader onto his shoulder, stumbling over the debris and skilfully dodging the creature gorging on my beloved Betsy in the great hall.

Several more beasts drop in from the shattered skylight and I watch one of the decorative chandeliers shake, then fall to the floor as Carter somehow evades the explosion of glass crystals filling the hall. Smithy, draped over the Corporal's shoulders, covers his face as Carter's back gets peppered with the ornate shrapnel. Nevertheless, he pushes on regardless.

"Quit your dallying Corporal, we haven't got all day, you know." I must say the young man looks built like a pack mule, traversing the open floor with ease and dexterity is if he were a rugger player playing a game in Twickenham, pushing his way through the rubble with ease as the beasts bears down on him and I wonder if he dabbles in the game of the Gods.

"Cambridge Blues?" says I, as he squeezes through the doorway.

"Oxford Blues Sir!" the oik replies with a wink.

"My sympathies, Corporal," I sigh, bolting the metal door closed behind them both. "Smithy, are you okay dear boy, you look like you've taken quite a beating?"

"I'll survive Sir," he grunts from aloft Carter's meaty shoulders.

The electrical illuminations flicker as a loud explosion shakes the surrounding foundations, sending pieces of masonry crashing to the level below, and I see Nancy gliding her way down the metal staircase balustrade into the dimly lit chamber far below. Her footsteps echo in this vast chamber and I wonder what exactly Tesla has hidden down here in the foreboding gloom as chunks of stone fall and splash below.

More unearthly beasts?

"Are you okay down there?" my voice reverberates against the hollow cavern walls as we descend the stairs cautiously into whatever madness Nicola Tesla has created beneath the earth.

"…ang on Swarley, lets me get me bearings…" Nancy replies from the darkness, her shoes scuffing the floor as she searches in the gloom for a light switch. I hear her rummage around, clunking levels all over the place, searching for the control panelling.

"Is that wise, Sir?" Smithy ponders as we hear what sounds like mechanical generators humming to life.

"I thinks I've found something down here, Swarley." Nancy calls up and I start to worry myself about what she is activating.

"Is that wise, my love?" I convey Smithy's concerns, speeding up my footfalls, eager to see what exactly the woman is doing down there as another switch clunks to life.

Above us, the huge hanging glass filament balls energise to life like swamp gas, casting an eerie illuminating glow upon Tesla's hidden laboratory and I stare on in wild disbelief at the stalactites' shadows dancing upon the ceiling.

The chamber is vast, my eyes lingering on its size. I see what looks like a man-made dock chiselled into the cave floor and a rippling lake with stalagmites poking up through the blackened water.

Nancy is standing by the rock-face next to the row

of electrical fuse handles as I approach and embrace her, her gloved hand still resting upon the last wooden lever looking like a prop from a Mary Shelley's novel.

"May I?" says I, lowering the last of the levers and relieving her of the Enfield slung around her chest. From over on the far wall of the chamber I hear a rumbling as two huge hanger doors begin to open high on the cliff face. Mechanical winches grind as the door separate slowly like curtains on a theatrical stage. We watch as the moonlight floods in through the opening, hoping that none of the winged demons are still swooping in the surrounding area. The light from the enormous moon casts its silvery glow down onto the water, glinting off the aluminium objects stored inside as the thunder cracks rumble in the far-off distance.

Exposed copper wires hang in neat rows contouring the exposed walls, disappearing into more wondrous apparatus mounted on the cave walls. Transformer pillars buzz as power surges throughout the Laboratory equipment and I see the very same Faraday cages I witnessed Tesla delivering to the Titanic's deck earlier this week. Several strings of smaller, brighter filaments, light areas cluttered with large copper instruments and magnificent looking vehicles standing tall, the likes of which I had only read in illustrated penny press publications.

Shining, rivetted panels of aluminium contour, a cylindrical contraption mounted on mobile platforms like ammunition for some sort of massive cannon. Pullies rigged to the ceiling seem attached to the contraptions nose cone, where I notice the pulley system spanning the cave. The skin of the object seems unfinished in one area, exposing the glistening golden screening within the metal frame of the craft. It's like nothing my eyes have ever witnessed, a gleaming golden idol standing there like a futuristic monument.

To my left, brass port holes line the side of some sort of large elaborate aquatic craft docked alongside the water's edge like a metallic skinned beached whale about to dive into the murky water again. I presume this is a warship of sorts, an ornate iron clad ready for war.

To my right, a behemoth of a bronzed panelled vehicle sits by a cliff wall, with a large twisting, circular, boring blade embedded into the granite rock face. Around the top is a sealed cabin with more port holes fitted around a viewing gallery.

I turn to Nancy, "the Sergeant Major requires your attention, my dearest," and she nods making her way over, her red hair shining in the moonlight as she smiles at Carter who is now unbuttoning his bloodied tunic, revealing his toned torso. She is practically swooning at the blasted fellow's swollen, glistening chest.

Damn you, Carter, put it away for God's sake.

He is the perfect specimen of a soldier and I feel the envy creep into my thoughts as I stand by the water's edge inspecting my own tired, haggard features. I turn and walk to the edge of the dock where the aquatic contraption lay moored and peer into one of the brass portholes. The bags under my eyes are heavy with six months battle luggage, my hair thinning and flat against my forehead.

I turn to Nancy and Carter, shaking this new uncomfortable feeling rising in my belly as I peer through the old war face, staring back. Is this what envy feels like? Is this what others have felt whenever the Great Swarley Paxmore once entered the room, chest puffed out and cheroot in mouth.

I swat the notion away as fast as it appeared and turn my attention to the vessel. "Could you even imagine the likes of such things," says I, peering inside the secured ship. "It looks like some sort of sea faring vessel Smithy, an Iron Clad perhaps? I can see the ship's wheel through there although I can find no obvious doorway." The interior draped in a deep red velvet.

Revolting.

I run my finger over the rusted patinaed name plate rivetted on the vessel and stand back. Each spectacle is more wondrous than the previous, and my jaw slackens, questioning Tesla's sanity. The madman had built himself a fleet of vehicles straight out of a Jules Verne novel.

"What in damnation is all this Swarley?" remarks Smithy, as Corporal Carter lowers the Sergeant Major onto a wooden chair by a desk in the working area of the lab. Smithy winces as Carter removes the bloody tunic from his own angry wound.

"I'm buggered if I know Smithy," says I.

More confounded pounding and screeching echoes from above as Nancy blinks from her trance, inspecting the wounds on both my men without setting her eyes on any more of the mind- blowing apparatus. I, however, am left to ponder upon his madness, gathering a mental inventory of these magnificent machines. I must say, Tesla may be insane, but the fellow has certainly got some stupendous imagination.

"Clear the desk, Corporal. If you'd be so kind, let's get the Sergeant Major lying down so I can tend to those wounds of 'is." I catch that saucy minx Nancy smiling at our buff Oxford ox, pulling the first aid bag from around her neck and reaching for his water bottle lid. Their hands barely touch as he offers her his water pouch. Damn it, he's all but naked standing before her as she inspects his swollen muscular pecks for injury. And I feel another twang of jealousy ripple.

Carter, I note with a scowl, is more than happy to obey my buxom Goddess and nods, sweeping an arm over the trinkets and rock samples upon the wooden desk, knocking parchments, sea charts and other paraphernalia to the floor, while Smithy lumbers from the chair, aided by Nancy.

Although concerned about this, I find I am too busy to render assistance as suddenly my eyes are drawn towards the large free-standing object, standing next to the two familiar looking massive electrical capacitors dispensing forks of blue meandering electrical discharge. I make my inspection of the area, realising the climb out is far too steep to reach the open hanger doors situated way up on the cliff face. Resigning myself to finding alternate ways out of Tesla's lair, I head back toward the live contraption situated within what looks like the laboratory area, while Carter inspects the large crew quarter and storage area.

As I make my way over, I am suddenly startled by the machine as it releases several magnificent static bolts of visible voltage arcs high into the cave space.

"Good god Smithy, take a gander at this thing!" My

eyes are wide now.

"Watch yourself Swarley," Smithy yells out, "remember what happened in Blackpool Sir." Nancy calms him and softly returns him back down on the table with a forceful hand.

I do indeed remember what happened back in Blackpool, what with all that teeth vibrating and horrendous screaming from those who attempted to shut down the damned device.

"I am well aware of the contraptions bite Smithy, fear not, I'll keep my distance."

I'm curious though, to see if this in fact the same piece of apparatus I destroyed back in Blackpool, because if it is, then Tesla needs to answer to many more war crimes than I thought. Slowly, I make my way over to the very same contraption we blew up during the Blackpool Tower invasion.

I stand pondering on this strange machine, with its intricate wrought iron metal steps leading up to the entrance to a hollow space, and peer inside, not daring to cross the threshold. The large, vented cocoon shaped cabinet is lit up like one of Tesla's exaggerated Faraday cages. Looms of wiring and gas filled vacuum tubes adorn the copper interior and ceiling space. On the floor is a metal plate where more copper wires intertwine, reminding me of the wiring loom wrapped around the hull of the Titanic before she miraculously vanished into thin air. The whole contraption buzzes with the static charge as the electro lights inside pulse brightly at brief intermissions. I am aghast at the sight of this familiar booth glowing, as if awaiting its next heinous order. I raise the

Enfield cautiously to the panel and cock the chamber, readying my aim as the contraption crackles to life.

I am suddenly aware of an object flying from the electrical doorway with a crack and bouncing toward me, clunking on the ground as it cartwheels to a halt by my feet.

"What the devil…" I hunker, stepping back as another is thrown my way, then another.

Bending down, I realise to my wonder the objects are in fact bullion bars.

"Gold, Smithy, they're bloody gold bars!"

"Who the devil is in there?" I order, raising my weapon and peering inside. But I find, to my disbelief, nothing inside, merely an empty cavity where the rear wall shimmers slightly.

On the ornate control panelling outside the electro booth are two brass ringed dials approximately sixteen inches in diameter, each one with its own set of status dials within the four compass points of the circle. A yellowing baker light dial below each of the brass ring has elaborately etched encoded descriptions at each point: a boat, a spade, a door and a cannon. The brass dial to my right has only two settings: to the top is the word ACTIVATE DOOR, to the bottom is the word DEACTIVATE DOOR.

I note that the current pointers on the brass dials are idling on the DOOR symbol and the ACTIVATE DOOR instruction.

"SWITCH THE DAMN THING OFF SWARLEY!" Smithy exclaims as the room vibrates.

"It's all under control, Sergeant Major. I think I may

have found our way out of this predicament. I think I have found a doorway out."

"Surely it can wait Sir, come rest for a moment Swarley, catch your breath." Smithy pants, "Carter has found us some food."

A reasonable request, as I for one am famished.

"An excellent idea, Sergeant major." Says I.

I tear off another piece of the bread crust from the rations Carter had recovered and take another mouthful of water from Nancy's water pouch. I watch as she attends to Smithy, who is staring up, blissfully unaware, at the full moon through the hanger doors as the noises still screech from the building above. The huge tear high in our night sky drifts westward like a shroud over the moon as we watch on, fascinated by its erratic movement, the thunder still rumbling on like a distant marching troop over a wooden bridge.

"What do you think that contraption is for then?" I point towards the huge cylindrical bullet shape object sat gleaming on the conveyor belt. I note the scaffolding planks around her, where it looks like some final work was being carried out on her exterior panelling.

"Dunno, Sir, artillery ordinance perhaps?" Carter shrugs, staring at one of the large navigational maps discarded on the floor. Nancy checks Smithy's dressing and walks over to Carter, casually placing a hand on his shoulder as she peers down at the map in his hand as the walls shudder above again and I watch as her bosoms jiggle slightly.

"Is that Spain?" she asks, and Carter nods.

"It would take some high calibre cannon though, to fire that thing skyward I mean sir." His head barely rises from inspecting the yellowing map in his hands as he points out several destinations to Nancy.

"Indeed, it would," says I, pondering the actual barrel size it would require launching such a bullet. "Perhaps, if we found the cannon, we could blow ourselves a hole out of here?" I recall reading several of Jules Verne adventures as a boy and cast my mind back to one such adventure involving an impossible cannon and a journey to the moon in such a capsule similar to was sat in front of us. Had this mad scientist actually invented the damn prototype to launch such a craft? Had he built himself his very own Columbiad?

The dials on the electrical booth have me thinking. If the boat symbol were to activate the strange looking vessel docked in the water and the Spade was indeed to activate the drilling vehicle in the rock face, what then was the cannon symbol indicating?

Surely not the launch of a space rocket?

"What's so funny, Swarley?" Nancy queries as I choke on my bread.

"Nothing, my dear. I think I may have been hit on the head harder than I thought during that ruckus. But if I'm not mistaken, that object over there is actually a space capsule intended for travelling to the moon." Carter looks up. The gold bar he has been fondling is now resting on his lap.

Nancy laughs, but quickly realises I am deadly serious, and I spring to my feet. "Swarley, you can't be serious," Nancy protests.

"Oh, but I am serious. I think that craft there is a prototype vehicle designed for travelling to the moon," I spin around pointing at the craft. "And what's more preposterous is I deduce that vessel in the water there is a submersible capable of travelling many leagues under our vast oceans." I spin again, this time pointing to the behemoth tracked vehicle. "and that monstrosity over there is designed to burrow deep into the Earth's crust and journey the lava lakes beneath our feet." I puff out my chest at that fine revelation.

"Are you off your rocker, Swarley?" Smithy looks on, dumfounded.

"Quite the opposite. I fear Sergeant Major and I intent prove it to you!" I spin once more to face Corporal Carter, who now has the interest of my Nancy as she peers over his shoulder at the gold bar in his lap. This gets my goat up once more.

"Corporal, could you assist my curiosity for a moment, please?" I nod over to the apparatus that stood humming on the floor and Carter nods, showing me the sea chart in nurse Nancy's hand.

"Sure Captain Paxmore, say could I show you this sir, it sure is quite intriguing." he holds out the items in his hand for me and I take the parchment, studying the symbols upon it.

"I haven't the foggiest Corporal, is it foreign?" says I, still rather jealous of the man's ability to excite my Nancy.

"Hieroglyphics Sir, From ancient Egypt. Looks like

28

inscriptions from the Valley of the Kings." Carter smiles.

"What of it, Carter?" says I as he follows me to the control panel

"Dunno, Sir, but I spent a bit of time excavating artifacts in Egypt before the draft to fight the invasion and it looks similar to an archaeological dig location that I was part of years ago. And I found this too." He holds up a sea chart for me, showing a plotted a course from New York to Alexandria. "Looks like Tesla was planning a visit to Egypt."

"Corporal, I fear now is not the time to be planning excursions. I'd rather you concluded your detective work and assisted me on more pressing arrangements." I cut him off dead.

"Whatever you say, Sir, it's just something I thought may be useful." he folds the parchments away and hands the maps back over to Nancy, catching up with me.

"Another time perhaps Carter, for now I need you to stand over by that device over there." I point to the large electrical pod. "Don't worry, Corporal, I have a theory."

Carter makes his way over to the extravagant conjurors box, perplexed, turning once again to Nancy, who can only watch on confused.

"I need you to examine inside doorway when I activate the control panelling here," says I standing by the control panel podium.

Smithy, now slightly drowsy from the medication, watches on with Nancy as I slowly turn the dial around to the symbol marked with the gun and set the opposing dial parameters to ACTIVATE DOOR. Carter slowly places a hand into the chrome shell and listens intently as the walk-in Faraday booth buzzed and crackles before me. The contraption lights up and began sparking, rippling voltage cracks enveloping the caged surface as the vacuum tubes glow.

"See Anything?" I yell over the hum, and Carter shakes his head. "No Sir."

"Damn and blast the infernal contraption." I was sure I had the dials cracked.

There was only one thing for it. I had to examine my theory closer and investigate the doorway from where the gold bars emerged from.

I take a deep breath and turn to Smithy before stepping up the metal stairs, hesitating before I stride inside the caged contraption and plant my feet upon the metal plate wrapped in copper wiring. I watch as Nancy hitches her skirt to reveal her fancy bloomers, running over to my side and we embrace.

Oh, my sweet, sweet intoxicating Nancy. I take a moment to drink in her loveliness.

"Swarley, I need to tell…"

"Shhhhh." I place a finger on her sweet lips.

"For King and Country Sweet Nancy."

"You're off your bloody rocker, Swarley!" Smithy interrupts as we break our embrace.

"No Smithy, I intend to prove to you that this contraption has something to do with accessing those vehicles and that Tesla has created a machine capable of teleportation."

"Teleportation, 'ave you gone mad, Sir?"

"Quite the contrary Smithy, these bullion bars arrived through this door from somewhere and I having witnessed what Tesla was capable on the deck of the Titanic, t'is not such a blind leap of faith really when you weigh the facts up."

"Weight the facts up? Nancy tells him he is off his bleeding rocker if he thinks that Tesla has built himself a contraption that can send a man through a magic doorway. He'll be roasted alive!"

"He's right, Swarley, what would I do without you?" I hold Nancy tight as she swoons in my arms.

"Oh, my dear sweet Nancy. Fear not, science is the way forward, you'll see." I puff out my chest, tickle Nancy's lips with my old moustache, and prepare my fate. But then a curious thought appears in my head. What indeed would she do without me? Or rather, who would she do?

Corporal Carter. That's who she'd do for a fact. I wager my warrant on it. Suddenly the appeal of the adventure into the unknown is lost on me as I turn my attention to over to that rugged, handsome bugger, Carter.

It was at that point, coincidently, Carter interjected, suggesting that he should be the one to step up and cross the threshold as a test subject.

Did he just wink at my Nancy?

"Now that's a fine idea, Corporal, you lead the way and I'll follow." I step back down, allowing Carter to take my position without so much as a moment's hesitation.

"WAIT SWARLEY. IS THIS WISE?"

Smithy shouts as Carter climbs inside the faraday cage and stands upon the metal plate.

Now Nancy is swooning all over that studly young

buck, pleading with him to remain. Damn her womanly ways. But who can blame her, he is rather a fine specimen of a man.

"Quite so, Sergeant major," says I, trying to maintain a hold on my decorum. "Keep your eye on that contraption." I turn the control dial once more, this time setting the pointer to the prototype setting and the ACTIVATE DOOR position, nodding to Corporal Carter as he kisses Nancy one last time.

"Good luck Carter," says I, as a part of me, I confess, wishing the young gigolo harm.

"Take this Bullion bar and throw it back through once you reach the other side." says I, handing the fellow one of the discarded bars of gold.

The light on the dial activates and the intense humming fills the cage as Carter salutes me once more and nods, "It's been an honour to serve with you, Captain Paxmore." He flinches as he steps through, disappearing in a flash of crackling light.

"Damit Swarley, you imbecile. You just incinerated Carter, just like those men in Blackpool."

The sense of guilt sweeps over me as I beg to differ, the light fading inside the cage as an image is formed, just for a moment. The same image I witnessed when Tesla disappeared on board the deck of the Titanic. The very same flickering filament that lingered, then formed the image of another place beyond the cage as a figure slowly fades from view and Carter walks through into the unknown.

After a moment though, the bullion bar is tossed back through, tumbling to the floor, and I manage a sneaky grin.

"Have faith, my good man…" I give them both a wink, checking the activation dial, and followed Carter, stepping onto the plate and walked through the crackling Faraday cage into the light.

I feel the sudden tingle throughout my entire body, the hairs on my neck prickling as my teeth vibrated. Then there is only the blinding light… and the smell of my singed moustache hanging in the air.

***

It takes a moment to gather my thoughts, standing there blinking frantically as my belly lurches and my teeth throb. But after a moment, I can control the vertigo and stop the swaying. When my sight returns, I'm astonished to find myself standing outside on the deck of the Titanic once more, the chill of the sea air engulfing me and the sound of the crashing waves below. Behind me, the door of the Faraday cage swings slowly, as a familiar rotten stench hits my nostrils. To the Starboard side of the ship, under the gloom of the greying sky, I watch another impressive naval ship approach, carrying the Union jack upon its immense top deck. I had never seen such a well-armed vessel in all my life.

My attention, however, is interrupted as I turn to the deck once more.

"YOU!" I bluster, straightening my aching back as our eyes meet upon the wooden deck. "HOW THE BLAZES DID YOU…" I turn back around again, noting I have just emerged from the very same Faraday cage Tesla had used to fire off his harpoon into the Wardenclyffe tower earlier today.

"Enough, Captain Paxmore. I have little time to explain to you the how's and where's of my experiments." Nikola Tesla begins, his slight European accent sounding condescending as usual. "Suffice to say my experiment worked and now I have more pressing matters to attend to if you will be so kind as to move aside and let me pass."

He stands there sporting the shiner I had given him earlier, holding the electrical cattle prod we used to tame our dragon rides to Carter's neck, his finger poised on the device's trigger. Carter strains, his eyes darting to the two large canvas bags of bullion bars by Tesla's feet.

"Sorry Sir, he jumped me before I could get my bearings Sir."

"I believe you are familiar with this device in my hand and I do not need to remind you of its ability to incapacitate that misfortunate victim about to witness its discharge."

I stand there utterly gob smacked. Nikola Tesla. The man who instigated this whole nightmare. The man who opened the heavens to the deathly people eaters.

"Now if you would be so kind as to stand aside and let me through with my experimental equipment, I can get on with my mission given to me by my President, to rid this world of the evil that threatens to destroy everything we have worked so hard to create." I watch him slide his spectacles back up the arch of his nose and guffaw.

"The only evil that threatens to destroy our world is that madman President Roosevelt, and I have no intension of standing down," says I.

"Captain Paxmore, I assure you my intentions are nothing but genuine. President Roosevelt has given me the task of destroying the portal after reconsidering his original plans of taking control of the natural phenomenon."

"Natural phenomenon… balderdash!" I pointed to the lumbering ship flanking the battered hull of the Titanic, its huge cannons towering over its deck. "You call this a natural phenomenon? And where the hell are we Tesla?"

"That Swarley is the question I have been asking myself over these last few hours while repairing my device. It seems however we should not be asking where the hell are we, but rather when the hell are we?" He smiles, "it seems old boy, due to some rather fortuitous circumstances, I have created a machine capable of traveling through the very dimensions of time itself. A machine that can break the barriers of time as we convey it. We need not look at time as being linear anymore."

I thought my brain was haemorrhaging hearing those words. Did he say he had built a time- machine?

"Wait a minute Tesla, are you telling me you made a time machine… out of the Titanic?" I guffaw.

"I rather think I have Captain Paxmore." He smiles back, awaiting the plaudits as the gigantic gun turret of the vessel swings towards us.

"It seems Jules Verne was rather a fine oracle, don't you think? I suppose you have seen my other work. In fact, all my inventions are rather impressive, wouldn't you agree, like the Faraday transporter?" Tesla notions to the cage behind me.

"Are you suggesting we travelled through time in that contraption?" I point back to the Faraday cage.

"It wasn't actually designed for travelling through time, merely a means to teleport from location to location-" he shrugs, "-but during the immense high-voltage surge I expect the mechanics were frazzled, causing this rather unique conclusion; A jump forward in time." Tesla looked rather pleased with himself. "I imagine that the cage back at my lab tripped during the power surge and you somehow stumbled upon the voltage fuse, reactivating the power connection again."

"Balderdash!" I retorted, stepping forward to apprehend the madman. "what utter poppycock!"

"And yet here we are, Paxmore." Tesla faltered, taking a step back as I approach and Carter makes his move swiftly, snatching at the cattle prod from the scientist, wrestling the conjuror to the floor. But tesla is quicker, stabbing Carter with the prong and sending fifty thousand volts to his spasming body.

"You bloody scoundrel you." I lurch forward as Carter slumps against Tesla's canvas bags. it startled Tesla, his eyes darting from Carter back to me. "You really have no idea what's going on, do you, Paxmore. You simply fumble your way through the greatest invention on Earth. I'm amazed you actually found your way through the Faraday doorway."

That remark rather took me aback.

"Well, it's hardly rocket science, is it Tesla," says I.

"Actually Paxmore, that is exactly what I was working on before you interrupted me-" Tesla replies raising a hand to me, "-so if you will be so kind, I need to continue

36

my work before we are lost amongst this dazzling sea battle. Your man servant will be fine. Allow me to continue and I will oblige you in entertaining your questions once we return through the doorway."

A barrage of explosions above cause me to flinch and I make a quick deduction of my situation as the large battleship flying the Union Jack on our starboard side draws closer. The conclusion is, I quickly realised, is that we need to be back on the other side of the cage door, and back inside his laboratory, before the doorway is lost.

"Very well, Tesla," I begin as another almighty boom explodes from the ship closing in.

"We have to move now." Tesla says as we watch the plume of smoke arc high over the Titanic. "If you would be so kind as to help me with my equipment, I'll explain all when we return to the other side."

I watch another projectile explode from the massive gun turret.

"What the devil are they shooting at, don't they know who we are?" I ponder aloud as my eyes follow the projectile up and over the Titanic.

"They are not firing on the Titanic Paxmore," Tesla scrambles to his feet pointing a finger port side and I follow his aim toward another ship on the horizon, "According to the radio messages I intercepted, Captain Paxmore, they're firing on the Bismarck."

"The Bismarck? What kind of name is that? It sounds Bosch to me."

Tesla shrugs, "Quite, it seems we are, or rather will be, at war with Germany."

"Well, about bloody time!" says I.

I reach down to check on Carter, who is muttering to himself as Tesla lifts one of his bags of equipment and knocks over the second heavy bag with a clatter.

I watch as several items spill onto the deck as another salvo of explosions burst from the British vessel.

Tesla's face blushes slightly as I see more gold items spill from the fallen bag.

"Before you jump to any conclusions, I can explain Paxmore," he stammers.

"What's there to explain, you're a bloody bandit, a common pilferer." says I, lifting one of the gold bars from the deck.

"Nonsense Paxmore, if you would just let me explain," he continues to make his excuses, but I am having none of it.

"You are nothing but a thief… a time bandit, robbing that does not belong to you. Why, I have a good mind to thrash you myself for your blatant thievery."

"Listen to me Paxmore, the gold belongs to a man called Morgan, a financier of my work, and I need it to complete my invention back at the Laboratory. Without the gold I cannot…"

"Don't sell me a bleeding dog Tesla, I know when I'm being lied too." I've heard enough nonsense and swing out at the scoundrel, hitting him square in the sauce box. Tesla drops his booty as he rocks on his feet clutching his bloody lip, stumbling for the Faraday cage as another barrage of explosions fills my ears and shakes the Titanic violently. More cannons roar onboard the starboard British vessel as the deck erupts in a ball of flames.

"Dammit Tesla, get back here and fight me like a bloody man."

But he has already crossed the electrical threshold in another blinding charge of light.

Another of the Bismarck's returning shells hit. The Titanic shudders, and I realise I'd better follow that bandit Tesla back to the lab while there was still an open doorway to flee too.

Carter, the damn lush, is out cold and a bloody ox to carry. I struggle my way back to the cage as I feel the Titanic lurch once more.

My back refuses my orders to pick up the pace and my knees quickly join in the mutiny as I try to lift that damn Carter to my shoulders.

"Carter, you brute, wake up damn you!" My arms ache as I pull him onto the plate and we both fall through. I clinch my teeth tight, using what strength I have left, hoping the contraption still works with two commuters travelling at once and we can still return to Wardenclyffe. Around us the Titanic explodes as the Bismarck's shells reign down on her, fiery balls of combustible gases rupturing and ripping the ocean liner in two, but the ship carrying the union flag continues to fire.

I feel that damn rattling in my teeth as the Faraday cage vibrates, enveloping us in a bright, blinding light, then the whooshing sound fills my ears once again.

"Swarley?" I hear the gasps from Smithy as I am thrown from the crackling Faraday cage, tumbling down from the contraption through the smoky clouds. Nancy screams as I stumble, steadying myself against the control panel, and watch her as she recoils, eyes wide. Even Tesla himself stares on, aghast, as I try to make my feet obey the simple command to walk.

"What in merry hell have you done Tesla!" Smithy looks on mortified as he clutches Tesla around his neck, preventing his escape.

I turn to see what has happened to Carter. Was he burnt in the explosion? Did he lose a limb as the Titanic broke apart beneath us? Because apart from the headache and the slight ringing in my ears, I feel fine. To be truthful, I feel better than I have for many years.

But Corporal Carter has gone, the Faraday cage nothing but a frazzled mess of flopping molten metal, sparks of electric flambo cracking against broken metal casing as the voltage bolts arc across the shattered coils.

"What the hell happened to Carter Tesla? Where has this contraption of yours sent my man?" I lurch forward from the smoking machine; my feet feeling like they are responding to someone else's commanding them from inside my head as I reach out to throttle the scientist with my bare hands.

"Argh, what abomination is this." I cry out, staring down at my naked body.

"Good god, what the hell is that thing!" My John Thomas looks like a huge swollen eggplant. "Damit Sergeant Major, I seem to be sporting an injury."

Nurse Nancy swoons into the arms of Tesla as Smithy gulps, while I stare down at what one could only describe as an appendage, you'd normally see in a prize

40

stallion's studding paddock.

"Looks painful, sir." Smithy coughs, removing his neck choke from Tesla and frowns, not knowing quite where to look as he takes Nancy from Tesla and places her to the floor.

The veins on my neck pop like climbing ivy, my body rippling as the muscles contract and throb, feeling the power surge inside my bones. Even my back feels free again as I stretch my arms out in wonder. My legs bulge, my knees bend easily, even the arthritis in my fingers seems to have gone. My whole body vibrates as I let out an almighty cry.

"WHAT IN DAMNATION HAVE YOU DONE TO ME TESLA!" The words echo around the cave as I contort and scream.

Captain Paxmore Sir, what the hell is going on?

His voice is quiet, panicked like mine as I lower my voice.

"Corporal Carter?" I turn, searching for the boy.

Yes Sir, what's going on?

"Carter, where are you, man?" I search the laboratory, confused.

I'm here Sir.

He lifts an arm from the smoke, only it's attached to me.

"Argh!" says I.

"Tesla... what kind of devilish possession is this?"

Tesla stands mesmerised because he knows exactly what is happening to me.

"Remarkable, I think you know already what has happened, Captain Paxmore." He removes his spectacles and rubs them on his sleeve. "I can only conclude that both you and Corporal Carter have fused together during the teleportation and become one entity. Quite marvellous really."

He looks past me and inspects the debris as he moves forward.

"The gold Paxmore, did you get the gold?" he seems more concerned about his stolen goods than our confusing predicament. But I'm too busy staring down at my new appearance to reply.

What does he mean, what the hell has happened to us Captain?

I ignore Carter's spectral voice as I stumble forward towards Nancy, lurching like Frankenstein's monster towards the shimmering lake.

"Gold. What the hell does gold have to do with my predicament Tesla. What the hell can gold do to help this affliction?" I hold out my bulging arms for him to see, but he dismisses this as if I have a rash or some other petty ailment.

Sir?

Tesla turns, his eyes blazing. "Because without the gold I cannot finish my rocket ship. Without my rocket ship I cannot fly to the anomaly and seal the damn thing up. If I cannot seal up the damn anomaly, then the world, as we know it, is doomed. That's why I need the gold, Captain Paxmore Sir." He spits the last words out in contempt.

I stop for a moment, gathering this information up and turn to the rocket ship on the platform; its unfinished hull leaning against the scaffolding.

"So, it is a space rocket then, like Jules Verne wrote about?"

"A similar concept yes," Tesla sighs, looking up at the moon though the open hanger doors, "but without the gold to reflect the Suns radiation I'm afraid the cooling system I have invented will not last the journey."

Sir? I hear Carters voice again.

"You need gold to cover the ship?" says I, slightly lost watching Smithy lift Nancy from the floor as she comes too, fanning herself with Carters folded sea charts to stop herself from swooning again.

"Indeed, I do Paxmore." Tesla replies defeated, walking over to disconnect the fuse panel and begins closing the hanger doors above. "And unless you have a treasure map to locate the vast amount required to smelt down and use, I fear my mission from Roosevelt is already over." The two huge doors slowly screech as they wheel slowly together.

Standing in the Lab in my new birthday suit was quite liberating, but I can feel the chill of the night air entering from the open hanger doors as they closed and I reach down for Nancy's hand as she looks on bemused.

We watch as the moon disappears behind the closing doors, hope of an adventure to the moon fading before it had even begun.

Sir! Carter interrupts as Nancy wraps a blanket around my torso like a toga.

"Just a moment Carter!" I reply, still trying to get my head around Tesla's information.

"I'm so terribly sorry Nancy." I give her a longing look.

"Is he gone?" she asks me, her lip quivering.

"Not at all my sweat, he lives on… in here," says I clutching her hand to my chest, "and he says he wants nothing more in this world than to hold you tight."

Nancy wraps her arms around me tight, sobbing slightly into my tight torso.

"Oh, my poor Howie." she sobs, and I realise I'm back in the game.

"So," Tesla pipes up, "unless you can pull a barrel full of gold bullion from that clap trap of yours, I'm afraid my space travelling invention remains a mere prototype."

"Why can't we just go back and recover the gold from the Titanic then?"

Tesla frowns, "My dear Paxmore, I'm afraid that horse has bolted."

I spin on my heels to confirm this; the faraday transporter is a smouldering mess.

"Swarley..talk to me for Christ's sake Sir!" Carter screams in my head as Nancy affectionately squeezes me.

The maps, the maps of the Valley of the Kings and the tombs!

"Carter asks what of the Egyptian Tombs?" I finally pass on his query as she looks up.

"Ah yes, a pipe dream," Tesla smirks, "the search for Tutankhamun's gold. A futile endeavour Paxmore. Just like Eldorado I fear."

I nod as Carter explains inside my head.

"What If I were to tell you I knew of a man who knew where to look?" I smiled.

Tesla stares intrigued.

"Do tell Paxmore, for a man with knowledge of the area could indeed separate the gossip from the folklore." He moves in as I beckon him closer, tapping the side of my head.

"Say hello to Corporal Howard Carter, Tesla!"

So, after several hours of interpreting Carters wishes from inside my head, a plan was coerced from the fellow and we loaded up Tesla's wondrous submergible contraption docked on the water and readied ourselves for another fine adventure into the unknown.

"Valley of the Kings Swarley?" Nancy ponders staring down at the map in the captain's wheelhouse, stroking my rather swollen bicep. "Do we know how many leagues under the sea this journey is?" I pick up one of Tesla's many books from his fine collection upon his shelves and laugh, "Well I hope it isn't this many my darling. I don't think Carter and I have the stamina for twenty thousand."

Nancy gives us a subtle wink, "Then what are we waitin' for Captain Paxmore, I believe we 'ave some unfinished business."

"Smithy," says I, as I run my fingers through my thick, new golden locks. "You and Tesla have the bridge."

"Aye, aye Sir." Smithy salutes as Nancy leads me below deck.

The saucy mare.

MISS ADVENTURE

BRANDI HICKS

Ash looked out across the vast expanse of the deep blue sea before him. The salty ocean air whipped his long mane of ebony tresses around his face and coloured his cheeks a rosy pink. This is what he lived for.

Until his brother Cinder woke up, anyway.

"Aye, don't we have any rum left on this blasted ship?"

"No, Cinder, ye drank it all last night whilst trying to shoot pelicans."

Cinder stroked his ruddy stubble and scratched inside his trousers unpleasantly. He darted port side and heaved the contents of his stomach overboard. He wandered back toward his brother, wiping his mouth on his sleeve.

"Right. When will we be docking again? I've been informed we're out of necessities."

"By necessities, do ye mean rum? As in: I just told ye the rum is gone?"

"Semantics. When will we dock?"

Ash let out a heavy sigh. "If the wind keeps, we should reach Tortuga by sundown."

Cinder's face perked up. "Tortuga, eh? I should hope we'll be staying a while. 'Tis my favourite place, it is."

"We'll be there as long as we need to hire more crew, get supplies—"

"And rum…"

"Yes, and rum." Ash rolled his eyes. How he and Cinder were twins and complete opposites was beyond his comprehension. "Can ye make yerself useful and swab the deck? If we want a crew, we need ole' *Miss* to look worthy." He patted the helm lovingly, polishing away a spot of dirt.

"Well, ye see, there's this hammock over here and…" Cinder's voice trailed off as he climbed into the hammock and instantly started snoring.

Ash rigged the wheel to stay on course and set about getting the ship ready for a crew. The last bit of crew left a fortnight ago at Port Royal, and due to Cinder's lack of motivation to do… anything...it was getting harder to maintain the *Miss Adventure*. Between Cinder's attitude, mixed with the fact they hadn't found treasure in quite some time, it became a struggle to keep a crew for very long. Ash had thought for certain that at least Freyja would have stayed, seeing as she was bedding Cinder, but his brother messed that up, too.

Cinder was still snoring as they approached Tortuga. "Aye, Cin, we're heading into port." Cinder didn't budge. Ash walked up next to him, leaned right into his ear and yelled, "LAND, HO!"

Cinder flipped out of the hammock, landing his backside on the deck...hard. "Ye could've just said so." He stood, gingerly rubbing his arse. Ash chuckled to himself and walked back to the helm.

"If ye want to make port, ye better help. Go ready the anchor."

"Alright, alright," Cinder grumbled.

"Now!"

"I'm goin', don't be getting yer knickers in a twist."

Although Cinder was lazy, he at least knew what he was doing. When he actually decided to help with ship duties, he got things done quickly and efficiently. As the *Miss Adventure* pulled into harbor, Cinder dropped the anchor and tossed the mooring lines to the dock worker. Tortuga, of course, had no port authorities to worry about.

"Try to stay out of trouble, or at least don't get caught. I'll find ye when we're ready to ship out."

"Aye, and ye need to try to loosen yer britches. Why not try the whorehouse while we're here." Cinder clapped Ash on the back and shook with laughter, then sauntered away whistling, heading toward the nearest pub.

Ash desperately wanted a drink himself, but even more than that, he wanted away from Cinder for a bit. He decided to take a walk down Merchant's Row, where various vendors had stalls set up to sell their goods— both legal and..questionable.. He kept his hand on his bag of gold that hung from his hip, and a wary eye out for pickpockets.

He perused the different booths—a man with an eye-patch and a grisly beard was selling dried meats of dubious origins. A female had trinkets that glittered like gold and claimed she would enchant them upon purchase, and musicians strumming a sea shanty. None really caught his eye until he happened upon the most beautiful woman he'd ever set his sights on, which instantly put him on guard. Her onyx hair fell in waves over bare shoulders, though the front was pulled back from her face by a band of crimson that matched the dress she wore. Her eyes were an enchanting emerald green, her skin the colour of honey, and her lips like the juiciest cherry. No woman that attractive should be in Tortuga, let alone mixing with pirates.

"My eyes must be failing me, Miss. I could swear ye are a Siren, but even they dare not come to Tortuga."

"Aye, Sailor, if you heard me sing, you'd know better than to think me a Siren," she chuckled.

Even her laugh is beautiful, Ash thought. "And what might ye be selling in this scourge of a town?"

She stood then and came to circle around Ash. She was a good foot shorter than his six foot two, her slight frame curving in all the right places, and her scarlet Spanish-style dress swaying gracefully with her hips.

"I don't know that you're the type o' man that could appreciate what I'm selling." She gave him a seductive wink.

"Ah, I didn't realise ye were selling *that.* I mistook you for a proper lady. Well, as proper as a lady can be in these parts."

"You misunderstand me, Ash. I'm no whore. I just don't think you're man enough to handle the treasure I can offer."

Ash took a step back from her. "How in the seven Hells did ye know my name? Who are ye? And ye must not know me very well—I'm plenty man enough for any treasure, even one a witch can offer." He puffed his chest out for good measure.

"I'm no witch, either. And I know more than you think. I know you and your brother, Cinder, need a crew. I know you grew up in a shipyard. Your mother died birthing you both and your father resented you for it, eventually leaving you and your brother to fend for yourselves. And I know you have the mark of the gods."

"H-how do ye—"

"It doesn't matter how I know; it matters what I know and what I choose to do about it." She ran a bangled hand across his back as she continued circling him, making him dizzy. "Ash MacCorran, how would you like to find the treasure every man, woman, and child long to have?"

"And what be that ye sorceress?" he slurred.

She circled him still, picking up speed. He was feeling woozy, his vision blurring around the edges. The world around him started fading away. The only thing he could see were pools of emerald; the only smell was a rich, earthy mix of saffron, rosemary and a hint of vanilla; and the last thing he heard was the voice of an angel…

"You will find your destiny. I will help you seek a wish."

"What would I wish for…" Ash's voice sounded distant to his own ears.

The woman stopped suddenly and leaned in to whisper in his ear. As she did, he vaguely noted that her breath smelled like the sea, the wood of the *Miss Adventure* and a scent from long ago that he couldn't quite place.

"You don't make the wish,"—she nibbled his ear — "it knows your desires, your heart and mind, and will give it to you. You just have to find it."

The last of Ash's vision tunnelled like a wave coalescing into the sea. And he had a brief feeling of drowning before he collapsed at the feet of the woman whose name he didn't even know.

Cinder sidled into the first pub he came to, a smarmy smile plastered on his face. He walked up to the bar and slammed his hand on the rotting wood, laying down a gold piece as he did.

"Give me rum until I can't stand and then give me some more."

Cheers came from all around at hearing such an order. Cinder was imbibing in his first mug of liquor, beaming, as he felt a tap on his shoulder.

"Aye, what can I do—" a fist to his jaw stopped him mid-sentence. "What the feck was that fer?" He looked up and saw a slender woman in an olive-green slip of a dress, curly, untamed red hair flowing wildly to her shoulders.

"Ye know what the feck that was fer, ye ungrateful,

cold-hearted imbecile!"

"Maureen! Good to see ye again. It's been a while, yeh?"

"A while? A while! It's been three feckin' years! 'I'll be back soon, Mo, then we can be wed.' 'Tis what ye said, ye big oaf! And I was dumb enough to believe ya!" She struck him in the chin again with a force he didn't think was possible, one of his teeth knocking loose.

"Mo, ye know me better than that. Ye know I live on the sea and can't be settlin' down."

"Then don't make promises ye don't intend to keep!" Maureen turned around and stormed out of the pub as laughter echoed around Cinder.

Cinder turned back to his mug to partake in more liquor to wash the taste of embarrassment out of his mouth. He tried to act tough, like he didn't really care, but he thought he loved Mo. As much as he could love anyone, that is. His theory was that he wasn't good enough for a woman to settle down with. He couldn't keep from looking at other women, couldn't keep his pants up when a female glanced his way. And he loved his sea-faring adventures, even if he had to put up with Ash's up-tight arse.

He was drowning these thoughts in his second pint of rum when a beautiful female sidled up to sit next to him. So beautiful, in fact, he almost dropped his alcohol. She had hair as black as a starless midnight, eyes as lush green as any jungle canopy, and bronzed skin that just begged to be touched.

"Aye, sailor. How bout buying me a round?" Her voice alone could seduce the pants off any warm-blood-ed man.

Cinder raised his hand to signal for a drink. "Barkeep, get the lady whatever she wants."

"Whatever I want, you say?" A devilish smirk flashed across her angelic face.

"Aye, ye tell me yer name, and I'll give ye whatever ye ask fer."

The woman trailed her finger down Cinder's arm. He could almost swear she was purring. "Ah, but my name isn't important, is it? Only what I can do for you."

Cinder puffed out his chest, trying to put his manliness on display. "And what can ye do for me, little lady?" He winked salaciously.

She pressed against him, the red satin of her dress gliding over his bare arm. Her whisper of a voice tickled his ear, "More than you could imagine in your wildest dreams, Cinder MacCorran."

Cinder pulled back, shocked. "And how in the feck do ye know my name?"

"I know more than you think. I know you envy your brother, Ash. I know you drink to forget the beatings you endured as a child, while Ash went by unscathed." Cinder started to protest, but the woman quickly shushed him. "Oh, I know you love Ash, though you wouldn't ever admit it to him. You don't blame him. You just want revenge for a past that you feel shaped you into something worthless. But my dear, you are far from worthless."

"And how do ye know that? Are ye a witch?"

"It doesn't matter how I know; it matters what I know and what I choose to do about it." Cinder didn't

54

notice the woman move, but suddenly she was standing behind him, her hands pressing on his shoulders, her mouth on his ear, her scent invading his nostrils. He smelled lavender mixed with the salty ocean air and a hint of something more exotic. Jasmine, perhaps? The smells were drowning him, and he didn't want to come up for air. His vision tunnelled. As he fell off his barstool, the last thing he saw was the jungle green eyes of a mistress he knew nought about.

Ash awoke, disoriented. He tried to gauge his surroundings, but he was having trouble focusing on any one thing. The room was lit only by the dusky sunlight coming through a window, hues of pink and orange dancing around. The smell of vanilla wafted in the air, mixed with the powerful aroma of sage. Then his gaze settled on an all too familiar sight. Cinder across some pillows strewn in a corner, drool trickling from his agape mouth.

Ash muffled a groan, then his gaze flicked to the opposite corner where the enchantress from Merchant's Row sat at a table, gazing into a candle flame.

"See anything interesting?"

If he surprised the woman, she didn't show it. She just continued to look at the small fire as she spoke. "Interesting to some, not so much to others."

Ash slowly gained his balance and stood, making his way toward the table.

"What's your name, woman?"

"Sibyl."

"If ye wanted me back at your place, Sibyl, ye could've just asked." He sent her a grin, but she didn't even peer up at him. "What are we doing here anyhow?"

Sibyl nudged a chair with her foot. "Would you please sit down and shut up? Has anyone ever said you talk too much?"

"I tell him that daily, actually." Cinder slurred as he started rousing.

Ash plopped into the offered chair. "Excuse me for wanting to know what the feck I've been kidnapped for. It's not e'ery day I'm drugged and hijacked to a gorgeous woman's home."

"This isn't me home, and I didn't hijack you. I saved you. So, once again, shut your mouth"

"Saved me from what, exactly?"

Sibyl threw her arms up and huffed. "Holy feck! You do not listen well, do ya? Fine, you both are being followed. Ever since you stepped foot on Tortuga, a shadow lurks behind both of ya. More you, Ash, than Cinder. I told you, you're marked. That doesn't go unnoticed, whether or not they know what they're seeing."

"What do ye mean, Ash, more than me? What's he got that I don't?"

"That's what you took away from what I said? That your brother is being followed more than you? You're jealous of *that*?"

"Ne'er said I was jealous," Cinder mumbled and rubbed the back of his head in a nervous tic.

"The gods tend to show favour to twins, for whatever feckin' reason, and you two seem to be a prime example of that. Add to that the turmoil you've been through

56

since losing your mum, and it just compounds. You need to find your Pa."

"Oh, we could find him easily enough. Just go to the nearest pub once you hit port on Dalkey Island, he'll be sidled up to the bar." Ash leaned back in his chair, propping his feet on the table and his hands behind his head.

"Sorry to be the one to tell you boys this, but that ain't your Pa."

Ash chuckled, "Okay, Sibyl, now yer just spinning tales. He may be an arse, but he's still our Pa."

Cinder looked curiously at Sibyl. "Now wait a minute, Ash. Let's see what she has to say." He walked over to the table, placing palms down and staring at her with open interest. "What say ye? If that ain't our Pa, who is?"

A wicked smile crossed Sibyl's face as her eyes clouded over white. Ash fell back out of his chair, crashing hard and swearing harder. Cinder blessed himself by making the sign of the cross.

"Aye, boys, you need all the holiness you can get. Your Pa is the Devil of the Seas—Davy Jones himself."

Cinder went nose to nose with Sibyl, her eyes still as white as snow. "Yer tellin' me, our Ma, may she rest in peace, got tangled with Squid-face? There's no way that happened."

Ash stood, anger and confusion filling him because something in what Sibyl was saying rang true.

"Cin, think for a minute. How many times did the old man make off comments about raising bastard sons?"

Cinder rubbed the stubble on his chin. "I just thought he was insulting us."

"How 'bout when he'd refer to Ma as a whore?"

"Burned my arse, it did. But still, just an insult."

"Remember that night he came home piss drunk—"

"T'was every night."

"I'm talkin' about the night he knocked yer tooth out. He said the devil was in us, that no part of us was his."

"Aye," Cinder nodded sagely. "Suppose I do remember that." He poked his tongue through one of the holes where a tooth went missing after a well-placed right hook.

Ash continued, "So, what say ye, Sibyl? Why do we need to find ole Mister Jones? And I think it's about time to tell us how exactly ye know these things."

Sibyl's eyes returned to their normal green, and she nodded. "I'm an Oracle. I came to Tortuga from Delphi to wait on you two eejits. Now, you need to get your crew together. Cinder, you need to ask Maureen to join."

Cinder held up his hands in defence. "Oh, no. No, no, and hell no. Ye saw her with me. She wants nothin' to do with me."

"She'll come. Just ask. Ash, at Merchant's Row, you'll find a man by the name of Tiberius. And then back at the pub, one of you will need to recruit two more. A woman by the name of Mary and a fellow that goes by the name Pythos. I'll be joining you as well."

"Fine. I don't want to be on this rot of an island any longer than need be. Let's get to it. Cinder, get Mo, and for all that is good, try not to piss her off."

"'Tis an easy thing to do. It is. I can't make any promises." Cinder stomped and huffed toward the door.

"Watch yer back and we'll meet at the pub to get the last two."

"All the supplies you need will be on the ship by the time you get there."

Cinder turned on Sibyl. With a look of intent gleaming in his eye, he pointed his finger square at her. "Don't ye forget the rum, ye Seer. Or ye know what'll happen."

Sibyl just rolled her eyes. "Gods forbid someone sees you sober."

Cinder grumbled as he made his way toward Maureen's small apartment in the town's centre. As he raised his hand to knock, the door swung open.

"'Bout time, ye big oaf. I thought ye'd be here a while ago, I did."

Cinder watched as a flurry of red curls pushed past him with a small trunk dragging behind her.

"Huh? What are ye doin' Mo?"

"I'm going to yer ship. Isn't that what yer here for? The Seer told me days ago, ye'd be here. She did. How else do ye think I knew when ye'd be at the pub?"

"Well, yeah. But—"

"But nothing. Let's go."

Cinder shut Mo's door behind her, mouth still agape. He shook it off and shrugged, "That was easy enough."

Ash strode down Merchant's Row like a man with a purpose. He surveyed everyone he came across, wondering how he'd know this Tiberius when he saw him. He stopped at a booth with a strange-looking vendor selling compasses. The man was short and impish, with a turquoise and grey beard. His eyes were violet, and he had rings through his nose, lip and a half dozen in each ear.

"You're searching for something; you'll need help to find. This compass will help look for what you have in mind."

The merchant presented Ash with an ornate device, gold with delicate swirls cut into the lid. Inside the mechanism, the needle glistened silver and each directional marking had a different gemstone—north was an emerald, south was a ruby, sapphire for east and amethyst for west.

"How much?"

"I don't deal in money when it comes to *special* sales; but a voyage I need, to tell more tales. Quiet as a mouse I'll be, take me sailing across the sea."

"Do ye cook?" Ash quickly held up his hand before the man could answer in another rhyme. "Aye or nay will suffice."

The man thought, then nodded. "Aye."

"Be at the docks by sunrise, *Miss Adventure,* is me ship." Ash took the proffered compass and tucked it snuggly in his jacket pocket.

The full moon was beaming down from the midnight sky. Ash was getting tired. He'd questioned many men on the whereabouts of the man called Tiberius, but people just skittered away at the name.

Ash decided to take a break from his search and leaned against an old, dilapidated brick building, out of sight from the main row. His eyelids were getting heavy, and he didn't notice the two shadows looming in the darkness in the alley beside him.

One of the men emerged from the vacant street, grabbing Ash and pinning his arms behind his back. The other brandished a dagger at Ash's throat.

"You be the one the Seer was going on about?" The smell of stale ale wafted from his mouth, inches away from Ash's face.

"I don't know what yer talking about, ye gobshite." Ash spat at the man.

"You're at the wrong end of me dagger to be talking like that, you fool. I don't see what's so special about ya. Surprised you haven't pissed your pants already."

The man was too intent on Ash to see a giant of a man sneak up behind them. Though the one holding Ash slackened his grip, he froze in place. The giant held his finger to his lips, motioning for Ash to keep his presence quiet. Before Ash could realise what was happening, the man had both men by the scruff of their necks, dangling them in the air, kicking and screaming.

"You should not be so mean to people, especially those who are marked by the gods." The large man walked the two vagrant pirates to the nearest watering trough and dropped them in, brushing his hands off as if he'd just thrown out the smelliest of trash.

Ash watched the man walking back toward him. Surely a god among men based on his stature alone. He had golden tattoos that reflected in the moon's glow, dancing over his cocoa coloured skin. His biceps bulged, protruding from his tattered vest, and a single carring glinted in the night. The whites of his eyes stood out from the darkness of the rest of him, his rich, hazel irises gleamed. His teeth were pearls piercing the night, made visible by a jolly, wide smile. The giant offered his hand to Ash.

"I am Tiberius. I've heard you've been looking for me."

Ash stammered his acknowledgment. "Y-yes. The Oracle, she said…"

Tiberius let out a hearty laugh that shook him. "Ah! Sibyl! She's up to mischief again, eh? Come! Let's go get some libations before we ship out! I'd like to get to know my new Captain." He clapped Ash on the shoulder and started leading him toward the pub where he was to meet up with Cinder.

"How did ye know to find me?"

"Word travels fast in Tortuga, my friend. Plus, Sibyl asked me to keep an eye on you in case of any trouble." He wagged his finger at Ash. "You, Captain, have a lot of enemies. I've been picking them off you since you docked."

"I guess I owe you a round or five, then."

Tiberius just shook with his booming laugh once more than the awkward pair clambered into the drinking establishment.

Cinder watched as a waif of a girl wiped the bar down, and then poured five pints of ale in succession, sliding them to their patrons with a flourish he'd never seen before. His mouth was open in awe when Ash and Tiberius walked up to him.

"Where's Mo? Couldn't ye leave the barstool for ten minutes to do yer part in this?" Ash condescended.

Cinder shook himself from staring at the barmaid. "I took her to the ship three hours ago. Don't be an arse. Some of us don't take so long to do our job." He eyed Tiberius with a wary look until the man flashed a smile and laughed.

"I'm Tiberius Chisholm." He stuck his large hand out to shake Cinders.

"Cinder MacCorran." He couldn't help but let out a chuckle himself, finding the new crewmate's jolliness infectious.

They ordered drinks and were watching the tawny haired bartender fill the mugs when a man covered in snakeskin tattoos approached them. Cinder's hand immediately fell to his scabbard, resting on the hilt of his sword. He noticed Tiberius took a protective stance beside the brothers and smiled approvingly.

The snakeskin man put his hands up in a defensive gesture. "Aye, mateys, I mean ye no harm. I was told to look for the twins, that I could be part of their crew. Ye be twins, no?"

Ash stepped forward. "I'm going to guess yer name is Pythos?"

"That's what they call me, aye. Me given name is Jack."

"Well, Jack, let me buy ye a drink before we get started on our adventure. We still have one more person to look for."

The men took their drinks to a table in the room's corner so they could survey everyone. They watched as women in various states of sobriety threw themselves at the unsavory lot of pirates. A few even approached their table, mostly eyeing Tiberius.

Cinder grumbled as yet another female left their table after Tiberius politely turned her down. "How the feck are we supposed to find this Mary person? All the others came to us. Why hasn't she?"

Ash shrugged his agreement and frustration, then made a sudden movement. He stood on his chair and yelled, "AYE! Who goes by the name of Mary?"

A half-dozen women raised their hands and looked at Ash appreciatively. Ash climbed down and picked his way through the crowd to talk to the Marys.

Cinder wasn't looking at them, though. He was still watching the mousy bartender, and how her face dropped when Ash announced his question. She was pretty, in a plain sort of way, but it wasn't her looks that drew him. He couldn't take his eyes off her, and now he knew why. That was Mary. He walked over to the bar, where she was diligently scrubbing a spot of dirt that wasn't there.

"Hi, Mary." Cinder's gruff voice came out more tenderly than he anticipated.

"Don't know what you're talking about, sir. May I get you a drink?"

"Mary," he implored.

The girl huffed and threw her cloth on the countertop. "What, Cinder? I don't want to go with you and Ash. I know what Sibyl said, but I don't want to leave. I'm just fine right here." Just then, a man approached and before he could get a word out, he wretched all over the barstools in front of Cinder.

"And what did Sibyl say to ye?"

"She didn't tell you?"

"It would seem not." Cinder inched closer to her, as close as he could get with the counter still between them. He didn't want to kiss her, but he wanted to hug her, protect her. He just couldn't understand why.

"Oh, for feck's sake. I'm your kid sister."

Cinder turned to face the bar room where his brother was unsuccessfully interviewing a heavy-bosomed woman full of more drink than sense. "Uh, Ash? Ye may want to come over here."

Ash ran a hand through his hair, scratching his head, trying to figure things out.

"What do ye mean, yer our sister?"

"Well, you see, when a man and a woman…"

Ash held up his hands in protest, not wanting to hear this young woman discuss the ins and outs of, well, in and out. "I know that part, but how, ugh! Who's yer Ma and Pa? "

"Me Ma lives in the village. I never knew me Pa, but according to Sibyl, it's Mr. Jones."

Cinder, standing protectively in front of Mary, piped in, "So why don't ye want to come with us?"

"I've been doin' just fine here without me Pa. Or you two, for that matter."

As if to emphasize how not fine Mary actually was,

a bar patron decided that was the opportune moment to come grab Mary's arse and try to cop a feel of her bosom. Cinder immediately threw himself on the man, pounding his fist into the man's face. Mary dumped a pitcher of ale over the two.

Cinder stood, wet from the alcohol, picked Mary up by the waist and threw her over his shoulder. She began to kick and punch his back.

"Put. Me. Down!" she cried.

"Aye, boys! It's time to head to ole *Miss*." Cinder marched out of the door, Mary still over his shoulder, and headed to their ship.

After a few days at sea, the motley crew got into a groove. They worked surprisingly well together, despite their different backgrounds. Ash was still Captain, of course; Cinder the First Mate, though Tiberius acted more like it. However, Cinder was putting forth more effort than he normally did, perhaps because Maureen would nag him until he did. The strange, turquoise-bearded man, named Rogan LaCroix, turned out to be an excellent cook...just extremely annoying with his constant rhymes. Sibyl stayed in the Captain's cabin mostly, studying a map she said would locate Davy Jones.

Each night they'd sit around a table on the deck, drinking rum and spinning tales. Rogan's yarns, though irritating, were always the most spirited.

"There's no way that be true, LaCroix. No woman in her right mind would bed ye, let alone three at once!"

Cinder laughed heartily, draping his arm across Maureen's shoulders—which was happening more frequently.

"I tell you no lie. I'll swear to it till I die." Rogan chugged his pint of rum in one swig.

Mary laughed. Her mood had changed as soon as they were on the open sea. Ash looked at her curiously, seeing so much of himself in the young girl. The shift in her demeanour was obviously due to the sea, and that was something Ash could relate to.

"Tell the one about Mr. Jones, LaCroix." Sibyl sashayed to the table, taking a shot straight from the bottle.

Rogan shivered at the mention of Jones' name. "Ye best be quiet saying that name, Seer. He might make us all disappear."

Ash sat up on the edge of his seat, eyeing Sibyl but talking to Rogan. "Mr. LaCroix, I think you need to tell us that tale now."

"Aye, but don't say I didn't warn ye; if I spin the story, by the end of the night it'll be Jones ye see.

"There was a girl, quite a bit like young Mary, that in her heart, Davy Jones she did carry. She loved him with a passion deep, promising his love to keep. One day, he left her for the sea, vowing on his return, he'd bend to his knee. The lady fair did wait, watching the sea, awaiting her fate. But he stayed gone too long, that Mr. Jones, and when he returned, he found her sickly, skin and bones. The plague and the men had ravaged her, left her to rot in her bed. Davy Jones found her lifeless and bloody, and he went out of his head. He put a curse on the land, and on his heart as well. He hid away his treasures and swore to raise hell. He attacks ships and sailors with a vengeance, declaring his own penance. To find his treasures lost, seek ye Mr. Jones, and pay ye the cost. Or kill him true, with a creature's blood of blue."

The crew was silent around the table. None had even raised their mugs while Rogan spoke his story. Once the silence grew deafening, Cinder boomed out a shaky laugh.

"LaCroix, ye have a knack for spinning yarn, that's for sure!" Everyone nervously laughed with Cinder, paranoia creeping around the edges of the ship.

Sibyl stood behind Ash and placed her hands on his shoulders, making him jump. She reached down into his vest's breast pocket, pulling out the compass Rogan had bargained with for passage.

"Tell this you want to find Davy Jones."

Ash looked at Sibyl incredulously. "Ye want me to tell a compass that I want to find Davy Jones? What's it going to do? Speak directions to me? Make him magically appear, will it?"

Sibyl slapped Ash on the back of his head. "Do as I say! Quit questioning everything."

Ash huffed, looked at Cinder, who was currently tonsil deep with Maureen, and sighed. "Fine. Aye! Compass! I wish, for some godforsaken reason, to find Mr. Davy Jones!"

Nothing happened.

Ash opened his mouth to tell Sibyl what a crock of shite it was when a loud clap of thunder boomed across the sky.

"LaCroix! Take the girls below deck!" Cinder shouted as a torrential rain started.

"I'll fix the rigging, Cap'n!" Tiberius tried to yell above the weather's din.

Ash raced to the helm, finding the wheel lock snapped and the wheel spinning furiously.

Cinder ran to help Tiberius with the sails, but a wave came abreast the ship and knocked him into a mast, rendering him unconscious. Tiberius raced to try to rouse him. Cinder woke as Tiberius pulled him away. A bolt of lightning struck the main mast, toppling it over.

Then, as fast as the raging storm had started, the entire sea and sky went eerily calm. The men gathered near the helm, looking around for any signs that the storm may start again.

Tiberius pointed out in the distance, "Over there. What is that? Is that a ship?"

"That can't be, it's moving too fast, it is." Cinder pulled out a nautical telescope. "Feck me. It is, and it's aiming to ram us."

Ash frantically turned the ship's wheel, hoping to outmanoeuvre the on-coming boat. "Nobody hits the *Miss Adventure*. Tiberius, get the cannons ready."

"I'll help!" Mary had appeared, as quiet as a mouse, behind Ash.

"Get back below deck!"

"I'm going to help, and you aren't going to argue." She followed Tiberius below to ready their weapons.

Ash turned the ship broadside to have the cannon's face their new enemy. "Are ye ready?"

"AYE!"

"Aim! Fire!"

The loud boom of the cannon fire rocked the *Miss Adventure*. The cannonballs whistled through the night air, striking their intended target true. The small crew cheered and readied the cannons once more, waiting for the enemy to show signs of damage.

"FIRE!" Ash yelled.

Again, the ship rocked, as the volley hit home.

But the vessel continued on its path straight for them.

Soon, it was close enough for Ash, and his mates, to see aboard the ship. Except they saw...no one. No one save for the captain at the helm. A tall man with a long, black beard that hung to his broad chest, steely eyes set on Ash.

No.

He was looking past Ash.

Behind him.

At... Sibyl. Who was smiling a wicked grin.

The captain started walking toward the edge of his ship and then vanished. Ash and Cinder looked at each other, bewildered. Then they each felt an icy hand clap each of them on the shoulder.

"Aye, my boys! I finally get ta see ya!"

"How the feck did ye get from there to here without…" Cinder's perplexed tone faded when he turned to be face to face with the oversized man.

The men became even more confused as they watched Sybil take the man by the arm and spin him around to give him a passionate kiss. Mary came to stand next to Cinder, looking aghast at the sight before her.

Ash was fuming. "Do ye mind telling us what's going on here? Who the feck are you?"

"Who am I? Who the feck am I! Son, I am the Devil of the Seven Seas. I am the drowning god. I am your Pa. I am Davy Jones."

"And Sibyl, what of ye?"

"I needed you here. Our family is now complete." She stroked Mary's cheek, but Mary recoiled from the touch. "Your mother didn't die during childbirth, and your mother doesn't live in the village. You're all my children, your father is Davy Jones. Rogan's story was mostly accurate, except for the bit where I died. They left me for dead, that's true, but Davy came to me just in time. He took me to a powerful sea witch," her eyes clouded over, and her arms raised above her head. "She gave me gifts beyond my wildest dreams. I'm an Oracle, yes, but so much more."

To showcase what she was saying, the waves raised above the *Miss Adventure*, hovering over top of them, waiting to crash down and drown them all. Sibyl made flourishing movements with her hands, and the waves parted and returned to the calm ocean. She clapped her hands together and thunder roared in the cloudless sky. Then she walked—nay, floated—port-side, and leaned over the railing. As she straightened, a giant, crimson tentacle snaked around her waist. Tiberius took a step forward, making to defend her, but Davy Jones held out his long arm and quietly chuckled.

"Nay bother, my friend. Tis only the Kraken."

"Only the Kraken!" Tiberius shouted and moved again to go toward Sibyl.

Jones just laughed louder. "I'm telling you true,

she'll be just fine. She's named him Sebastian."

As the crew looked on, the colossal squid lifted Sibyl into the air, tossing her from arm to outstretched, slimy, sucker-filled arm. She giggled and flew like a bird. Finally having enough, she motioned for the large cephalopod to place her gently back on the ship. She stroked its tentacle in a loving goodbye, and it slunk back into the depths of the ocean.

"The last gift I'll show you is one I want to offer you, my children." She turned to Jones, looking at him longingly. "My dear, will you help me show them?"

"Of course, my love."

Cinder rolled his eyes at the show of love. By this time, LaCroix and Maureen both appeared on deck. Maureen clung to Cinder's side as he held her tightly.

Sibyl and Jones embraced once more.

"Look, we get yer in love or whatever you want to call this strange…" Cinder's lament trailed off as he watched Davy Jones pull a dagger out of its scabbard and stab Sibyl in her back. The blade pierced her, all the way to its hilt. Blackness oozed from where it stayed.

She turned to face them all, a smile on her face. The dagger stuck out of her chest; the blackness dripping down the front of her as well.

"There are very few ways to kill me and Davy. We are, in essence, immortal." To emphasize this, she pulled the dagger the rest of the way out of her chest cavity. The sizable hole it made started knitting itself back together immediately. There was one very noticeable thing, though.

Mary gasped, "You have no heart. Literally! You

have no heart!"

Sibyl laughed, "Isn't it beautiful? Now that we're together, we can do the ritual to give you each immortality, too. Isn't that the most sought-after treasure? Isn't that what every true pirate craves?"

Ash found his voice first. "Yer a monster. We don't want to be like either of ye. This isn't a treasure, it's a curse."

"Ash, my first-born, don't be a fool. We can rule the Seven Seas, together as a family, for all of time."

"As a family?" Mary started hysterically yelling. "A family! You abandoned us! We thought you were dead, that we were alone. What kind of *family* does that?"

Sibyl moved toward Mary, but Mary inched backward into Cinder and Ash. "My dearest, we couldn't raise you. Look at us. We live by the sea, we're not natural."

"We don't want any part of ye or yer world." Cinder spat.

"I'll kindly ask you to disembark me ship now," Ash placed his hand at his hip, fingering the grip of his sword.

"There's no need for that, son. Ye saw how blades go through us, they won't serve ye well here."

Recognising the truth in the words, Ash moved his hand away from the sword. His mind was whirring, trying to come up with a solution to his current predicament.

Ash looked to the faces of each of his companions—Tiberius, his golden tattoos reflecting off his dark skin, staying steadfast in his loyalty to him; Mary, shaking with nerves but holding her head high with tears in her eyes; Maureen, her flaming locks blowing in the sea breeze, her strength and willingness to fight showing in the straightness of her spine and glint in her eye; Cinder...Cinder had grown a lot in the few short days they'd been out to sea, and Ash couldn't have been more proud to call him brother now; and the strange fellow, Rogan LaCroix, stroking his colorful beard, staring off port side where the Kraken had been. Looking at the dwarf of a man, the pure simplicity of a plan smacked Ash across his face.

"LaCroix…"

"Aye?" A shadow of a smile played at the man's lips as the conversation quietly passed between the two of them.

"What should we have on the menu tonight?"

"Calamaro, Cap'n."

"Aye." Ash agreed and elbowed Cinder, who, admittedly, wasn't that quick-thinking. Ash nodded to where the giant squid had been and understanding dawned on Cinder's face.

"What about the trick with the ink monster? Can I have that, too? Could be mighty useful in battles." Cinder walked to the edge of the ship. "Or is that a onetime thing ye have? All for show?"

Sibyl scoffed. "All for show? Let your Ma show you how things work. Give me your hand."

Cinder offered his hand to the Oracle, and she sliced it with the same dagger that had skewered her chest, still covered in the blackness of her blood. She spat into his palm where the cut opened and rubbed some of her life source in. He clenched his fist and screamed a blood-curdling yell, doubling over in agony. When he stood upright, his eyes turned milky white.

"Cinder! No!" Maureen wept and tried to go to him, but Ash stopped her.

"Call to the sea, my son. Call forth Sebastian, he'll be happy to see you and listen to your commands."

Cinder stretched out his arm toward the open water, the waves started rippling around at his gesture. Within seconds, the tentacled being emerged, half boarding the boat, tipping it sideways. Everyone slid port-side, Ash grappling to have his sword at the ready.

The beast let his arm splay across the deck due to Cinder's command. While everyone was still getting their bearings from the sudden shift in power and of the vessel, Ash wielded his cutlass, striking the creature's limb, soaking the blade in blue blood.

The screech that followed was ear piercing, dropping everyone on deck to their knees.

Everyone except Sibyl and Ash.

The two faced off against each other, rocking as the Kraken flailed back into the water to tend to its wound. Rogan, Mary and Tiberius held Davy Jones.

"You're no match for me, son. Just accept your fate."

"My fate is still mine to decide, witch."

"My darling, your fate was written in the stars the night you were born. You are destined to do amazing things."

"For a seer, ye sure do miss a lot."

From behind Sibyl, Cinder, eyes now a flaming red, drove his own dagger straight through her back to pierce where her heart should have been.

Sibyl laughed. "Are you a complete idiot? I showed you that this cannot…" Her voice trailed off. She looked at Ash, the smile on his face widening.

"Ye best not try to outsmart the twins touched by the gods. Ye won't ever win. My blade wasn't the only one to pierce that pet of yers." He walked over to where Davy Jones sat tied to the mast, courtesy of Tiberius's strength. "I'd say it was a pleasure to meet ye, Pa, but quite frankly, I prefer the drunk arse back on Dalkey Island."

Ash's cutlass pierced through Jones, who stared seething at his son. The crew worked together to throw the corpses overboard, into the vast expanse of Davy Jones' Locker, the irony not lost on any of them. Ash walked back to the helm, taking his place behind the wheel.

"Cinder! Help the crew clean up this bloody mess, we need ole *Miss* looking good for when we dock next."

Cinder rubbed the back of his head, glanced at Maureen and said, "Well, ye see, there's this hammock over here and…"

Ash smiled to himself and laughed. He looked out across the vast expanse of the deep blue sea before him. The salty ocean air whipped his long mane of ebony tresses around his face and coloured his cheeks a rosy pink.

This is what he lived for

THE GOOD SHIP SCOOBIE

EMMA K. LEADLEY

The good ship Scoobie was one of those vessels with few original parts and many replacements, but the Captain and her crew loved her. She provided shelter, solace and was the most hallowed pirate airship in the known world.

Scoobie was sitting on the ground, wheels down, hatch open, and for all intents and purposes, looked like a vessel idling. Inside was a different matter.

"How's the furnace?" asked Captain Reynard, into the speaking tube, his voice booming down the metallic interior and coming out loudly in the engine room.

"Firing up nicely, Cap'n," came the engineer's reply. "How long til' Gunner comes a-running?"

Reynard squinted out the window, looking at the sun's trajectory and noting, with a sigh, how peaceful everything looked. That would soon change. He glanced down at the instruments in front of him. "I reckon we've got eighteen minutes until we're wheels up."

"Right-ho!"

Reynard paced in the cockpit. He had full faith in his crew, but until any job was *fait accompli,* he couldn't help but worry. Sixteen minutes later, he heard the sound of alarm bells and from the resonance of the noise, those bells were on the move.

"Get ready for take-off!" he shouted into the tube, scanning between nearby buildings for any sign of Gunner. He popped up the periscope, giving their landing site a full three-sixty, but still… nothing.

The surface below the ship rumbled. Only slightly, but enough that the vibrometer gave a pronounced reading. *Dang*, Reynard muttered, then raising his voice: "We gotta go. The tanks are coming!"

He raced aft to help with the take-off, coming face to face with both Greaser and The Boy.

"What about Gunner?" The Boy's eyes were wide. New to the ship, he wasn't used to combat, and fear showed in his face and shaking hands.

"We'll pick him up later. Balloon up, NOW"

Frantic banging and cranking echoed through the ship's bodywork as they got to work. With the turn of dials, pneumatic valves on the roof opened a hatch to release the hot-air balloon and with a pull of a lever from Greaser, it filled with angry heat from the furnace.

Reynard turned to close the hatch and saw Gunner legging it across the square, his twin pistols flashing blue with electric charge from the static generator. "Wait!"

"Lift-off!" shouted Greaser, the balloon inflated.

Reynard tossed a rope out to Gunner. "Sorry old boy, best I can do!"

The Scoobie shot upwards into the sky, Greaser and The Boy continuing to shovel fuel into the furnace and maintain the lift. In the front cabin, Reynard wound up the wheels and set course with the wind behind them. The ship made good headway, and he knew they would be safe from a chase. No-one ever expected a vessel as nimble as The Scoobie.

Now he could find out what happened to Gunner. Turning a few dials, the periscope swung on a band around the ship and he could view the underbelly. A taut rope hung and, following its line down, Reynard allowed himself a wry, thin-lipped smile.

Gunner had entangled himself in the rope enough that he was with them, his pistols no longer flashing with live sparks, and he inched up the rope. He was low enough to swing precariously and kept looking round to check for spires and weathervanes or other impediments to his climb. The movement of the periscope must have caught his attention as he looked directly into the lens and glowered.

Ha! If looks could kill, thought Reynard.

Swinging the periscope back round, Reynard started looking for a landing spot. In the distance was an area of land in between several wooded areas, big enough for the sort of landing they'd need. Again, he smiled. Gunner would forgive them eventually–he always did. And the crew would always tell him to run faster the next time once he'd calmed down. An angry Gunner was not the one you gave useful advice to.

Fixing the rudder in place with the steering pedals chocked, Reynard made his way back to the furnace. "You can slow down now," he said. "Gunner's dangling below us and we need to drop him down before putting ourselves down. Then, you'd probably want to look scarce a while whilst he works out his issues."

Greaser nodded. "Tell us when you open the balloon hatch," he said, and winking at Reynard, added, "and by how much." Both men laughed.

The Boy looked confused. "If you let us down too fast, that wouldn't be good for Gunner, would it?"

"No," Reynard said, and walked off, still laughing. Back in the cabin, he checked his calculations and, turning a wheel, cranked open the valve at the top of the balloon. The Scoobie started drifting down at a nice slow angle and, keeping his eye on Gunner, saw his crewmate would understand their intention.

Minutes later, the ship emerged over the first of the treelines, the tree tips grazing Gunner's feet as he himself prepared for landing. Reynard opened the balloon hatch to maximum and with a lurch, The Scoobie dropped another couple of metres. The passenger dropped and rolled back towards the trees in a practised manoeuvre. "Gunner away," said Reynard into the tubes. "Prepare for full landing."

He rocked a switch and the landing springs rolled into place, The Scoobie dropping to a stationary rest in a mere few bounces. Hard touchdown. Moments later, Gunner yanked the hatch open and blazed in.

"What the hell you playing at, Reynard? You bastard! That's the last damn time you dangle me on the end of a rope. You will bloody well wait for me next ti—"

"Oh, thank goodness you made it unscathed, old boy," said Reynard, reaching to pat the shoulder of the angry crewman. "Now, I know you've been through a fair whack, but why not come with me, have a snifter and tell me what happened." He put his arm round Gunner and led him to the cabin, winking at both Greaser and The Boy watching from back aft.

Secure in his cabin, Reynard poured a generous glass of port each and pulled out a box of cigars. "Gunner, my dear…"

"Don't you try to mollify me, you fiend," said Gunner, his lips twisted in a scowl. He reached out and took a swig of port, slamming his glass down and, whilst Reynard refilled it, took one of the cigars. He sat back, cutting the end and waiting for an offer of a light.

"I got the key, by the way," he said, a wry grin spreading across his face. "We're all set."

Later that night, The Scoobie drifted silently back over Birmingham. The hustle and bustle of the day was gone and now, gas lamps guttered under the starlight and nary even a tom cat was to be seen.

Captain Reynard adjusted the pedals and steering until they were in position over the roof of the Midlandia Bank. "Ready when you are."

Gunner swung open the hatch and he and The Boy rappelled down in parallel, a grappling hook on the end of each of their ropes. Once on the apex of the roof, both men quickly unhooked and went in separate directions, looking for suitable fixing points. The overhanging decadence of the architecture proved to be its downfall, and, with a hiss and a clunk, the grappling mechanisms firmly fixed The Scoobie in place above them. A second set of hooks attached long coils of rope to similar positions on the overhang.

"Time to prove your worth," said Gunner to The Boy. "The Captain knows who he's hiring, but you gotta show the rest of us he's right."

They both turned to the large glass dome that was the bank's centrepiece. In daylight it bathed the foyer in a soft, golden light that made the internal marble surfaces shone. Right now, it was their planned entry point.

The Boy walked round the dome, stopping to tap on each pane. He rocked back and forth on his heels as he did so, muttering to himself. Finally, he crouched down and chalked an outline round his chosen pane. He pulled a small pouch from an internal pocket and it quickly grew as he unfolded it. Tens of clockwork spiders streamed out, arranging themselves in an equidistant pattern within the chalk marks. They threw out streams of silken thread to each other and with a sudden tug, The Boy swung the glass out of the frame, entirely held by his arachnid menagerie.

Gunner gave a low whistle. "So, the Captain was right," he said. "You really can build magic with your bare hands."

The Boy barely glanced at him before throwing his rope into the foyer below. "Anything to look out for?" he asked, getting into abseil position.

"Nothing I heard of," said Gunner, doing similarly. "Besides," he tapped the pistol mounted on his hip sling, "Gunner by name, Gunner by—"

There was a slithering noise, and The Boy was near to the ground.

"Damn him," muttered Gunner. "I'm supposed to be in charge here."

An angry barking came from below and he swung down, gathering speed as the rope slipped through his leather grip. At the bottom, he'd already unslung his pistols and was looking for the source of the noise when he saw The Boy stroking a sleeping dog laying on its side.

"Saved some of dinner and laced it with sleeping powder," he said, in reply to Gunner's raised eyebrows. "Might have used too much…"

Gunner stalked off. "C'mon then," he shouted. "No need to waste time."

The Boy grinned and followed, his footsteps echoing in the large space. His hurricane lantern cast looming shadows as it lit the way to the vault. They'd practised this route again and again, but the shadows seemed to taunt his way, making him second guess himself until he caught up with Gunner.

"Remember, we take everything now and sort it later." Gunner took the key from his pocket and turned it in the large, rounded door in front of them. It swung smoothly open, but his face fell. "Well, damn me. That ain't on the plans."

An inner door blocked him, tall iron bars reaching from top to bottom and horizontal supports running across to make the gaps too small for any human to even contemplate squeezing through. Gunner put his hand on a bar and pushed. The door remained resolutely shut. "Well, I don't know what we're going to do now—", he said, gawping as it swung open.

The Boy stepped back, putting his pouch carefully back in his pocket. "Steal the money?" he suggested and strode inside with a swagger, oblivious to Gunner's scowl.

The two men took little time working through the vault, one from either end. They emptied everything into a series of bags and The Boy used his clockwork devices to pick any locks that refused to fail under Gunner's hammer.

"Ooh, pretty," said The Boy, twirling a string of pearls round his fingers. "Me ma would like that."

Gunner raised an eyebrow. "We don't keep any of the goods. Remember?"

The Boy's face fell, but then he grinned. "Least this time, I get a share of the money. Now that I'm proper Scoobie crew."

"Aye."

They continued in silence until they met in the middle. Gunner grinned. "Ready?"

"Ready."

Half an hour later, the two men were both back on board, the auto-haulers having made light work of lifting both them and their bagged cargo away. They'd re-locked the vault doors, and once The Boy had stroked the dog goodbye with a plaintive, "but why can't we take him with us?" they'd lifted out and even replaced the glass pane to hide any obvious sign of infiltration.

Now, with dawn breaking, they drifted at low altitude over the west of Englandium, heading towards The Borderlands. They sat round a table, each with a glass of port, The Boy with a glass of orange.

"We'll get to our safe house in just over an hour, at my estimation," said Reynard. "Which gives us time to get some shuteye when we get there and sort out the haul at leisure once we're rested."

The rest of the crew nodded, agreeing with his proposal. He was rarely wrong, and his team trusted his word and his judgement.

"Good work tonight, men," Reynard continued. "If this is as big as we think, we can have a couple of months down time before we even need to even think of the next job."

"Here's to The Scoobie and her crew," said Gunner, raising his glass as the contents sloshed inside his glass.

"To The Scoobie," they all repeated.

"And may she always keep us saf—"

A violent rocking sent everyone to the floor, then to one wall and the other. The air filled with sounds of everything that wasn't locked down, falling and shifting.

Gunner lost his glass. "What the absolute Hell?"

"What the blazes?" shouted Reynard, reaching for a nearby grab handle in an attempt to stand. "Gunner, you go aft, I'll go for'ard."

"On it, Captain!" shouted Gunner, crawling on his

knees as he unhooked a pistol.

The ship thrashed from side to side and a roaring cacophony froze them all in fear. The sound was unlike anything made by man.

"Is that… is that, a…?" The Boy started.

"Spit it out," whispered Greaser. "I've never heard anything like that in my life."

"Dragon!" shouted The Boy, curling into a tight ball. "It's a dragon!"

"Don't be ridiculous," said Gunner, matter of fact. "We've not got any reason for a dragon to come close, let alone attack."

"He may be right, old boy," said Reynard, his knuckles whitening with the effort to stay on his feet. "I mean, what did you pick up at the Midlandia?"

"Aw, shucks. Must've grabbed too much gold in there."

They held on as the ship tilted and rocked from side to side. Reynard made it to the cockpit but came back, gripping to the sides with a tight grimace. "Steering is gone, I'm afraid. We're just going to have to wait this out. I do hope it's not a sea dragon."

The Boy whimpered. "You mean we'll drown?"

"Hopefully not, my dear fellow. We have some buoyancy devices somewhere, I'm sure."

They all wedged themselves in tighter and sat in glum silence. Gunner had grabbed the bottle of port as it rolled past, and The Boy munched solemnly on a hunk of yesterday's bread.

Greaser tossed his spanner from hand to hand. "What if we throw out all the gold?" he asked, hope rising in his voice as it broke across the quiet in the cabin. "I mean it, the dragon, will leave us alone then, won't it?"

"Ship's steering's broke though," muttered The Boy. "We need it to put us down else we might as well be dragon meat."

"Oh."

Minutes later, they felt like they were falling and, as a man, scrambled again for purchase against anything that would hold.

"Brace for impact," said Reynard in a chipper tone, belying the shake of his hands. "Then we can sort out this ruddy mess."

The almighty crash winded everyone, leaving them gasping for breath. The wall of the ship caved and buckled and the screech of metal on a rough, solid surface forced them to clap their hands over their ears. It continued, pinging them from side to side, slowing gradually to a halt.

"Well, we're on land, I guess," shouted Gunner above the din to no particular person.

With a great shudder, The Scoobie came to a grinding halt.

Reynard sprang to his feet despite the chaos. "Lighting, we need lighting. Find the lamps," he shouted. Greaser and Gunner split in different directions and The Boy sat up, looking round in confusion.

"Did we die?" he asked, deliriously. "There's a light over there. A light. Is it a tunnel?"

"Shut up, you idiot!" hissed Gunner. "It's the Captain coming back. You don't want him to think you've gone soft in the head."

"Right, crew. Let's see what state we're in." Reynard pulled the lever for the external hatch and the pistons sighed. Nothing appeared to move, so he booted the door with a strong smack from his right foot. It crumpled to the ground, a couple of feet below them, illuminated in light from a distant source.

Securing a rope to the inside of The Scoobie, Reynard jumped down, swinging his lantern from side to side. It was dim and dark, the air full of dust, but the light illuminated a large cavern.

"Are we in the belly of the beast?" whispered Greaser, peering from the hatchway and ducking back in again.

"I don't think so, old chap. I believe that's daylight up ahead," proclaimed Reynard, striding towards the light. "We're not in it, we're ahead of it. We struck lucky."

Gunner jumped down and followed, pistols ready to fire. The Boy shrugged and trailed after Greaser to check out the engine damage.

Outside, Reynard and Gunner stood at the mouth of the cavern. The dark edges ramped down into a pit and, above them, widened out. Various ledges cut into the substrate formed a continuous, spiral ramp down. It was piled with coal at various points and over the far lip, a tall chimney belched thick, grey smoke.

"Well, Gunner, my old boy, I do think we could've done far worse. It's just a coal pit. We can escape this."

"Depends on the ship's damage," muttered Gunner, his eyes darting all over the place. "And not forgetting we have a gold-hoarding beast to despatch."

"Now, now. Less of that. If we can persuade the beast to let us go by leaving a pile of gold, we can take enough coal to make it up and then some. Look at this place!" Reynard gestured wildly with his arm. "It's all fuel. Think how much money we could save."

Gunner grunted his acquiescence. "Yeah, okay. But where is the creature?"

Gunner and the Captain headed back to The Scoobie, peering into every crack and crevice for sign of the dragon that had dragged them there. Nothing roared, flamed, beat its wings or otherwise gave an indication of existence.

"We'll mend the ship and sort a plan," said Reynard. "Better to keep busy and all that."

Back on board, they found Greaser, and The Boy hunched over an array of mechanical parts with a welding tool. Both were animated in their movements and didn't notice the intrusion.

"That'll do it!" shouted The Boy, releasing the object they'd been working on. It scuttled out of the cabin and started climbing the walls.

"What on earth have you unleashed there?" asked Reynard. "I'm supposed to be in charge and you're releasing potential havoc on my ship. Not without my permission, for goodness' sakes."

"It's a beetle, or something like. It uses the sounds of the hull to detect where there's a weakness or breakage and repairs the damage. It's like a bigger version of the lock pickers, in theory."

"Ah, very good, I suppose. A bit more conviction would help, though! Gunner and I have checked the exterior and nothing seems too badly amiss. How's the engines?"

Greaser sighed. "The beast managed to pop the balloon hatch but the balloon itself is intact so we can use that and create lift with the heat from the furnace by channelling it through the side vents in front of the wings if we need."

"Even better. We can leave when we're ready then." Reynard grinned and looked at his men. None of them returned the gesture. "What?"

"The dragon."

"Ah."

Gunner spoke up, "I've had an idea." His lip curled. "The darned beast isn't here right now, but no doubt it'll be back, and it'll want our gold. I suggest The Boy uses the autoloaders to fill us up with coal whilst he keeps an eye out for the danged creature. Greaser can keep mending the ship and me and the Captain can pull the gold out, to leave as tribute."

They all nodded, reluctantly.

"Right then," said Reynard, clapping his hands together. "Let's get to work."

Everyone pitched in and soon, Greaser was helping The Boy with the autoloaders, happy The Scoobie was in the best possible condition. They cleared the spiralling path of coal, stashing it anywhere they could on board.

Their final load sorted; Greaser let out a low whistle. "Well, we're not going to need fuel for a while. Saved us a fortune, I guess. Tit for tat. Coal for the lovely things in life."

"Everyone ready?" asked Reynard. "Gunner's just depositing the gold and then we can be off."

"Ready, Captain."

Both Greaser and The Boy took position, ready to light and load the furnace. Greaser pulled a series of levers and twisted valves to direct the heat and air flow.

A vague thump came from the side hatch and Gunner shouted, "ready."

The Scoobie started wheeling out the cavern at low speed as Reynard pressed a sequence of foot pedals. With the jets and rudder in position, he steered a course, clearing them of the darkness.

The early morning was bright, with a clear sky and the sun already warming the air. Greaser was the only one who didn't blink, his googles already protecting his eyes from the orange burn of the furnace.

"Ready, Greaser?" asked Reynard through the speaking tubes.

"About two minutes, Captain. The balloon's expanding now."

The Scoobie filled with the familiar banging and cranking of the balloon's inflation mechanism and Greaser switched the direction of the heat upwards whilst The Boy turned dials. With the final pull of a lever, the balloon shot up from the ship's top surface, filling with heat.

"Why are we not lifting?" hollered Reynard, as The Scoobie teetered precariously on the slope.

"We're heavy captain. We need the balloon to be at max fill and we're doing everything we can."

"I'm putting down the landing springs," said Reynard. "Give us some extra bounce."

"What? You're crazy!" Greaser shook his head and continued shovelling coal into the furnace chute.

The Scoobie bounced awkwardly, and they all felt the rocking sensation as the balloon and springs found a resonance until… they lifted. And bounced. Again and again until the ground was below them.

"Woop!" shouted Gunner, from his position at the open hatch. "And we're away—Ah shucks. Reynard! Eyes on the port side, level with the horizon."

In the cockpit, Reynard swizzled the periscope to come face to face with their nemesis. The dragon had returned.

It hovered in the space between The Scoobie and the cavern and with wings outstretched, it dwarfed the ship, casting it into shadow with just one wing. The dragon barely moved as it kept pace, scales glistening, intelligent eyes assessing them.

Reynard gulped.

"Why's it not in the cave?" whispered Greaser through the tubes. "We left the gold in the cave, didn't we?"

His voice rose as he approached midships, where Gunner stood at the hatch. "Didn't we?"

"Mostly," grinned Gunner. He'd roped himself to the ship and was dangling out the hatch door, keeping a close eye on the dragon. "It's a magnificent beast, I'll give it that."

"What the hell?"

Gunner reached into a sack and pulled out a few small coins. "Watch this!"

They all watched the coins fall. Gunner, Greaser and The Boy crowded round the hatch as Reynard leapt from the cabin.

The dragon's head snapped downwards, watching the coins as they landed. But it remained next to The Scoobie.

"Okay," said Gunner, in a slightly less confident tone. He pulled out a bigger handful and tossed it out wide.

The dragon watched too, then flew inwards to look Gunner directly in the eye.

"I think it wants more," whispered The Boy, voice quaking. "Please, give it what it wants."

Gunner grabbed a larger handful, coins spilling over his fingers, and dropped it downwards. Then, took the sack and tipped it, angling his chin defiantly at the dragon.

The dragon swooped and roared, and the last The Scoobie's crew saw of it, before heading for a good sleep, was it gathering up its new treasure.

"Gosh, that was too much excitement for the day, wasn't it chaps?" Reynard said through the tubes. "Stiff drink, anyone?"

ADVENTURE AWAITS

RAY GUNN AND THE MARTIAN REVOLUTION

DAVID BOWMORE

Cornelia, Queen of Earth, emerged from HMSS Thatcher on a palanquin born by service-bots at each corner. The distant light of Sol cast a long, distorted shadow as they carried her to the city dome. Shimmering light panels protected the regal entity from any unwanted attention.

An honour guard lined the route as the royal procession approached the city-dome. The President of New Sydney and several dignitaries bowed in unison as the service-bots lowered the litter to the ground, allowing Cornelia to walk forward.

"Welcome to Mars, Your Majesty," the President said. As with most Mars born humans, he stood more than six feet tall.

"President Magnuson."

"Ma'am. May I take this opportunity to say that

honour us by choosing to stay here in New Sydney for this most auspicious of occasions. Our facilities may not be all that you are used to, but what we lack in luxury, we make up for in hospitality."

"Show me to my rooms."

"Of course, Ma'am." Magnuson fell into step beside the Queen, guiding her towards a track-car, the door of which was already open, but he steadied it, nonetheless. She said nothing as she took her place in the back seat. Magnuson joined her on the seat, facing. During the twenty-minute journey, he kept up a running commentary on points of interest in which he thought Her Majesty might be interested.

The Queen let him talk without response.

The upper levels of the dome housed suites of the highest grandeur. However, they were few, and therefore a certain amount of reorganising had taken place, including the President moving out of his living quarters for the royal visit.

"A banquet is to be held in your honour this evening, Ma'am."

"I am aware of the itinerary, Magnuson."

Magnuson activated the door, and the Queen passed through with little acknowledgement. He returned to the track-car with a feeling of dread firmly installed in his gut.

The banquet saw more than three hundred leaders, diplomats, and scientists of Mars gathered along with their spouses, significant others and offspring, seated at dozens of circular tables. Queen Cornelia occupied the centre of the top table with President Magnuson on her right. Floating vid-drones recorded the entire event.

After the meal, during which the Queen put up with more of the president's fawning ramblings, she stood to address the gathered dignitaries.

"It is with great hope that I see the advances you have accomplished here on Mars," she began. "It is an astounding achievement when one considers how little the original settlers had. Indeed, the planet has much to offer humankind as we step farther into the galaxy. You and your forebears should be very proud."

She waited for a minute as a gentle murmuring of approval trickled around the room.

"However," she said with a harder edge, "if humanity is to truly conquer the vastness of space, then we must do so in unity. Under my guidance, we shall rise as an empire. It is with this intent that from this day onwards Mars will no longer be an independent planet with its own political structure, but a key player in the new Human Empire. In less than a year, we will have new outposts on the moons of Saturn. In ten years we will be an interstellar race."

"I'm sorry, Your Majesty, but are you revoking our independence?" Magnuson asked.

Cornelia turned a cold blue eye on the president. Her people did not, as a rule, interrupt. "Indeed I am."

The Mayor of New London stood, "This is outrageous. We've been independent of Earth for more than two hundred "

"And you have not built any defences to guard against an invading force."

"You… you… you can't come to our planet and make these demands—"

"Shoot him," she said.

One of her guards, an eight-foot-tall bronze warrior-bot, raised its arm to release a beam of red light that caught the mayor in the centre of his chest. He grew bright orange before popping; blood, skin, and body parts landed on the people nearest him. Several people fainted. The mayor's wife voiced a scream that came from the depths of her soul as she looked at the finger that landed in her drink. Her husband's blood dripped from her face.

Queen Cornelia looked to one of her aides and said, "Now."

A second later, the glass of the dome roof shattered, showering the shocked diners in sharp and deadly shards. Troops swooped in, expertly bringing themselves to the floor with ion-powered jet packs.

Casting her gaze over the other important guests, the Queen asked, "Does anyone else wish to object?"

An ashen President Magnuson shook his head.

"Good," she said, before ordering half of the people present killed.

Raymond Gunn waited in a backroom with other non-essential personnel. He picked at the cold food on the bamboo plate. He certainly would prefer one of

Nelly's special Shiner's Diner steak burgers. Everyone knew Nelly served food in beta section.

But tonight, Ray's task was to pilot the leader of New Dallas, her family and important staff, to and from the banquet. Not one of them recognised him. Why should they? He was just the pilot. But he remembered better times when he'd been a boy and his father had held a seat on the senior council of New Dallas. Back then, he'd been schooled in a small class for the elite's children, as had Rachel, daughter of the New Dallas' leader. Even after fifteen years, she still had the biggest eyes Ray ever remembered seeing. She was polite enough, but their respective stations in life now put her far above that of a lowly solar glider pilot like Ray.

He wondered if she ever remembered their childhood games on the playground, or the promises of marriage when they grew up. He pushed these thoughts of romantic involvement firmly from his mind. There was no point in torturing himself over the what-might-have-beens of life.

His six and a half feet frame jumped from the lounger at the first blaster shot. Others around him starred at each other in bewilderment. The piercing sound of shattering glass quickly drowned out the screaming. The distinct sound of plasma shots added to the panic. He dashed for the door with two other pilots, Williamson and Stodardt, his pistol already drawn, hearing panic coming from the banquet room further along the corridor. Some dignitaries, bloodied and injured, were stumbling their way towards them. The commotion was dying down as he and the other pilots arrived at the banquet hall. Smoke from overheated blasters rose from the ends of barrels brandished by warbots and human troops alike. Gore covered every available surface. Some guests wandered around in a daze or hid under tables. A vid-drone floated before the Queen, with a pale-faced President Magnuson by her side. Half a dozen jet pack wearing troops stood in a semi-circle, guarding their queen.

Using an upturned table as a shield, Ray dropped to his knees. More pilots rushed into the room, some heading straight for Queen Cornelia, but Ray focused on scanning the room for Rachel or her family. A plasma bolt zipped passed him, turning Williamson inside out and splattering Ray and Stodardt with his remains.

Ray saw Rachell being corralled with dozens of other stunned survivors by jet pack wearing troopers and bronze warbots.

The Queen said, "I think they realise who's in charge now. Don't they, Magnuson?"

The President nodded his head and said, "We submit." Looking at the floating vid-drone, he said, "There will be no resistance."

"Good," Queen Cornelia said. "People of Mars. I intend to make the human race great again. Follow me and we will all prosper, but I warn you, rebellion will be met with brutal retaliation."

Dismissing the vid-drone with a wave of her hand, she said, "Those of you who came rushing in under the presumption that something was amiss, throw down your weapons. You will not be harmed."

Ray looked at Stodardt, who shrugged his shoulders. Ray's gun clattered as it slid along the floor. They both stood with their hands held aloft.

Two pairs of jet packs rushed to restrain them.

"You will both be tried and executed in due course," the Queen said.

"What? But you said—"

A punch from the jet pack silenced Stodardt. They were thrown to the ground in front of the other prisoners. Rachel helped Ray to his feet. He looked into her big eyes and smiled a weak smile. The colour had gone from her face and she looked about ready to pass out. Stodart tried to stem the flow of blood from his broken nose.

"Thank the Gods, Rachel. For a moment, I thought you might have—"

"You know me?"

"Sure. I'm your pilot for the evening, Ray Gunn. It's my job to look after you."

"Of course. I'm sorry I didn't recognise you."

"Where are your parents?"

"Dead... I... think."

The tears she had been trying to hold back spilled over the rims of her eyes. He held her by the shoulders and looked into those big watery orbs.

"I don't know how, but I will think of a way to get you out of this."

She shook her head and pointed at the gore surrounding them. There was nothing else he could say, so instead, he drew her into his arms. She wept onto his shoulder.

Before long, the survivors of the massacre were being roughly marched into the corridor. Destination, the city jails on the ground level. The corridors they traipsed along were narrow, forcing the guards to thin out in order to cover all the prisoners.

Ray, realising he could do little to help the girl from a cell, and even less from a grave, came to a decision. He whispered in Rachel's ear, "I going to make a break for it. Coming?"

She looked at him with bewildered eyes and said, "What?"

He told her again.

"Are you mad? You'll never make it." She shook her head in disbelief.

"I'm dead if I stay. I have to try."

"I don't think I can."

"I'll come back for you. Promise."

He tore his eyes away from hers and broke into a sprint as they were passing a junction to another corridor.

Blasts scorched the walls as he slid around a corner. He picked himself off the floor and once again was running at full speed, took a quick left, a right and then another. The upper levels proved easy to navigate, being—as usual—always fairly deserted. But he imagined the lower levels would be in chaos after seeing the devastation of the banqueting hall. No doubt, a whole battalion of jet pack troopers and killer robots would be enforcing control, subduing Dome Security and destroying passers-by. But they wouldn't know the dark areas of a city like New Sydney. Once his mother had moved to the dome to escape the shame of his father's disgrace, Ray had easily found friends in low places.

He could hear the heavy tramp of booted footsteps behind him. He skidded to a halt by a service elevator. Used his genetic pass to gain admittance and was whooshing to the ground floor in seconds. He halted the descent a minute later and got out. A service door led to an emergency stairwell. Back up a few floors. Now he would have time to think.

He wasn't far from level thirty-five, which connected with beta dome via an enclosed walkway. Once in the smaller dome, he made his way to ground level. Nelly lived above Shiner's Diner. Shiner, her husband, had died ten years earlier, but she found no reason to change the name.

Sticking to the shadows, he eventually found himself looking into her security eye.

"Let me in, Nelly."

The door slid open, he slipped in. It closed with a swoosh.

Seeing the drying blood on his clothes and face, she said, "Gods, Ray!"

"You've seen the news."

"Yes. You didn't really attack her, did you?"

"What do you mean?"

"It's all over the news channel. You and the others attacked the queen after she made her announcement."

"No, no, no. That's not what happened at all. We arrived after we heard ion blasters. And it's not a rematch I relish the thought of. I need to get out of this uniform and into civilian clothes. Do you have any of Shiner's?"

"I dunno, Ray. He was a big fella and look at you."

"Better than the other way around."

Nelly smiled. She must have been nearly seventy years old, but today she looked a picture of vitality, even with her old school spectacles perched in her nestlike hair.

"You'd better refresh too." She pointed to the washroom.

Once the door had closed, he deposited his uniform in the recycler before stepping into the refresher. Three minutes later, he wandered into the bedroom, naked as a baby.

"Sorry, Nelly. I dumped the uniform," he said as she averted her eyes.

"I've laid out some of Shiner's day clothes. They're not very fashionable, I'm afraid."

She left him to dress and a few minutes later, Ray emerged from the bedroom looking like a new man, albeit in loose-fitting clothes.

"I've been thinking," she said. "If you wait here for an hour until it's a little quieter, we'll go down to the diner. Then I'll take you through to the back of the kitchen where there's an access hatch to the service tunnels?"

"Are you sure?"

"And more than that, there's a little town I know from way back called Dustville. Real friendly folks."

"How will I find it?"

"Easy, cowboy. I'm coming with you."

"No, no, no."

"If you expect to keep the clothes of my dead husband, then you ain't gotta a choice."

"What about the Diner?"

"Way things are looking; they'll take it from me anyway."

He looked at the viewer for a minute. The apartment

was bereft of windows, but the viewer displayed a live feed as seen from the top of the dome. Not only was it a beautifully clear night, but he could also see the Queen's navy hanging in the air. Shuttles moved between larger ships like insects buzzing around wild camels.

"You're probably right. I don't think it will be very safe living in the dome from now on. She's quite mad."

"Damn right I'm right. Now sit down and eat some stew."

With a Shiner's Diner cap pulled low over his eyes, Ray walked into the eatery behind Nelly. Troops from the junta were already making themselves at home. They boisterously claimed the entertainment centre, demanding drinks and food from a service bot that scooted between the kitchen and the troopers, desperate to keep up with their demands.

Ray sat as far from them as possible.

"Coffee?" she said.

Ray nodded. Gods knew if he would ever taste the best brew in New Sydney again.

The news screen in the corner flashed his image with the word WANTED stamped across it.

"Dangerous fugitive and leader of the rebellion, Raymond Gunn is wanted for the attempted assassination of Her Majesty, Queen Cornelia," the reporter said.

"We have to go, Nelly." He wiped sweat from his neck with a bamboo napkin.

"Slow and steady, Raymondo. We've only just got

here. Relax for ten minutes."

It was the longest ten minutes of Ray's life. Eventually, Nelly said, "Come into the kitchen." She led him to a storage area and, using a magdriver, retrieved from a drawer of odds and sods, loosened the lower screws of a ventilation grille, creating a flap they could squeeze into. Then, using the magdriver again, she re-secured the grille. A hundred yards along the ventilator, they came across a downward shaft. Nelly's torch, also retrieved from the same drawer of assortments, showed them it was not too deep; Ray judged it to be about fifteen feet. At full stretch, he would have a few of feet to drop. Then he reached up to help Nelly down.

"Which way?" he asked.

"Follow me."

Ancient red lights that automatically switched on as they approached prevented them from walking in complete darkness.

Now they were free to talk.

"If the reports of how she controls Earth are true, then things don't look good for Mars," Nelly said.

"You can see it in her eyes—madness, total madness.

"Mad as a marshfly on heat, we used to say when I was a girl."

He smiled. "I didn't know you were from one of the settlements. Tell me about Dustville."

"It's the town where I was born. I left when I was seventeen. I wanted the big city life, but there was nothing wrong with my hometown. It was just quiet. Real friendly folk, much friendlier than people of the dome when I first arrived."

"I hope they're still friendly."

"So do I, but we'll tread carefully at first, just in case." She raised an eyebrow.

They had to slow their pace as the old woman grew tired.

The tunnel was long and lined with tubing and wires and fans that barely moved the stale air. Doors led to gods knew where and sometimes they walked under ventilation ducts similar to the one they had entered the tunnel by. Other corridors criss-crossed, but they stuck to their original bearing, heading in a straight line to wherever it might take them.

After several hours of walking, the service tunnel narrowed before ending in a flat wall. The only point of interest was the large puddle of water they stood in.

"Great. What a waste of time?"

"Upwards and onwards, Raymondo," Nelly said.

He followed her gaze up a long pipe that an old, rusty ladder ascended. They began the climb. He followed as she huffed and puffed her way up to the small speck of daylight.

The grate that covered the shaft entrance made enough noise to wake the first settlers as it hinged open, but soon they both lay panting on the pale grass. Then she started to laugh, and he joined her, holding her hand as tears of fear and joy streamed down their faces.

Several miles behind them, the dome of New Sydney glinted in the early morning light.

Ray had often seen many of the dots that made up the Martian villages from his solar glider, but this was the first time he had seen one up close. The dwellings, originally carved out of the Martian stone by plasma cannons, looked haphazard and uncomfortably.

Mars had only been capable of supporting life for about a hundred years. Many people had fled the cities and their control the instant it became known that the air was breathable and that the ground was fertile enough to grow crops. However, it was a less ordered life. Rumours were rife with the way people lived; tribal elders led the towns, small battles took place for territory, women gave birth to mutated babies.

Ray and Nelly walked under a wooden signpost with a swinging board - Dustville.

A camel and a genetically enhanced long-haired horse tied to a hitchin' post outside the saloon, raised their heads towards the strangers. A dusty service bot sat in a rocking chair; its electronic eyes swivelled as it watched them pass through the swinging saloon doors.

The bar tender poured liquor from a bottle into three small glasses for the men at the bar. An antique jukebox rattled away in the corner. Ray didn't know where Luckenback, Texas, was, but it sounded a far better place than Mars right now.

"What can I get ya?"

"Do you take city-creds?" Nelly asked.

"City boys are ya?" He answered his own question. "Sure ya are. No one wears silks like that out here in the dust. What ya running from, girls? The law?"

"It was a simple question deserving of a simple an-

108

swer," Nelly said.

"Jus' tryin' be friendly, ma'am. Your city-creds be good here, though like most other dusters, we prefer, silver, gold or good old-fashioned barter."

"Then we'll take two of those," she said, indicating the bottle still in his hands, "and a room for the night if you have one."

The barman gave them a shifty look. "You two a thing, then?"

Ray couldn't help noticing the hand that poured the drinks made a mechanical grinding sound that made his teeth itch. The drink slipped into the glasses, and then quickly disappeared as the two fugitives downed the burning liquor.

"It's been a long day, chief," Nelly said, "and we need a square meal and a bed to rest on, that's all. I don't mean to cause offence. And we'll have more of that good stuff. I haven't had rye that good in fifty years."

The dusty service bot sauntered in and leaned one elbow on the bar. An old, jagged dent along above his right ear revealed itself as he took his hat off.

"Trouble, Billy?" it asked in metallic tones.

"No, Sheriff," Billy replied. "We're just getting to know each other. You know how it is."

"Don't forget the register, Billy," the sheriff said, before once again returning to his seat on the boardwalk.

"Yeah, I need your names for the register if you're stayin'," Billy said with an apologetic smile.

He slid the book over and passed them an old fountain pen.

"Print and sign here please."

Billy looked at the names and let out a thin whistle between his teeth.

"I thought so. You're Nelly Ranger as was. Always was a short tempered, so an' so, weren't ya?"

"And I remember my dad giving you a hiding once or twice, too. Still managing to stay just the right side of the law?"

He smiled and shrugged his shoulders.

"We'll catch up later, Billy," Nelly said, making for the stairs and their room.

Nelly lay on the bed, fully clothed, her eyes closed. The room was better than Ray had thought it would be. A window let natural light in but kept the cool of the night out. A phosphorus glow emanating from one wall, filled the room with an eerie light well into the evening. A small box by the bed played more old Earth music. In many ways, this simple room was better than those of the domers, as Billy called the inhabitants of the big cities. It had fresh, non-recycled air for a start.

Ray sat on a comfortable sofa.

"What are you gonna do about rescuing that girl?" Nelly said, her eyes still closed. "You did promise her, didn't you, or did I hear that bit wrong? You got out quick and I can't blame you, but that girl was alive last time you saw her, and she'll be scared. Are you going to leave her and all the others to that madwoman's mercy, or are you going to do something about it?"

"I know I have to do something, but I'm not sure

how. I think we should go back down and let your friend know what's happened. They might have some ideas."

"I'll be down in a bit."

Back in the bar, Ray ordered a long drink going by the unappetising name of swump.

"Good, ain't it?" Billy said.

Ray nodded his head and wiped froth from his upper lip. Then, seeing the glint of metal on the boardwalk, he asked, "How come a service bot is your sheriff?"

"Made sense a few years ago. And after a little re-programming, we got a bot what does what's right for the people o' the town. He don't take no camel shit off o' no one. And you should see how fast he can shoot."

"But service bots aren't programmed for that sort of work. There not military," Ray said.

"There's always a work around. The sheriff shoots low velocity ions that don't kill or even break the skin's surface. But you have a hell of a headache when you wake up, believe me. I been in the receiving end of it once or twice in my younger days."

The bar being empty Billy came around to sit next to Ray.

"So, mind telling us dusters what all the fancy flying ships is for? We don't get ta hear much out here."

"The Queen of Earth is paying a royal visit," Ray said, wiping foam from his lips with the back of his hand.

"Whoopee-do. And how much is that costing?"

"The whole planet. She's revoked independence and slaughtered just about all the most important people in the three cities."

"Never." Billy whistled between his teeth.

"And if you ask me, it won't be long before she comes after all the outlying towns and settlements."

"Can she do that?"

"She can do what she wants. She has a whole space fleet to call on, with backup from Earth whenever she wants it, and we have nothing."

Billy downed his slump and then called out to the sheriff.

The sheriff came in slowly, his finger raised, ready to shoot hot ion.

"Don't be like that, Sheriff. There ain't no trouble here. But I want you to listen to what the boy, here, has to say."

"What you think 'bout that, Sheriff? Is it right?" Billy asked after Ray finished telling the story.

"It is true. She has no legal right. Therefore, this is an act of war. I can assure that I will, as my protocol programmes demand, defend the people of Dustville."

"Hey, do you need a deputy? I'd stand with you and I can do more damage than you. I got no qualms about sending Earthlings back to the mother world in pieces. And I bet Teddy Masons at the hard&software store will make a stand too."

"You're both crazy."

"I am following pre-programmed protocols."

"Whatever. But—"

"No buts," Billy said. "This is our planet. It's time dusters and domers stood shoulder to shoulder. Do you think we should have a town meeting, Sheriff?"

"Yes. I will find the mayor and spread the word. We will meet here in one hour."

112

"You'll be at the meeting, won't ya', Ray. Tell 'em how bad things is?"

"Sure, I'll tell them," Ray said.

Ray walked back to the room he shared with Nelly to inform her about the meeting. She sat by the window, with her eyes closed, letting the wind cool her.

"I thought you were coming down."

"I've been remembering. I was once a sergeant for Dome Security. My dad inspired me. He was the Sheriff here in Dustville when I was a girl. He would do something about all this because it's simply wrong. We all know it's wrong, so we have to fight back. And for you, that means saving that girl of yours. I'd come with you, but I'm just too old. I'll only slow you up."

"Come downstairs. The new sheriff is calling an emergency town meeting, and he'd like us to be there."

"Sounds like his head is screwed on right."

After hearing Ray's story about the massacre, the residents of Dustville prepared themselves. By contrast, the Queen's troops were complacent, content in their superior firepower.

Two solar powered all-terrain trucks rolled into Dustville, kicking up dirt and dust in their slow wake. Two bronze warbots and four humans rode on each of the vehicles. Two of the human troops wore jet packs.

The sheriff's rusty knee joints creaked as he stood

up from his usual position outside the saloon and meandered into their path.

"All newcomers must sign the register," he said.

This brought a mirthless chuckle to the human troops, and one called out, "Move aside, tin man, before we roll right over you."

From his vantage point in the room he shared with Nelly, Ray saw the sheriff raise his finger and point. The human troops looked at each other. The driver of one of the track carts advanced the vehicle, intent on mowing down the loan challenger.

The end of the sheriff's finger flipped up and he let pale blue beams of light streak across the short distance. In seconds, he'd taken out the entire human complement of one truck. At the same time, Billy stepped out of the jailhouse with an ancient plasma cannon on his shoulder. Half a second later, the other truck turned into a ball of molten metal and screaming death. One of the warrior robots raised its weapon, but the sheriff had no protocols to restrict the level of harm he could administer to non-humans and a red beam from his other hand severed the head from the body.

Ray and Nelly helped the townsfolk bury the dead Earthmen. Stripped of their uniforms and weapons, the four surviving troopers were deposited in the cells of the jailhouse to await trial. Ray had no desire to see them dancing at the end of a rope.

Everyone knew that more troops would come—and in greater numbers—once the invaders realised that the patrol was missing. For this reason, the people of Dustville were already making plans to move out. Billy and the sheriff were keen to keep Mars an Earthling free zone. Teddy Masons and his son were attempting to reprogram one of the military robots. Nelly joined the townsfolk, actively encouraging them to resist. For her, it was the right thing to do. It was what her father would have done.

The beginnings of a rebellion.

Although tempted to join them, Ray had something to do first. He had a promise to keep that would mean sneaking back into New Sydney the way he'd left it. With the sheriff's permission, he stepped into a trooper's uniform, strapped on a sidearm, slipped the shining helmet on his head, and buckled a jet pack to his back. Billy's bionic hand gave a firm but creaky hold as he said goodbye.

"Are you with us, Ray?"

"Of course, as soon as I free Rachel, I'll find you."

"Thank you, Ray. We are with you too," the sheriff said.

"Dome Security was always lax, always lazy," Nelly said. "That's the weak point."

"You be careful, too."

"I've outlived two husbands. And I don't plan on meeting the maker just yet. You be sure to come to us."

Then she drew him into a tight embrace. He didn't ever want her to let go.

Trying to get to grips with the flight controls, he flew to the ladder that led to the underground tunnels.

❧

Hoping he was well within the city boundaries, Ray stopped at a service door. It opened easily, and he stepped into the backstreets of the city dome and found it as he'd never seen it before. Quiet, dark, empty. A city under curfew.

Avoiding the enemy while trying not to look suspicious, he made his way to the city jails. As trouble was a rare occurrence in New Sydney, the jails were small and not intended for mass occupation. He prayed to all three gods that Rachel, after forty-eight hours, would still be alive.

Two Martian guards, collaborating with the enemy, inspected his singed I.D.

"What happened to this?" the unusually short one asked.

"Trouble in one of the outlying towns. Soon as I got back, I was told to fetch the prisoner, Rachel Firstman."

"You're a bit tall for an Earthling?"

"Are you questioning me?" Ray's right hand resting easily on his ion-blaster.

"No, sir. Just trying to be vigilant like they said we had to be."

"You." He pointed at the taller guard. "Take me to the prisoner."

The cells were dark with no natural light and crammed with 'political' prisoners. Rachel was in a cell with at least a dozen other inmates. And there were dozens of cells.

It had only been two days since the Queen's announcement, but Ray barely recognised Rachel as she sat in the corner hugging her knees. With dried tears on her face, and her expensive cloths torn and ragged, she bore the look of an exile rather than one of the elite. The other occupants of the cell fared no better. And by the stench of the place, they didn't have access to toilet facilities.

The guard called her name. One of the other prisoners kicked her in the back. "Oy, Princess. They want you."

Using the wall for support, she climbed to her feet.

Ray, afraid she might recognise him and give the game away, remained silent. The guard used his shock stick to deter the residents from approaching the metal bars. Each had already received the crippling shock and consequently backed away from the limited but effective weapon.

Rachel's approach was too slow for the jailer.

"Hurry up," he said, grabbing her by the hair and dragging her from the cell.

"I'll take her." Ray guided her by the arm as she left the cell on legs that shook.

The jailer resealed the cell door and walked behind them, jabbing at the occasional outstretched hand with his shock stick.

Rachels's legs finally weakened, forcing Ray to catch her as she fell against the corridor wall. It was then that she looked into the eyes behind the vizor.

"You!"

Ray looked up at the guard whose eyes flared as he realised, he'd been duped. From his crouched position, Ray stood up fast, bringing a clenched fist to the underside of the guard's chin. The cells immediately became a deafening uproar as hundreds of prisoners cheered the quick and effective knockout of their treacherous jailor.

As Ray helped Rachel to her feet, she said "What about the others?"

"We can't save everyone." He wanted out of the hell hole as quickly as possible.

"But they're going to be executed." Then turning to her former cell mates, she said in a loud voice, "It's Ray Gunn. I said he'd come back for us. I told you I knew him."

A chant started to spread along the mass of dirty, stinking humans, "Ray Gunn… Ray Gunn… Ray Gunn."

Ray, thinking he might live to regret the action, took the keycard from the belt of the unconscious guard and handed it to one of the outstretched hands. Stodardt looked back at Ray and they shared a smile. It wouldn't take the prisoners long to free themselves. He hurried Rachel along; they needed to be clear before the riot started.

The last thing he saw as he looked back was of a mob of people surrounding the guard.

The farther from the cells they travelled, the more Rachel seemed to gain strength. He swiftly guided her towards the service door he had used to re-enter the dome. They stepped through straight into the path of a patrol and found themselves staring down the barrels of a dozen ion blasters.

"Where are you going with her?" the troop leader said, stepping forward.

There were far too many of them for Ray to do anything else but surrender.

VOLUME 2

Cornelia, Empress of System Sol rested upon a recliner. On her well-manicured right hand, she wore a golden dragon ring with ruby eyes, which entwined around the three outer fingers.

A service bot stood to her left, holding a tray with a glass of champagne on it. Behind her and slightly to her right stood Magnuson, a fine sheen of moisture glistening on his forehead.

She eyed the two prisoners before her.

"So, you are Ray Gunn. Now that we have you, the rebellion will fall."

"It has nothing to do with me."

"But the uprising is in your name; in the city and the outlying towns," Magnuson said.

In one flowing movement Cornelia stood and backhanded Magnuson across the cheek, drawing blood with the dragon ring.

"That's the last time you speak without permission. Take him away and remove his tongue," she ordered the two guards. Once they had dragged the former president away, the empress was left dangerously exposed, but all Ray's hope of escape ended before they had begun. Warbots were only on the other side of the turbo-door.

Rachel looked up into Ray's eyes. His hand trembled as he took hold of hers.

"Now, we must consider how to dispose of you both?" Cornelia said, turning to lift the glass of champagne from the service bot's tray.

"Publicly, I think." She turned her back on the bot

and the corners of her mouth lifted in a cruel smile. "Yes, we will send a very public and very bloody message that will squash any further thoughts of revolt."

The knee joints of the bot creaked almost imperceptibly as it took a step forward.

The sheriff winked at Ray as his forefinger flipped open.

"Why are you smiling?" Cornelia asked.

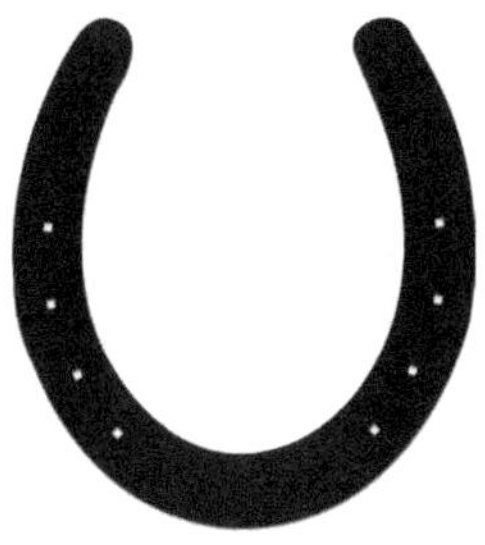

A HEART & A HORSESHOE

S.O. GREEN

Coming to Morocco had been a stupid idea. Redheads didn't belong in Africa. Even SPF 50 wasn't keeping Hel from looking like an overripe tomato three weeks out of four. Granted, that one week left her with a braw tan, which meant it was time to go out on the pull.

Bars in the city were total sausage parties, and Hel had spent the first month wondering where they were keeping all the lassies. She'd been hoping for a wee holiday romance with a girl with dark eyes and silky black hair. Nae joy.

Tonight's oasis of debauchery was a European-run joint, lit mostly in neon, and the beat pulsing out the speakers was still going to be banging in her head when she woke up in the morning, hopefully in someone else's bed. Hel—resplendent in boots, combats and a 'Made in Scotland Fae Girders' t-shirt—ordered whiskey in a pint glass and cruised the floor until she found what she was looking for. Eye contact.

The brunette at the bar had her hair swept over one eye and a quirk on her lips, like she'd seen it all before. Hel wondered if she'd care to subject that notion to scrutiny. She was wearing a blouse, slacks, and neckerchief, like a Girl Scout leader. A memory crawled out of the dark hole of Hel's alcohol-soaked brain and, suddenly, some things started to make a lot of sense.

To be fair, Akela was pretty hot.

"Alright, hen?" she asked, sliding up to the bar. "Do you believe in magic? Because I've got a wand you can play with."

And, obviously, there were all kinds of things wrong with a chat-up line like that, but it was a hell of a conversation starter.

"Needs work," the lassie said, but she didn't stop smiling.

"You'd be surprised."

"Really? You think so?"

It was probably wrong to be into someone who seemed so thoroughly unimpressed, but Hel couldn't help herself.

"Hel," she said, with a bow.

"Short for Helen?"

"Short for Fucking Hell."

Whatever *it* was short for, this lady certainly wasn't. She rose off her bar stool, and Hel's eyes followed her up and up and up. Had to be almost six feet. Well worth the climb too, probably.

"Michelle," she said. "So, what do you do around

here, exactly? Other than lean on *terrible* pickup lines?"

Hel shrugged. "Security."

It was a fancy way of saying 'I knock folk on their arses for money'. She'd been part of a firm, but the rest had gone and fucked off to Algeria, where folks needed more security.

Pish, because she was banned from Algeria.

"Do you work for a company or do you take free-lance contracts?"

"Why? What part of you needs securing?"

Her new friend laughed. "You're a strange woman."

"I get stranger when I've got a drink in me," she said, and drained her pint glass.

"Maybe we should get a drink in you then. And see what happens."

"Fuck aye, hen. Let's make an evening of it."

She flagged down a bartender. Short she might have been, but she was not easy to ignore. Red hair was rare enough around here, but most of the women weren't built like brick shithouses. She could carry a keg on each shoulder in case she fancied a proper drink.

She ordered them a bottle each and paid, because chivalry. She was ready to find them a table when she realised some arsehole was horning in on her racket.

Arsehole du jour wore a black leather jacket over dusty desert camo, like he'd just wandered in out of the dunes. His hair was trending grey, and he hadn't shaved in a few days. Rugged, if you liked that kind of thing.

Honestly, Hel didn't.

She was close enough to hear the conversation over the bass, but not so close he'd put them together. She kept it that way, for now.

"Michelle Scot. My name's Douglas Finster. My employer would like to have a few words with you."

"Really? And who's your employer?"

"I have a car waiting outside. You can discuss it with him."

Michelle laughed like she wasn't subtly being coerced. "I'm afraid I'll need more than that."

"He thought you might say that. Which is why he authorised me to tell you that the silver cask didn't contain what he thought it would."

"Oh? So, what did it contain?"

Finster reached into his jacket and pulled out a plastic bag like he was starring in CSI: Sahara. There was a shrivelled ball of human muscle tissue inside, mummified with age. He dumped it on the bar and the nearest revellers shirked away with cries of disgust that barely registered over the *thump-thump-thump* vibrating in the Day-Glo air all around them.

"You should probably put that back where you found it," Michelle said, entirely unmoved. "It belongs in a museum."

"My employer also authorised me to bring you to meet with him by any means necessary. Do you understand what that means?"

"I think I can make a good guess."

Even so, she didn't move to accompany him. He grabbed her around the elbow. She just glared at him.

And, while Hel hadn't been quite so turned on in a while, the third wheel was a mood killer.

"Hands off the lady, pal," she said, shouldering between them, which was pretty easy when you had that much shoulder. "Didn't your mother teach you how to treat a lassie?"

He reached back into his jacket, and she didn't think he was going for another heart. She caught his wrist, trapped it against his chest, then smashed him in the face with the bottle still in her other hand.

Contrary to what popular culture will tell us, alcohol bottles don't break on impact with a human skull. Instead, Finster's face was the part that broke.

He slammed backwards into a table, the occupants of which scattered like sand in the wind. He collapsed in a bloody heap, upsetting beer bottles.

Everyone else started to back away, except for the two girls and one guy wearing jackets over their desert camo, who all came at her in unison.

"Fuck, he's got friends. Didn't see that coming."

She torpedoed her bottle at the nearest. He tried to dodge and took it in the shoulder with a grunt. She grabbed a glass off the bar and hurled whatever was in it at the blonde lassie, who covered her face and didn't notice Hel's foot until it sent her hurtling backwards into her pal.

Then the bald woman punched her in the jaw, and she went slamming into the bar. You knew it was going to be a good night when you could taste blood.

"Check it out," she jeered. "This one's got balls."

"That makes one of us, hen," Hel said, and kicked her between the legs.

No matter your biological makeup, the toe of a steel-capped boot still hurts.

Hel turned back to Michelle and wiped the blood off her mouth. "Your place or mine, love?"

"We might need to take a rain check," the other woman said, nodding to the three men blocking the back door.

"Any ideas?"

"Upstairs."

She leapt the bar. Hel followed, pausing just long enough to snatch up her other bottle. For a single moment, she saw how the other half lived. Honestly, she didn't know how they resisted the temptation with it all *sitting* there.

"I'll come back for you," she told the bottles, and chased Michelle through a door and up a flight of narrow stairs that smelled of smoke and rosewater.

They ran through a private suite that wasn't in use, but which featured a TV bigger than Hel's apartment and a stripper pole, then into a back office. Michelle threw the window open and looked out over the nightlife pulsing away. Ignorant and uncaring of the turn Hel's night had just taken.

Hel looked down and saw the canopy below and the hard-packed sand beyond.

"Pretty sure I watched an episode of Mythbusters that said we'll die if we try to land on that," she grunted.

"I'm going to climb down, Helen. Who just *jumps* out of a window?"

"Don't knock it till you've tried it, Mitch."

Michelle shook her head, still smiling, and folded herself through the window, putting those long, long limbs to good use. And while Hel could think of better uses, there was a time and place for everything.

She looked down again. "Fuck sake…"

She dragged her arse over the window ledge. Only for more of Finster's friends—for such a miserable bastard, he had an awful lot—to burst into the room. The beardy giant in front cleared the distance in two strides, floor trembling under him, and grabbed her by a fistful of hair.

Her bottle cracked his clavicle, and his grip loosened enough for her to flatten his nose with her forehead. That kiss was straight outta Glasgow.

The guy behind him drew his pistol. She let go of the window ledge, bounced off the canopy at an angle and cartwheeled into a dumpster that just happened to have a mattress in it.

"That was fortunate," Michelle said, as Hel scrambled out.

"Not really," she grunted. "Folk don't throw out mattresses for no reason."

Shame, because she'd really liked that t-shirt, but now she'd need to burn it.

Michelle wrinkled her nose. "We need to get you out of those clothes."

"Thought you'd never ask, hen."

Priorities. Hel checked her bottle was still intact, then made sure she had all her limbs. She heaved herself out of the dumpster.

"You're hired, by the way."

"Eh?"

"You said you were in security. It turns out that I'm in the market for a bodyguard."

"Braw. We can discuss my fee over a drink."

She tossed the bottle from one hand to the other. It disintegrated in the air as a bullet put paid to her plans for the evening.

"Fuck sake. I paid for that!"

Two more goons were advancing from the club's backdoor, subtlety spent, and pistols raised. Michelle grabbed her by a fistful of soiled t-shirt and yanked her into an alleyway across the street. People were screaming and running in all directions. The Moroccan nightlife disintegrating around them.

Finster's pals would probably have followed them, but a pair of jeeps swerved into the street ahead of them and a squad of Gendarmerie with bigger guns jumped out. Hel savoured the beautiful music of their arrest.

"Alright, hen. Back to my place. Then you can tell me what the fuck is going in."

"We lost Lownes and Boscoe," Letty grunted, slamming the safe house door shut. She yanked off her baseball cap, blonde ponytail spilling, and walked straight to the mini bar. "Gendarmerie caught them. Looks like the target and her fat friend got away."

The atmosphere in the hotel room Wolfe had secured for them soured like a glass of milk in the Moroccan sun. Their gear was still sandy from the dig site and half Finster's team were walking wounded. Now two of them were off the table completely. The insult to the literal injuries.

"She will resurface," Wolfe said. He was studying his pocket watch like he thought it would tell him the exact time said resurfacing would occur. He didn't sound remotely worried.

Finster didn't suffer from the same optimism. He'd vouch for his team. They'd run black flag ops throughout Africa and, yeah, they'd lost people along the way, but more than half the charter members were still with them. This should have been a simple bag-and-drag. Instead, it had turned into an absolute cluster-fuck.

Letty was still on her feet but Briggs had a fractured collarbone and a broken nose, Hall had a bruise the shape of a bottle of scotch stamped on his sternum and Nancy was sitting on a bag of ice with a face like murder. Now they'd lost another two men to the Moroccan military police. This mission was circling, and Michelle Scot was their only lead.

That and a shrivelled pump in a silver box.

Gerard, their medic, had finished patching Briggs' nose. Now he was inspecting Finster's eye and pulling all kinds of faces that were in no way encouraging.

"What's the prognosis?" he grunted.

"She fractured your socket, boss." Gerard scrubbed his forehead with his sleeve. "I'm gonna have to take the eye."

"Are you fucking serious?"

"You're gonna look like a pirate," Nancy sniggered.

"Glad you're finding this so entertaining."

Her expression darkened. "That cunt kicked me," she snarled, "in the cunt."

Wolfe shook his head and snapped his watch closed.

The click prompted the ten remaining members of the mercenary group, formally known as D-12, to look up in unison. He ran his fingers along his watch chain, the way he always did when he slipped it back into his pocket. Nervous tick maybe. He spoke into the sudden quiet.

"Perhaps we should……terminate our agreement, Mister Finster. I will make other arrangements."

"We ain't quitting," Nancy growled. She drew her knife and jammed it into the tabletop like it had sprouted red hair. "Not until I make a wig out of that bitch's ginger."

"My team has strong feelings about seeing the contract out, sir," Finster said, sitting back in his seat.

Wolfe nodded. Gerard prepped a morphine syringe. Finster rolled up his sleeve.

"And you know how it is. 'An eye for an eye'."

"Fancy," Hel decided, as they stepped into the museum. "Never been to a place like this on a second date before."

White marble and gold leaf; velvet rope and glass cases. A history made of bone and clay and bronze and stone, told in fragments. Civilisation in drabble form.

"*Second* date?" Michelle asked.

"Aye. First date's always in a bar though."

"And what makes you think we're dating?"

The arched eyebrow was a challenge Hel could rise to. "Should have read the small print. That's a non-negotiable term of my employment."

"Everything's negotiable, Helen. I suppose we'll just have to wait for your first performance review."

"Dinnae have to worry about *my* performance, hen."

After hours, the museum loomed, shadowy, and all that history looked just a little threatening. Not quite so much as the gun-toting mercenaries on their trail, but enough that Hel would have been gripping her pistol just a little tighter if she'd owned one.

Which, she'd explained to Mitch, she didn't, because waving a gun around had a tendency to get you shot. Folk who saw you armed only with what the Big Man gave you naturally assumed they had a chance of taking you alive. At least until you corrected their misapprehension.

What she'd picked up from her place amounted to a change of clothes, a tactical vest and a telescopic baton, which rounded off her earlier 'I've got a magic wand' joke quite nicely.

She'd wanted to ask why they needed to visit the museum after hours, but Hel had learned that wasn't how the 'security' gig worked. Nae questions, just looking big and fierce, which Hel was quite good at despite only being a baw hair over five feet.

Mitch had a key to the place, which made sense, since Hel had only just met her and was ready to give her a key to her apartment as well. She walked with purpose to an office in back of the ground floor and Hel followed, hands on hips, eyes open for Finster and his scum.

The office was lit. Hel sank her weight, expecting trouble. Instead, Mitch walked to the window and tapped on the glass. A man in a clean and pressed kaftan, bearded and head wrapped, looked up from the book he was reading and waved at her. His smile was enough to put Hel at ease.

"Abdullah," Mitch greeted, with a bow.

"Shalom Aleichem, my old friend," he said, matching the depth of her bow. "What can I do for you at this hour?"

"The box I gave you. I need it."

His smile flickered but held, and Hel wondered what the subtext was.

"Of course, my friend, of course. You are transferring it to another safe place, yes? It has been in my possession many years and it is time for it to move on."

Mitch shook her head. "I wish that was true, Abdullah, but no… Someone's searching for the cask."

The curator nodded and stepped aside to let them into his office. The smile had vanished. He unlocked a door in the back corner of the little room. Hel noticed his hands were trembling.

"How did they learn of its existence? How did they connect it to you?"

"The symposium, I would guess. I knew I shouldn't have given that lecture. One of the researchers from the University was asking a lot of questions about it. The one with the glasses and the tweed."

"Ah, Rufus. I cannot imagine he became embroiled in any intrigue. The man is a scholar, not a treasure hunter."

"I know. Which is why I'm reasonably sure he's already dead."

The room behind the office was an appraising room.

Lights and magnifying glasses on telescopic arms bolted to the table at the centre, shelves lining the walls, laden with locked metal boxes. Abdullah took down one box and set it reverentially on the table.

Mitch pulled out a second key—she must have been collecting them—and unlocked the box. Inside was…

"A fucking horseshoe? What, is it lucky or something?"

"Or something," Mitch said, and pocketed it. "Abdullah, where's Marya?"

"Roaming the corridors, most likely. She dislikes when I work late and she has no patience for the bureaucracy of my position, but she enjoys wandering among the artefacts of her people's history. She says it empowers her."

"Find her and go home. This isn't…"

There was a clatter in the office. Boots on white marble and impending arseholery. Hel heard someone snigger.

Abdullah shot a look at Mitch. She shook her head, but he was already turning to leave the appraising room. Hel went to follow, and Mitch caught her arm.

He flicked the light off as he stepped out.

"Gentlemen. And ladies. How may I help you this evening?"

He was smooth, she'd give him that. Half the folk she knew would have led with different questions. Like 'how the fuck did you get in here?' and 'how many black eyes are you wanting?'

"Shalom Aleichem, sir," someone said.

Not Finster. This man had breeding, and he had education. And, despite having no accent, he pronounced the Arabic like a native.

Mitch recognised the voice. Hel felt the skin prickling on her arm as they stood elbow-to-elbow in the dark. Not a good sign.

"I have recently unearthed an artefact during an archaeological excursion, and I wish to bequeath it to the museum. I wonder if you might be able to identify its origin for me. A silver cask containing the mummified remains of a human heart."

"An unusual item, certainly. Shall we see what we can find?"

Hel heard clicking, then the sound of a laptop booting. Rustling as the hired guns sat on the edges of the desks all around Abdullah's office. Sweating him.

One of them stepped into the doorway of the appraising room. Bald and limping slightly. Hel saw the woman's hand groping for the light switch and started to slide her baton free.

"Ah, here we are," Abdullah said. The hand retracted. "There is one historical tale that references a heart in a silver cask. Supposedly, it was the dying wish of Robert the Bruce, King of Scotland, that his heart be carried into battle against the enemies of his god. The heart was purportedly taken to Granada, where it was almost lost, but it was recovered and interred in…a place named Melrose Abbey in the early 14th century. Presumably, it cannot be the same cask."

"One would assume not," the stranger said. "But then, a person of cunning will prey upon our assumptions, will they not?"

"I'm afraid I don't understand," Abdullah said.

"That is quite alright, sir. I do not expect to find the answers from you but, rather, the woman hiding in the room behind you."

There was the sound of a struggle. Before Hel could stop her, Mitch marched out of the appraising room with her hands up. Honestly, seeing her give herself up to save a life was pretty fucking hot. Even if it *did* make Hel's job tougher.

Half a dozen guns cocked. Someone yanked Mitch into the light.

"Where's the other one?" Finster growled.

"Gone. We didn't actually know each other. She was just some ex-pat trying to get in my pants. As soon as she realised, I wasn't going to put out, she ditched me."

The message was pretty clear. She wanted Hel to stay where the fuck she was. Hardest thing she'd ever had to do.

"Hello again, Ms Scot," the gentleman greeted.

"Somehow, I thought it would be you. What are you going by now? Snake?"

"Wolfe."

"Right."

"No weapons," a woman's voice announced. Then there was a thunk that sounded suspiciously like a horse-shoe landing on a tabletop. "Found this though."

"I see. Then it would seem we are on the right track. I doubt you would have sought this out if you had not felt threatened by my progress. It is most encouraging."

"Don't flatter yourself," Mitch scoffed. "That's just a good luck charm."

"I suppose we will see, won't we? You will, of course, journey with me to our final destination. I wish to have you on hand, in case it becomes apparent that you have deployed further tricks."

"Wouldn't miss it for the world."

"What about the Arab?" Finster demanded.

"Loose ends must be tied," Wolfe said.

It was the only warning Hel got before she heard the wet plunge of a knife. Abdullah gasping for breath, Mitch growling. She clenched teeth, fingers itching. But he was already dead, and the only thing she'd get by stepping out there was her arse shot full of holes.

"We have a flight to charter," Wolfe announced.

The mercs filed out of the room, dragging Mitch with them. It wasn't looking good for Hel's job security or her love life right about then.

She counted to thirty—longest fucking thirty of her life—and stepped out of the appraising room. Abdullah slumped next to his desk, clutching a wound in his belly that had already dyed the bottom half of his kaftan crimson. Blood painted a red stripe through his beard.

"Hold on, pal. We can call someone."

"We both know that is not true," he whispered. He nodded to the desk, since his hands were busy. "The horseshoe. Take it to her."

"Seriously, what's the thing with the horseshoe?"

"There are some things you should not question."

"Sorry, pal. I'm an atheist. Kind of comes with the territory."

"Do this service for him and Allah will forgive you."

Hel snorted and slid the horseshoe into her vest. She

shook her head. "I'm sorry."

"We are all doing His work, in our way. And I have done my part. If you see my wife, Marya, tell her that I loved her."

Hel nodded. He drew a breath, and she wondered if he was going to say something else. Instead, he exhaled softly and slid to the floor.

She reached over and eased his eyes closed. "Fuck sake…"

She'd call someone about this once she was on her way to the airport, but she needed to get back home to Bonnie Scotland fucking quick-like. Wolfe had the money to charter a flight, and he had Mitch. All Hel had was a horseshoe.

She stepped out of the office and was halfway back to the door where Mitch had let them in when two shadows detached from an adjoining corridor.

One of them was wearing an eye patch.

"You owe me an eye, bitch," Finster snarled.

"I knew she was lying," Finster said, going all-out with the self-congratulation. "And here you are, hanging around like a bad smell. Like the man said, loose ends must be tied."

He kept his gun trained on her as his pet giant marched over and wrenched her raised arms behind her back. He looked like he was thinking of bashing her nose in to make up for the bloody gauze in the middle of his face.

Why was everyone so equity-minded?

The moment he had a grip around her wrists, Finster exchanged his gun for a knife. He grabbed her by the chin, pushed her head back and angled the point of the blade towards her eye.

"This is probably going to hurt a lot," he said. "But the good news is, I think this marble should wipe clean."

"Braw. Wouldn't want this to stain."

She kicked him between the legs, like she'd done with his baldy lassie. Only he had the equipment to make it *really* satisfying. Something gave way under the steel toe of her boot and he reeled back, croaking, struggling for breath.

The giant tried to grab her around the neck. She smashed her head backwards, flattening his nose by another centimetre. He let out a strangled roar as she twisted out of his grasp, whipped out her baton, and cracked it on the back of his skull. He didn't go down.

The general rule is, if they don't go down, keep hitting them.

It took half a dozen more hits before he was flat on the floor and no longer trying to fend her off. She stamped on the back of his head for good measure.

Then a bullet whizzed past her. She jumped and rolled. Finster tracked her with the wobbling muzzle of his pistol, his other hand cradling his bruised junk. His remaining eye had enough murder in it for at least two or three but, fortunately, no depth perception.

"No more fucking around!" he bellowed.

Someone obviously agreed with him because the next gunshot blew out the side of his head and turned his

138

brain into a red streak on the wall.

Hel put her hands up. The woman with the pistol wore a hijab, staring at her, dark eyes studying, considering, concluding.

"Marya?" Hel tried.

"Speak," she ordered.

"I came here with a lassie called Michelle Scot. Some cunt named Wolfe took her away. I've got her horseshoe. Abdullah said I needed to take it to her."

Marya's eyes narrowed, searching for the truth in the lines of Hel's face, which probably didn't look all that trustworthy on account of all the times she'd been punched. She kept her hands up because she didn't want to end up like Finster.

She glanced around. Hel realised she was probably looking for her husband.

"They killed him," she said. "But he said he loved you."

Marya scoffed. "I knew that already." She waved Hel up to her feet. "It is time for you to leave. You have a job to do and I must grieve."

With that, she shot Finster's giant friend in the head and wandered away, back towards her husband's office. The gun vanished into the confines of her robe.

Hel watched her go for a few moments, then did the only appropriate thing when faced with two dead mercenaries who'd been trying to kill her until a few seconds ago.

She checked their wallets.

❦

Wolfe ruled that they couldn't wait for Finster. It would be up to him to follow the rest of the group. His team were ill-at-ease taking orders directly from their client, but they obeyed all the same and the only one who openly complained was the shaved-headed woman, Nancy, who didn't seem to have a filter.

They rode out to the nearest airfield, where Wolfe chartered a flight to leave at dawn. Michelle sat on a bench across from him, hands fastened at the wrists with cable ties and a jacket draped over them so that her captivity would raise fewer eyebrows.

They didn't need to worry. The time wasn't right for her to act yet.

"You didn't need to kill Abdullah," she said, as they waited in the private departure lounge.

"Of course, I did. I cannot afford for complications when I am so close to reclaiming what is mine."

That was the closest they came to conversation. They'd always fundamentally disagreed on everything. It was a point of pride for her.

The only other person to try to engage her was Nancy, who sat with an arm around her shoulders and talked about what she was going to do to her once their boss had his prize. None of it was especially imaginative.

"And what makes you think you're going to live through this?" Michelle asked, when she took a breath.

Nancy yanked her head back by a fistful of hair and put the point of a knife under her chin. "Don't worry about me, love. I'm the one *holding* the knife."

Wolfe waved her off, but Michelle could see the flicker of amusement on his lips. He was seriously con-

140

sidering just letting Nancy slit her throat and leaving her there in Morocco.

She didn't tell him, but it would have been the smart play.

Instead, they touched down in the dreary, misty autumn of the Scottish borders around noon and she had to fight down a swell of nostalgia. A lot had changed, but she remembered the place.

And she *definitely* remembered Melrose Abbey.

It was a crumbling ruin now, and the mist gave it an eerie, haunted atmosphere. Grey and grim and silent. They walked through the stones, many illegible the identities of men and women who'd once lived and breathed, forever lost to time.

Nancy slashed angrily at her phone. Her calls to Finster rang out over and over, speaker making the warbling tone echo all around. Every time her boss didn't answer, Michelle felt her hope surging.

She'd gambled, involving Helen. It didn't mean it wouldn't pay off.

"That is enough, Ms Kruger," Wolfe said, after the tenth missed call. "It is clear that Captain Finster will not be joining us."

Nancy scowled at him but slid her phone into her pocket all the same. She dropped back in the line until she and Michelle were walking elbow-to-elbow.

"You're a dead woman," she hissed. "Your girlfriend too."

Michelle shrugged. "We'll see."

It had been a mistake of the old ways to inter artefacts of power in graves and tombs. Superstition had been enough to turn away most grave robbers. They made the few desperate or practical enough to ignore the warnings serve their purpose by serving as examples of the fate that befell thieves. Cursed.

But the old superstitions didn't hold true anymore, which was why Wolfe's men didn't hesitate to start digging when he gave the order.

They knocked down the plaque marking the heart's resting place and broke soil. Michelle stared at the inscription and sighed.

A noble heart may have no ease if freedom fails.

They worked for close to an hour until, finally, they dragged the silver cask to the surface. Nancy pried the lid off with her knife as Wolfe looked on expectantly.

"Aren't you even going to ask why he doesn't touch the cask himself?"

"Because he pays people to do shit for him, sweetheart. Plenty of people don't do their own dirty work."

She dumped the cask upside down. A length of rope spilled out into the grass, tied in a loop at one end.

"What the fuck is this?" Nancy asked, disgusted. She picked up the noose between two fingers. "Stinks like the fucking ocean. Seriously, we went through all that for *this*?"

"Naturally," Wolfe said, taking the rope from her unresisting hand. "You see, almost 800 years ago, a powerful demon was tricked into weaving this rope from the very sands by a cunning wizard. When the rope was completed, the wizard sealed it in a silver cask, knowing that the demon had poured much of his strength into its creation. Do you know what it would mean for the demon to rediscover its power again after 800 long years?"

Nancy considered what he'd said for a moment, then said, "Are you fucking crazy?"

Wolfe laughed. The sound made Michelle's gorge rise.

"My dear, you have been very entertaining. I believe I will extend the term of your employment indefinitely."

The noose leapt from Wolfe's hand like a serpent. It coiled around Nancy's throat before she could react and pulled taut. A choked scream escaped her and then she was on her knees, strength gone, skin greying.

The other mercenaries aimed their weapons at Wolfe. The coil of rope in his hand sprouted new nooses, each one seeking out a neck, ensnaring the other men and women who'd served under Finster before they could fire.

Michelle was already running, sprinting towards the ruined abbey, head down and neck itching for fear of a noose. The mist had turned red and pulsed with a steady, growing darkness. Wolfe's true nature, warping the world around him as his power grew.

She ducked through the shadowy doorway and then a strong hand yanked her out of sight of the nightmare unfolding in the cemetery outside.

"Glad you're not dead," Helen greeted. "Would have been a bit of a pisser bringing this thing all the way out here."

She twirled the horseshoe around her finger. Her grin was so bright Michelle could see it even in the darkness.

The moment Helen cut her loose, she snatched the

horseshoe up and started running, heading for the south chancel. Helen followed, probably as bewildered as Nancy had been. Hopefully, her education wasn't going to be quite so painful.

"Which part of Scotland are you from, Helen?"

"Me? I'm from Fife, hen."

"Then you've heard of Michael Scot?"

"The wizard? Aye, I remember a story. They said Alexander the Third asked him to send a mandate to the King of France to keep his pirates away. Said he flew there on a black stallion and, when it stamped its hoof, all the bells rang across the whole of Paris. After that, the King did'nae really care to refuse."

"Some of that's true."

Halfway along the aisle, carved deep into the stone, was a groove shaped like a hoof. Michelle placed the horseshoe and stepped back as the plinth fell and slid aside.

Underneath was a leather-bound book with a symbol scarred onto the cover that the uneducated might have confused for Satanic. Battered, and the pages were dog-eared but, as she lifted it from its resting place, her fingers remembered the grooves in the spine where they'd fit.

"How's that going to help us?" Helen grunted. "Aren't the best spell books made from human skin?"

"Yeah, but it smells after a while. And this is remarkably well-preserved for being almost a thousand years old, I think you'll agree." Michelle sighed. "Which makes two of us, I guess."

Helen stared at her, unamused. There must have

144

been so many questions, but she settled on, "Who the fuck are you, hen?"

"Do you believe in magic? Because I used to have a wand but now I don't."

Helen glanced down at the space where the book had been, then at the book, then at Michelle. She looked up through the fractured ceiling, where the crimson mist was beginning to smother out the weak sunlight.

"Now," Michelle said, "are you going to help me save the world or what?"

Hel had been out of her depth plenty of times in the past. Fighting that bus load of football hooligans on that bridge that had got her dumped in the river. Trying to work freelance security in a traditionally Arab country when she couldn't speak Arabic. Tonight, was probably going to go to the top of the list though.

Rolling, red fog smothered the cemetery. Wolfe's silhouette hovered above the gravestones, stretched and inhuman. The rope coiled in the air between his hands, writhing like a tortured snake, as it slowly unfurled, coming apart.

And, while Hel didn't know what the fuck was going on, she did get the impression that was a bad thing.

Mitch took a stance between Wolfe and the abbey and let the book fall open in her palm. She started whispering something. It sounded like a long passage of Arabic. Actually, it was a short passage, repeated over and over again.

Hel really hoped it wasn't a prayer.

The mist curled around her, puffs of white emerging. Hel felt a surge of hope. Then something moved between the gravestones, twitching, jerking.

The bald lassie, Nancy, corpse-pale and grinning like a lunatic. The rest of the team clambered to their feet behind her and started shambling towards Michelle.

And Hel guessed this was where she came in.

"Alright," she said, reaching into her bag for the half-empty whiskey bottle inside. "Round two."

The closest merc had his gun dangling from its strap around his neck. That must have been a neat trick, sneaking those through customs, since she'd had to leave her baton behind in Morocco. But, since he wasn't using that sleek, shiny rifle, she figured she may as well.

She grabbed it by the barrel and smashed it in his face. Pain didn't seem to matter, so she twisted the gun, cinching the strap around his throat. She used it like a string and him like a puppet, spinning him around. Then she bludgeoned his skull flat with her bottle.

He dropped, and she caught the lanky, blonde lassie in the teeth with the backswing. She tumbled between the tombstones and Hel was starting to feel like she had a handle on this when Nancy rammed her off her feet.

"Hope you're planning on putting up a fight, sweetheart," Nancy said, voice distorted, twisted where the noose had left its mark on her throat. "He likes it when they struggle."

"He's not my type."

Nancy cackled and Hel started to get the impression that, other than being dead, not a lot had changed for her. She pulled her knife and pounced, trying to push it through Hel's chest cavity. They fought for control, deadlocked.

"He doesn't care. I'll admit, it's a little cruel. You hold out as long as you can but the pain? It's unbearable. Agony. Like he's peeling off your skin and sliding his fingers through your bones. I gave up just to make it stop. Slid into that blackness thinking it was finally over. Only it wasn't over, was it? I'm still here. So I figure there's only one thing left to do."

She punched the knife closer to Hel's heart, leering with every fraction of an inch it slipped.

"Have some fucking fun while I can."

Hel twisted, rolling over. They wrestled, tumbling in the wet grass, punching, scratching, biting. Pity Nancy was such a mental; they might have been friends.

Hel came out on top, with the knife. Nancy held her off, but Hel was the heavy one. She leaned on it, adding her weight to the blade, until it sank into Nancy's chest, between her ribs, through her heart. Sand puffed out of her mouth and gushed between Hel's fingers, welling out of the wound like she had a desert sewn up inside her.

She stopped fighting, but she didn't die. She probably never would, unless Mitch could deal with the big, bad Wolfe.

She stood tall as ever, but the dead mercenaries were circling her, pressing hands and faces against the barrier she'd erected to keep them out. Sweat was pouring off her and the incantation she was reading seemed to be getting harder and harder to finish. Wolfe was looking far too pleased with himself.

Hel picked up the bottle where she'd dropped it, gulped down one final swig, and then tossed it at Wolfe's head.

Honestly, it surprised her when it thunked off the side of his skull. He'd been so focused on Mitch, he hadn't even noticed the little, redheaded ant scurrying around his feet. His concentration broken, Mitch found the gap she needed, and she took it.

The ground opened beneath Wolfe's feet with the roar. He slipped into the crack, lit by the burning glow from beneath. He looked up, features split in a snarl. The animal breaking loose.

"I buried you before," Michelle said, voice ringing out through the church ground. "This time, I'm burying you deeper."

Wolfe clawed for the rope that had fallen nearby. Hel moved it out of reach with her boot. He glared up at her but couldn't rise. Something was pulling him down. Hands, reaching up from the abyss to reclaim him.

With a growl, he vanished into the earth. Nancy finally went still. The soldiers gathered around Mitch collapsed in unison. Done.

Hel looked down at the rope.

"Don't pick it up!" Mitch commanded. "It's dangerous!"

Hel snorted. "I'm no' an idiot, hen. I wasn't *going* to pick it up. Don't get your knickers in a bunch."

"Oh," Mitch said, as she slumped onto her butt. "Good."

Hel ran to her and scooped her up. Then she realised her bottle was still intact and grabbed that too.

"Did you honestly stop for a drink on your way here?"

"It was a long flight, hen. I was drying out."

She took another gulp, then offered the bottle to Mitch. To her surprise, she took it, drained it to the last drop and wiped her mouth on the back of her sleeve.

"I've missed this place," she explained.

Hel, who didn't think she'd ever been in love before, wondered how you knew when it happened to you.

Maybe going to Morocco hadn't been such a stupid idea after all.

THE DESERT QUEEN

CHRIS CORNETTO

On the road ahead, white-garbed nomads watched from their horses, as motionless as desert ghosts. The setting sun lit them from behind, stretching their shadows into a long black claw.

"It's all right," Bastian said. "There's only four of them, and we're protected by the Sultan's Peace. He needs the trade as much as we do." He lifted his hat to wipe the sweat from his brow.

Milo slowed his horse and scanned the stony hillside, one hand on his sword. "Keep telling yourself that."

An uneasy murmur ran down the line of pack mules and their handlers.

"There." Milo inclined his head toward the southern ridge. "See that?"

Bastian adjusted his stirrup, to look without being obvious. South of the road, a plume of dust rose from the ridge to drift across the pink evening sky. So much for the Sultan's Peace. "Must you always be right?" he muttered. "Doesn't it get tedious?"

Milo gave a wry grin. "It's a curse, I know."

It was true that Ismail II, Grand Sultan of Muradeva, needed trade. With unbroken drought for almost a year, the crops had failed. His people were hungry.

But Ismail also needed the nomads. He had no reason to pay them between wars, but he could turn a blind eye to the occasional lost caravan – so long as the grain was delivered, and the caravan on its way home.

Bastian Torino's convoy, grain delivered to the city of Harreketh, was on its way home.

Farah of the Karda peered over the ridge. She waved for her men to still their horses.

Below, the caravan trundled on, oblivious to the Ghassan ambush. She couldn't tell but hoped her little dust cloud caught the convoy's attention. It was too late to spare them a fight, but that was never the point. She merely wanted them to be ready for it.

The Ghassan were worthless jackals. They would take the caravan, but the more of them dead or wounded, the better. There were near thirty of them, but maybe with enough casualties, enough fatigue, and caught by surprise… maybe she and her dozen riders could pry the spoils from their hands.

Maybe she could give her father the victory he so badly needed.

Rustam, her second in command, crawled to the ledge beside her. The man was twice her age and more experienced in battle, but kind enough to advise her without usurping her authority – the dust cloud had been his idea. He was a good man to have around.

"Did they see the signal?" he asked.

"I can't tell," Farah said, though she doubted they had. The caravan was slowing down, bunching up as it approached the four men in the road. Just as the Ghassan wanted.

The caravan master, a soft-looking southerner, dismounted, perhaps hoping to barter for safe passage. With another tribe, he might have struck an accord, but the Ghassan wouldn't settle for less than they could take. Hidden behind a rise, two dozen riders chafed restlessly, ready to charge.

Talking gave way to angry shouting. Sawad, the Ghassan leader, hoisted his curved sword in signal to his men. Without waiting for them to arrive, he attacked.

Farah expected the caravan master's head to fly from his shoulders. A shame. It was handsome, in an effeminate southern way.

At the last moment, Bastian rolled beneath the scything blade. He came up to catch the next raider by the wrist, wrenching him from the saddle. Before the bandit could recover, he punched him in the ribs with a dagger.

The nomad leader wheeled for another pass. He raised his blade and spurred his mount into a charge.

Bastian picked up the dead raider's sword. He stood his ground, knowing it hopeless to flee. He took a fighting stance, waited… waited… and threw.

The sword whirled through the air. The charging nomad ducked, and it sailed harmlessly wide.

But it did its job. With his eyes on the sword, the nomad leader didn't see Milo's heavy broadsword until it took him in the ribs, lifting him from the saddle. He was dead before he hit the ground.

The bandit's horse thundered on, absent a rider. Bastian felt the wind eddy around him as it passed. "What kept you?" he shouted to Milo.

Milo shrugged and looked over his shoulder to where two more raiders lay motionless on the stony ground. Their white desert robes bloomed crimson. "Just stopped for a quick nap. You all right?"

Bastian brushed himself off, checking for injuries. "I think so." He reached up, felt his bare head, then saw on the ground a bundle of trampled fabric. "But my hat wasn't so lucky."

"It was ugly anyway." Suddenly Milo snapped to attention, eyes wide and alert.

Bastian followed Milo's gaze to the cloud of dust, steel, and horses crashing toward them – not from the southern ridge, but the north. "Archers at the ready!" he cried, already sprinting for his horse. "Here they come!"

Farah caught herself holding her breath. "I can't tell if they're brave or just lucky."

154

"Bit of both is my guess," Rustam said. "They did us a favour, killing Sawad. If they weaken the Ghassan enough for us to take them, I'll give their bodies a hero's pyre. The god needs brave souls, even heathen outlanders."

Farah frowned at the scene below. More than a score of hardened riders charged down on two mounted men, eight lightly armed guards, and several terrified mule drivers. It would take more than courage or luck to see them through.

"What if we helped them?" she said without thinking. The Karda needed brave souls, too.

Rustam shook his head. "Bad idea. We'd be slaughtered with them."

Cries of battle, of pain and terror, filled the valley below. The archers loosed frantically, wounding only two riders before they panicked and broke. Half the defenders were down in the first clash. Mules bucked and reared, lashing at friend and foe alike. All was chaos, painted blood red by the setting sun.

Farah expected the caravan master to abandon his men and flee. Silently, she wished he would. His heavy horse would never outrun those bred for the desert, but what Ghassan would give chase and miss out on the plunder? She focused her will on him, urging him to run while he could.

But, for the second time that day, he surprised her.

"Over here, you sand-eating beggars!" Bastian

shouted. He flung a handful of sparkling gems, the profits from Harreketh, at the swirling raiders. "Come and get me!"

Milo flicked the reins and urged his horse on, pulling up beside him. "Sand-eating? That's all you've got?" He rattled off a string of insults that would make a sailor blush.

Between the gems and curses, the bandits took notice. Several peeled away from the caravan to give chase.

Bastian ducked low on his horse and spurred it to a gallop. Clouds of dust kicked up all around him, making breathing hard, forcing him to squint. He looked over his shoulder, the riders behind him a blur of shadows. "Did we get enough?" he called to Milo. If only they could pull away enough bandits, the guards might stand a chance.

"Shut up and ride!" Milo shouted back.

In moments the bandits were on them. Milo veered left then cut right, driving back a pursuer with a wild slash.

Damn, but their horses were swift.

Bastian spat sand from his gritty mouth. Wasting no more words, he drew his blade and swung his horse around.

There would be no escape, no survival. But, for the sake of his men – whether to save or avenge them – he would bring all he could to the hells with him.

The caravan master, tailed by his bodyguard,

emerged from the other side of the cloud of dust. Four of the Ghassan did not.

"Four!" Farah gasped. Her heart raced. "Did you see that?"

"Hush, girl!" Rustam said, but she wasn't listening. Her eyes were fixed on the scene below.

Dust cleared, revealing the bodies of fallen nomads. The survivors turned for another pass. The two southerners, hopelessly outnumbered, scorned fate and did the same.

Farah gripped the rock until it stung her hands. She wanted to cheer aloud, moved by the display of valor. She ached to draw her sword and teach the Ghassan a lesson of her own.

The two riders crossed and, just before impact, crossed again. The nomads wheeled aside to avoid a collision, sending a ripple of confusion down their line. It cost one a hand, another his head, and the southerners again passed unscathed. The odds, now two on six, were growing better by the minute.

The caravan, however, did not fare as well. The defence collapsed, and battle gave way to slaughter.

"Just a few more," Rustam calculated. "If another one or two go down, we could hit them when they dismount to gather the plunder. It should be dark by... Farah? Farah!"

On the next clash, to the shame of their ancestors, the filthy Ghassan had attacked the horses. *The horses.* Heart aflood with wrath and courage, Farah ran to her mount, all thoughts of strategy washed aside.

ADVENTURE AWAITS

Bastian staggered to his feet, dizzy, aching, and bleeding from more scrapes than he cared to count. He snatched up the sword he'd tossed aside as he fell.

Milo, clutching his left arm, flashed a grim smile. "At least it's not my sword arm." His weapon was nowhere to be seen, but he plucked one from the rider, now dead, who'd slain his horse. The other five bandits, still mounted, circled them warily. "It's been an honour, captain."

"Don't quit on me yet, Milo." Bastian backed against his old friend, sword at the ready, tracking the riders as they whirled around him. "If you can handle one, I'll take the other four."

Milo chuckled. He'd always been the better fighter, and probably still was despite the broken arm. "As you say, captain."

The thunder of hooves sounded from all directions, echoing off the hills. From the east came the rest of the bandit company, still ten strong and splattered with blood not their own. And from the west came another dozen nomads, one leading the pack in a furious charge.

Bastian swallowed hard.

Milo's back stiffened against his. "So, ah… who's gonna take the rest of 'em?"

Farah twirled her sword overhead, yelling defiance. Rustam's pleas to stop were lost in the wind behind her. She careened into the startled Ghassan line, leaning from her saddle, slicing left and right. She couldn't tell if she felled the men, but her blade trailed crimson spray.

Before the foe could surround her, the Karda cavalry drove into their flank, sowing chaos through the ranks of the larger band.

Farah wheeled back into the fray, catching sight of the southerners just in time. She crashed her horse into a Ghassan rider's, driving him back from the two men on the ground, and sliced his shoulder as they parted. She rode a circle around the outlanders, a living whirlwind, defying any to draw close.

But none did. Leaderless and overwhelmed, the remaining Ghassan turned tail and fled like the cowards they were. A cry of triumph went up among her men, ten of whom were still in the saddle, with one more dazed but alive.

As Farah surveyed the carnage, the battle fury faded. She cleaned the blood from her blade, trying not to dwell on how it got there. All around her were corpses, transformed by death from hated enemies into ordinary men, their faces as lean with hunger as her own people's.

It was the victory her father needed, to push back against Ember Mahdi. She told herself this over and over until the nausea waned.

Once composed, Farah rode to meet the southerners. She found the caravan master making a sling for the other, amidst a ring of meat that had been men. Again, the bile rose in her throat, but she swallowed it down.

"Since you haven't tried to kill us, shall I thank you for our rescue?" He arched an eyebrow.

"You may thank me for your lives, at least."

The man with the broken arm gave her a wary glare. He was tall and leanly muscled, his skin almost as sun bronzed as hers. His pale hair was a spiky, sweaty mess, but she could picture it cut soldier short. He carried himself like a warrior.

But the other man, the caravan master, reached for a hat that wasn't there, grimaced, and bowed to her. "You have our gratitude. I am Bastian Torino, of Ravencourt, and this is my friend Milo."

Ravencourt. It made sense. With his pale skin, long brown curls, and trim moustache, he looked every part the soft southern merchant. It was tempting to dismiss him as such, but she had seen him *fight*. There was steel beneath that softness.

He looked up at her with a brilliant smile. "And who, may I ask, is our saviour?"

Farah unwound her headscarf and let her hair fall loose. She wasn't vain but was satisfied to see the man's eyes go wide. "Farah, of the Karda."

"Farah." He paused and looked into space, as if searching his memory. "Like the desert queen?"

She nodded. It was a name handed down her mother's line, to honour her glorious ancestor. "And I thank you for the gift of these goods."

Bastian frowned at the white-robed nomads already pawing at their cargo. "Well, yes," he reasoned. "We find ourselves short on handlers, and some gratitude is in order. Let's arrange an agreeable division?" He was still embarrassed that he had compared the desert girl to the Farah of legend, a children's tale, and tried to hide his blush. Sunburn made it easy.

Farah also eyed the cargo, her mouth quirked in a way that looked almost apologetic. She was stunning, but he couldn't let that distract him. He and Milo were in very real danger.

"The division is a simple one," Farah stated. "We have liberated these goods from the filthy Ghassan, which makes them ours."

On reflex, Bastian opened his mouth to haggle for the return of some of his property. She silenced him with a look.

The journey was a total loss, but he had wealth enough at home to start over. The gems sewn into his sleeves would pay their way, if he could find somewhere to sell them. All he had to do was not die of exposure.

"Very well. But we lay claim to four of the horses." They had slain at least four raiders, and he knew the nomads' custom on rights of conquest. Without food or water, they'd have to run the poor beasts into the ground, but it might be possible to backtrack to Harreketh. Maybe.

"Agreed," she said to his surprise. "You may have first pick of the captured horses. I will take responsibility for their care until you are released."

"Thank you, but that won't be necessary. We'll be leaving right away."

Bastian felt a hand on his shoulder. He turned, and Milo shook his head. "She didn't say until we leave. She said until we're *released*."

Bastian whirled back to Farah, his hand on his hilt. His blade was halfway free of its sheath before Milo caught his wrist. All around them, watchful riders drew their swords.

Farah held up a hand for peace. She waited for the clamour to settle down before she spoke. "Think on it. Even if you fought your way free, you wouldn't survive the desert. You will be a guest of the Karda until such time as you arrange ransom."

"Or until the slave-buyers pass through the village!" shouted one of the nomads, unhelpfully. He gave them a wolfish grin.

In one fluid motion, Farah drew her blade and slapped it against the man's horse. It bucked and threw him, to the laughter of the other nomads. She, however, did not smile.

"Bind them," she said as she turned away. "Then let them choose their horses."

For the Karda tribe, peace was a time of hardship.

There was nothing peaceful about it. Without a common foe, eternal rivalries flared between the desert tribes. Without the sultan's gold, they raided each other to scrape by. Even in the best of times, there was never enough.

This was not the best of times.

After a short rest and a few hours' ride, Farah reached the oasis by mid-morning. Before they left, despite the objections of her men, they had buried the dead caravaners in heathen fashion. The Ghassan they left for the jackals.

The oasis, once broad and glittering, was a narrow pool ringed by sun-baked mud. Even from a distance, the waving date palms seemed to droop. It was too early for the day to be so sweltering, but there was no arguing with the heat.

At least the wells had not yet failed. When they did, so too would the Karda.

"Riders, my lady," Rustam croaked, his head bowed low over his mount. The words evaporated in a shimmer of heat. They had given much of their water to the mules, with little left for the men.

Farah didn't reply. The riders were no surprise; if anything, they were late. Anyone approaching the village could be seen from miles away, even those not followed by a train of plunder-laden mules.

The riches should have cheered her, but they did nothing to ease the knot of worry in her stomach. It had grown risky for her to leave the village. Though she needed to win wealth for the tribe, her father also needed her close – especially with Ember Mahdi whispering poison in his ear.

"Hail!" Rustam shouted as the sentries drew near. "Lady Farah brings her father gifts and captives, taken by steel from the Ghassan!" Her riders, though parched and weary, gave an enthusiastic cheer.

Guests, she corrected him mentally, *not captives*. Though the southerners were bound, she had promised them guest-rights. The distinction was not a small one – a guest could be held for ransom, but not sold as a slave.

The two sentries rode up and inspected the caravan, nodding their approval. "We'll escort it home, my lady," one said. "You… Perhaps you'd best hurry ahead." He frowned, avoiding her eyes.

Farah's heart sank. Without pausing to give further orders, she spurred her tired horse to gallop the last few miles to Karda village.

Behind her came the thud of hoofbeats on stone, the sound of a trusted friend. *Thank you, Rustam.*

With all eyes on Farah and her lieutenant thundering into the distance, Bastian tried again to wriggle his hands free. He had been working at the knot for hours, but only managed to chafe his wrists. The cord, tied to the saddle-bow, was too short for him to wipe the sweat burning his eyes. He missed his hat.

The desert was a stony, blasted waste, interrupted by a strip of green below a sandstone bluff. By midday, the ground would be hotter than a hearth.

At least they were riding, not walking. As promised, Farah had given him the pick of the horses, and she did not balk when he took the best. If anything, she seemed impressed that he knew which beasts to choose.

He also suspected her of giving him more water than she took for herself. Had she?

Bastian sidled his horse closer to Milo's. "Lovely weather," he rasped through dusty lips. Swallowing hurt. "Makes you miss the rain back home."

"In a rush to get back?" Milo wriggled his hands

discreetly to show they were free. Even with a broken arm, he had unbound his wrists and tied a sham knot to make them look still trussed.

He expected nothing less of Milo.

Bastian looked around at the forbidding landscape. Another bead of sweat trickled from his brow to sting his eyes. "Better not," he decided. He liked their odds better with the nomads than on their own, and, while it galled him to be their captive, he couldn't hate them. They had buried his dead. Though they owed him nothing, though it wasn't even their custom, *they buried his dead*. Decency like that counted for much.

Of course, he knew it was Farah who insisted they do so. The woman fascinated him. Something about her brought to mind legends of the desert queen, and it was more than just her name. She was beautiful, in a fierce and dangerous way. Just like the desert itself.

Farah galloped past the grove of date palms. She left her horse to graze in the shadow of the cliff and climbed to the village on foot. She passed through the warren of colourful tents that sprouted between the tumbledown walls of a bygone age. The ancient temple of Haephesto loomed over all.

Some of the tribe greeted her, but most looked away. She knew why. In her absence, the Ember had been whispering again – whispering of greatness lost and the god's wrath, of succession and conquest. The ball in her stomach turned to molten lead, and she hurried her pace.

Well behind her, Rustam huffed to keep up.

Of necessity, Farah stopped at the well to slake her thirst. Though she lowered the bucket as far as it would reach, it caught little water. She poured it down her throat and hauled up another pail, this time nearly empty. She splashed the tepid water onto her face.

As she did so, a shadow fell across her.

"Welcome back, sister dear." Naji folded his arms across his muscular chest. "You're just in time."

Farah spat on the bone-dry ground. "Me, sister to a craven jackal?" Even those words were too kind for her half-brother, spawn of father's concubine. Since childhood, he had preyed on anything weaker than himself. He would whip a horse bloody if it displeased him and did worse to men – when he could get away with it.

Naji's hand twitched to his hilt. With effort, he wrestled his scowl back into a gloating smile. "Come now. That's hardly a way to speak to your future emir."

She scoffed. "You, emir? Maybe when Haephesto's balls freeze off." For the flaming god of the desert, that would hardly be soon. "Father would never choose you."

Naji shrugged carelessly, flashing his jackal grin. "Maybe it's not up to the old man." He waved a hand and swaggered away.

Farah glared, itching to drive her dirk into his retreating back. If it weren't taboo to spill kinblood, she would have killed him long ago. It was nothing he wouldn't do to her, given the chance.

But, despite her anger, Farah knew something was wrong. *Why* was Naji so smug? Normally, he had the sense to mute his ambitions, to veil his threats in her presence. What was different today, to make him so brazen? What did he *know*?

"In the meanwhile," he called over his shoulder, "you should guard your impious tongue. Haephesto wastes no mercy on blasphemers."

Farah's temper flared as hot as the god's own fires. "Go, sing his praises with your own forked tongue, you worm! He knows your measure, and so do I!"

All around her, villagers focused intensely on their tasks, careful not to meet her eye. An old woman, though she pretended not to listen, made a sign to ward off evil. Under her breath, Farah cursed Naji and his sham piety.

Rustam staggered up to the well, panting and sweating profusely. One look at her scowl and he knew the cause. "Your brother?"

"Half-brother," she muttered, handing him the bucket and ladle. "Half a man, too, next time he gives me an excuse." She patted the dagger on her hip.

Rustam's frown spoke all he needed to say. Even without the taboo, it was unwise to pick a fight with Naji while Ember Mahdi championed his claim.

The balance of power between Emir and Ember was always tenuous. In hard times like these, people looked to the god for succor, and the holy man held the edge. If he rallied enough of the tribe behind Naji, father could be forced to name her brother heir.

Had he done so in her absence? The thought sent her into a sudden panic.

Farah sprinted toward her father's pavilion. She prayed her victory and treasure would tip the balance the other way, before it was too late.

Bastian and Milo knelt on the bank of the oasis, lapping water greedily. The shade of the palm trees, where the shore should be, was several yards behind them. The oasis was small enough to make a tribe nervous.

In his experience, nervous people could be dangerous.

"Nice of them to untie us," Bastian whispered, stretching his stiff muscles. Untie him, at least. Milo had simply handed their captors his rope.

"For all the good it does us." Milo surveyed their surroundings. "Since they have our horses and weapons, the desert's as good as a prison."

Bastian leaned over the oasis again to hide from the eyes of the guards. He splashed water on his face. "We should take a few days to rest, let them grow complacent. Wait for an opportunity." And maybe, in the meanwhile, learn more about Farah.

Milo nodded.

One of the nomads nudged Bastian with his spear butt. "Time to go."

Flanked by guards, Bastian and Milo scaled the cliffside path. Below them, stolen mules grazed among desert horses in the shade of the bluff. Beyond the shelter of the oasis, dry grass gave way to bleached stone. Nothingness stretched to a horizon that shimmered like waves in the beating sun.

By the time they reached the top, Bastian was sweating profusely. Without the shelter of the cliff, the harsh sunlight threatened to bake him in his own skin.

168

He touched a rock for balance and jerked his hand away, scalded.

Milo, of course, showed neither weariness nor discomfort. He gave a low whistle of awe that made Bastian look around.

He had expected a camp of tents and huts, and it was, in a way. The tents were there, but they were strewn throughout the ruins of a once-mighty city, centuries dead. Sandstone walls and pillars jutted into the sky, like the skeleton of a beast too giant to fathom.

A sprawling temple, still intact, dominated the landscape. It filled Bastian with wonder and dread.

"What do you make of it?" he asked Milo. "Think they still use it?"

Milo nodded toward a streamer of smoke rising from the temple roof. It was answer enough.

Farah gasped for air, burning inside and out. She heard the shouting before she even reached the tent.

Her father never shouted, never lost his calm. He never needed to. He could command with a whisper. Something was wrong.

She crashed through the door flap without bothering to lift it – and careened into the chest of Maluk, the Ember's personal guard. He was the largest man in the tribe, chosen for stature as much as skill. She bounced right off him.

Ember Mahdi looked down on her, his dark snake-eyes gleaming. Once, he had been Ember of a large city, before a temple schism sent him to the desert hinter-lands. "Ah, there's the rash young lady now. I'll let *you* give her the news." His white-bearded face split into a grin of crooked yellow teeth. Maluk held open the flap for him, and they departed.

Yusuf, Emir of the Karda, slumped at the table. He buried his face in his hands.

Farah picked herself up and rushed to her father, flinging her arms around him. "Father, tell me you didn't…"

Her father heaved a sigh, then fell silent for a long while. "The north well," he said finally, not looking up. "It's gone dry. It won't be long until we lose the south one, too."

Farah thought of the water, too precious to waste, she had splashed on her face. "We'll manage. We can haul water up from the oasis. It's not yet dry."

Yusuf placed his hands on the table, hands that never before had trembled. "For now, yes, but you ignore the larger problem. The wells are a symbol. The god has withdrawn his favour."

Farah grabbed her father's hands to steady them. "Those are the Ember's words, not yours. He doesn't speak for the god. He's a nasty old man, hungry for the power he thinks Naji can give him."

Yusuf shook his head sadly. "They're not just his words. He has the whole tribe speaking them. It has become their truth."

"So? You would make Naji heir, to please them?" She threw her arms in the air, disgusted.

"Not heir, child. Emir. Mahdi named the god's price

170

for keeping my throne, and I would not pay it."

Farah found herself trembling now, her voice unsteady. "What about the price of stepping down? The Ember will have Naji march to war with every tribe for a hundred miles, the zealous fool!"

"Yes, he will, but not to plunder. He aims to unite them."

Her eyes narrowed in suspicion. "To what end?" Mahdi craved power, but he barely hid his disdain for the backwards nomads. So far from the seat of power, no number of followers would satisfy his vanity.

Yusuf gripped the table hard. "To please the god, he would throw us against the very walls of Harreketh."

"That's madness!" Farah shouted. "It would be death for the tribe!"

Her father looked away, for the first time unable to meet her gaze. "Is he wrong?" he whispered; voice hoarse with emotion. "Are we not keepers of the faith? Does it not fall to us to correct the city dwellers, soft within their walls, when they grow decadent?"

"Correct them?" Farah spat on the carpet. "With fire and steel?"

"The god's fire!" her father shouted, startling her. Even so, it was almost a relief to hear him yell. "They suffer unbelievers to live among them, and we do nothing about it! Small wonder Haephesto has turned his eye from us…"

Farah couldn't believe her ears. "So you're letting this happen? You really think Naji could unite the tribes, let alone take Harreketh? He's a brainless butcher!"

Yusuf slumped again; his fire gone as quickly as it

had kindled. "No. But Mahdi could, in his name."

It all fit. The desert would never be good enough for Mahdi. "He's using Naji," she told her father. "He's riding the fool like a pony. He wants to be Ember of Harreketh."

"I know he does. Naji may be a fool, but I am not."

"Then why do you allow this? Do you think the sultan will sit idle when we sack one of his cities? Win or lose, this is suicide!"

Yusuf shrugged; a man defeated. How had he grown so old, so quickly? "Each day I pray the desert queen to intercede for us, that the god might send us rain. None comes. Is it not my fault? I know the price but cannot bring myself to pay it."

"What is the price?" she demanded.

"The price of rain has always been blood. He would have me prove my faith with–"

"With victory?" she blurted. "With treasure? Father, this is what I came here to tell you! We attacked a Ghassan raiding party, twice our size, and captured their spoils. Haephesto still favors us!"

Her father's eyes went wide, with a glow almost feverish.

"There's money, father, and more. There's silk, and honey, and wine, and–"

He waved a hand, cutting off her frenzied rambling. "And *prisoners*?"

"No… Well, sort of." She shook her head to clear it. "There are two, but I promised them–"

Yusuf stood and clutched his hands together, hugging them to his chest. He faced the heavens, his eyes

172

squeezed tight. "Oh, the god is good. This is wonderful!"

Farah cocked her head, confused.

"There are two ways to appease the god. Either I must give to the flames… that dearest to me…"

Though her father did not name it, Farah knew exactly what was dearest to him. Her chest went tight. To think he would doom the tribe, just to spare her?

"Or?" she croaked.

"Or I must step down, so a new emir can stoke the temple fires with conquered foes."

Farah's jaw dropped. Her tongue felt wooden, unable to form words.

"Don't you see?" Her father's face was awash with relief. "It need not be Naji! You have brought victory to the tribe, and prisoners when we most need them. Haephesto has chosen you to lead his crusade! *You* shall be emir!"

Long, long ago, a young girl rode out from the eastern steppes. A fearless warrior with a flaming sword, she united the tribes and brought the civilized world to its knees. She was a storm of blood and steel that left death in its wake.

But when the storm died down, the girl also brought order. She redrew the map and ended the feuds. She brought law to the lawless people of the desert. For a century, the land flourished under the peace she wrought.

Even rain fell generously in those days. Some said the god blessed her reign, others that he cared only for how she watered the sands with blood. Either way, it was a boon purchased by the death of thousands.

The taboo against kinslaying was one of the desert queen's laws. So was the one against guest-slaying.

The air in the temple was hotter than outside. In the centre of the hall, where Bastian expected an altar, two massive bellows pumped life into a burning forge. Heat billowed from it in tangible waves, the smoky breath of a living thing. The clang of hammers echoed from every wall.

The desert nomads were the best smiths in the world, and Bastian watched with unfeigned interest as they folded the steel a final time. "If I could bring a dozen such swords to Almadyn, I'd recoup all my losses. The lords would fall over each other for the chance to buy one."

"Good luck finding a dozen," Milo said. "I've only seen ones like that in a chief's hands."

"An emir's," Rustam corrected. He frowned but did not say more.

The warrior had been their chaperone since they reached the village, to protect as much as guard them. Everyone Bastian saw hurried about their business, their heads down as if a storm were about to break. The entire camp crackled with nervous energy.

"I heard of a caravan caught smuggling one of those blades," Milo said. "Eighty men put to death. Every last one."

Bastian whistled. It wasn't typical for raiders to wipe out a caravan that size, since it required coordination between tribes. It was more common to demand a toll, or to grab a few animals and run.

"Forging a shamshir is a sacred act," Rustam explained, "the sword itself holy. It binds the emir to the god, a symbol of his right to rule."

Bastian nodded, making a mental note to keep his hands off the sword. The fire pit roared with every gust of the bellows. "So why forge one now? Doesn't your emir already have a shamshir?"

Rustam remained silent, his eyes fixed on the glowing forge.

"Rustam!" shouted a woman's voice.

Everyone turned. Farah stood framed in the temple entrance; her dark eyes wild with fury. "We have to talk," she said. "Now."

Rustam looked to Bastian and Milo, then back to his commander.

"Bring them," she said. "This concerns them, too." She turned and dashed out the door.

They followed Farah to the edge of the camp, scurrying to match her pace. Bastian was first to catch up. Tucked beneath a bush, behind a low, broken wall, he saw his and Milo's swords.

"I'm leaving these here for you," she said abruptly. "At first dark, you need to leave. Steal a horse and go."

"My lady?" Rustam gasped, panting for breath. He sat back against the wall.

"Slow down," Bastian urged. "Perhaps you'd best explain?"

Farah paced, too agitated to hold still. "I erred in bringing you here. I thought the ransom money would give my father an advantage against our priest. But I failed. I'm too late." She kicked the stone wall. "No matter what I do, I've already lost."

Bastian pretended not to notice her wince as she limped the next few steps. Even frowning, she was beautiful. "How can we help?"

Farah ceased her pacing and stared at him.

"I'm serious." And he was, though he had spoken without thinking. "Milo and I can't just ride off into the desert," he improvised. "We have no supplies and don't know our way. As I see it, our best bet is to throw in our lot with you."

Milo eyed him sceptically.

"Don't say it," Bastian said. He knew he was a fool for damsels in distress; he didn't need to hear it. "You're right, but it changes nothing."

Milo shrugged and turned to Farah. "Well, you heard the man. What can we do?"

Farah shook her head. "Why? I stole your goods, brought you here by force. Now I'm giving you your freedom. Why won't you just leave?"

Bastian opened his mouth to speak, but Milo beat him to it. "You buried our dead," he said. "Those men weren't family, not even our friends, but they were our responsibility. And we failed them. We can't make that right, but you gave them rites and an honest grave."

Bastian nodded. His friend had spoken his own heart. "My lady, we are at your service."

VOLUME 2

In the years to follow, Farah often thought back to that day – to how a small kindness to a stranger, like a seed tossed carelessly to the ground, blossomed and grew. How it changed the fate of a tribe, and the course of her life.

In that moment, however, Farah rolled her eyes. "Yes, how very noble," she scoffed. "You don't even know what you're saying. My father would have me burn you on the god's altar, so I can be emir instead of my brother. Still keen to help?"

"I err…" Bastian squirmed. "I admit, it's not what I had in mind."

"Your father would make you emir?" Rustam asked. "Perhaps we should consider–"

She smacked the back of his head.

"I'm joking!" He rubbed his head and gave her a cockeyed grin. "Still, you'd make a good emir."

To her shame, Farah had considered sacrificing the men. The temptation was there – the chance to triumph over Naji and the Ember, devils take them both. The welfare of her tribe hung in the balance.

But she couldn't do it. She had named these men guests, and that bound her to them. No reign begun with the breaking of taboo could come to any good.

Of course, there were other reasons she couldn't kill them, ones she'd never speak. Her eyes traced the pleasing curve of the merchant's jaw, gritty now with stubble. The start of a beard made him less effete. "No, it's not worth it," she told Rustam. "Whether Naji or I rule, Mahdi will have us march to war for his own glory. The Karda die either way."

Rustam frowned. "So he would. But I would sooner die fighting for you than him."

"If I may?" Milo cut in. The man's eyes scanned restlessly, as if he were always on guard. "If we have until nightfall to make any decisions, why don't we go somewhere more private so you can fill us in on the situation?"

Farah nodded and led them across the village. Rustam kept watch as they huddled into her tent. Once inside, she told them of the Ember's plans and her conversation with her father.

Bastian held his chin, tapping a finger on his lip. "But this drought afflicts the whole region. It has nothing to do with your father's rule. Why does he need to step down?"

Farah snorted. "It's not even about the water. Mahdi's convinced the tribe that the god is angry, and that my brother will return them to glory. All he'll bring them is death."

"I get it, though," Milo said. "When things get bad, people look for a savior. It doesn't matter what he does, so long as he promises them everything."

Bastian tilted his head and stared at Farah, long enough for his gaze to make her uncomfortable. "So? Why not you?"

"Huh? What do you mean?"

"Why *don't* you become emir of the Karda?" he

asked. "Why not unite the tribes, just like the desert queen? Something tells me you could."

Farah closed her eyes. It was a tempting picture, her astride her horse, her army stretching to the horizon. Her holy warriors would sweep aside all of the Najis, the Mahdis, and even the fat sultan on his throne. She could remake the world as it should be. A new world built on the bones of the old.

Farah had known battle her whole life – she was good at it, even loved it a little. It was the part of her that scared her, that instinct to destroy. To become a queen, to become a legend, there was no room for doubt. The desert queen brought creation and destruction in equal measure.

But Farah couldn't do it. No matter how well she swung a sword, she couldn't close her eyes to the blood she spilled, to the hopes and dreams cut short by sharp steel.

It was the difference between her and Naji. To her, lives mattered.

"That was a different Farah," she said, smiling sadly. "I'm just me. I don't have it in me to burn the world down." She shrugged.

Bastian reached out for her hand, and she let him. His were calloused, and surprisingly strong. "Maybe that's not a bad thing?"

Milo coughed and shifted his seat. "I'll help Rustam keep watch."

"Not yet," Bastian blurted, to her disappointment. "I may have a plan."

The alarm rang out across the moonlit camp. Torches streaked back and forth as men and women grabbed their swords. In a swarm, they hurried downhill to the horses.

Bastian watched the chaos from the shadows of the ruins. The air was cool and dry, but the stones were still warm from a day baking in the sun. "Must be flattering," he whispered, "to see how eager they are to rescue you."

"Maybe they're just eager to kill the dirty outlanders who kidnapped me?" Farah smirked briefly before her face sank back into a frown. "Besides, some are my brother's men. They'd love to offer him condolences for my death."

"In that case," Milo said, "I hope they don't find Rustam. I rather like the guy."

Somewhere out in the desert, Rustam led horses in a wild moonlit gallop, creating a false track as he pretended to chase escaped prisoners. Once he'd been gone for twenty minutes, a warrior loyal to Farah had raised the alarm.

"At least it worked," Bastian offered, trying to buoy their spirits. Though Farah had agreed to the plan, she was plainly uncomfortable with it. Given what she risked, he could hardly blame her. "The temple must be stripped of guards by now."

Farah scanned the darkness, her mouth still knit in a frown. "No, not all of them. But we've wasted enough time." She pulled her hood low and took off in a crouch, not watching for him to follow.

"Come back in one piece," Milo said glumly. It galled him to stay behind, but his arm was far from healed.

Bastian clapped his friend on the shoulder. He wanted to say they'd be back in no time, but the words wouldn't come. It was too likely a lie.

He stumbled through the dark after Farah, the thin moonlight a blessing and a curse. He banged his shin on a rock and grunted, biting his tongue not to cry out.

"Quit fooling." Farah grabbed his shoulder and pulled him along.

Sconces burned on both sides of the temple entrance, spilling too much light to sneak by. "Nothing to it, then," Bastian said, mostly to convince himself. "Either they're gone or they're not."

"Less talk," Farah whispered harshly. She took one last look around, then edged along the wall and into the temple. Bastian, one hand on his hilt, followed.

Inside the great hall, all was silent except the crackle of torches. Though the bellows slept, heat still radiated from the dying forge. The finished shamshir, set with an ebonwood grip and freshly sharpened, sat carelessly on the anvil. It was all too easy.

Bastian held his breath while Farah crept along the outskirts of the chamber. The torches cast weird shadows over the floor, and the sword glinted in the firelight. As she reached for it, something moved from behind the bellows.

"Farah! Look out!"

"Thief!" roared a hulking shadow. It charged and, before she could dodge, crashed into Farah. She rolled with the blow and came up standing, the shamshir miraculously in her hands.

Her attacker was the biggest tribesman Bastian had ever seen. The giant hefted a two-handed scimitar large enough to behead a horse. It made Bastian's cavalry sword look like a table knife.

Farah and the giant squared off, blades at the ready. The guard towered over the woman by a head and more. Bastian swallowed hard and rushed between them.

"Idiot!" she shouted. "What are you doing?"

"I've got th–" His words cut off in a grunt as he parried the massive sword. The impact jolted his arms and forced him back a step.

Bastian danced back, giving his muscles a chance to recover from the shock. *Make him swing*, he thought desperately. *The sword's too heavy. When he misses, I'll cut in before he can–*

Steel crashed against steel, ringing through the hall. The giant's swings came hard and fast, and Bastian had no time to think, only to defend. He kept giving ground beneath heavy blows that jarred his arms and notched his blade. He felt the heat of the forge on his back, and knew he had to act.

The giant levelled a two-handed swing that would have sheared both blade and neck. Instead of parrying, Bastian ducked the blow and lunged for the monster's heart.

He was stopped short by a boot to the face. Lightning flashed behind his eyes, and again when he struck the ground. The world spun in circles of dizzy agony.

Bastian's vision refused to focus. He saw every-

thing in double, including the scimitar raised for a killing blow.

Farah stepped astride the fallen Bastian. She caught Maluk's descending blade along the length of her own – angled not to block it, but to deflect its momentum toward the floor. The giant scimitar struck the ground with an explosion of sparks.

Before Maluk could recover, she twisted her blade over his. She leaped back, raking her sword across the man's wrist as she withdrew. The priest's bodyguard howled and clutched his arm, unable to stem the blood pulsing from the wound.

The shamshir was *sharp*. It felt glorious in her hands, as if it had been forged to fit them.

Maluk bellowed like an enraged bull. He raised his sword high for a killing stroke, showing no sign of his wound save his crimson sleeve. With speed surprising for his size, he lunged and swung.

But he was too slow. No one in the tribe, even the mighty Maluk, was faster than Farah. She stepped inside the attack, as close as an embrace, and the massive blade came down behind her. Half the shamshir jutted from Maluk's back.

The giant's eyes went wide, and his sword fell from his grip. Refusing to die, he grappled her in a bone-crushing hug. With desperate strength, she wrenched the shamshir aside. Blood flew in an arc as it sliced free of the man's ribs.

Hells, but it was sharp.

Maluk staggered back, dead even before he fell. His body toppled onto the sacred forge, still hot from the day's labor.

Farah's pulse throbbed in her temples. As the smell of entrails and seared flesh hit her nostrils, she dropped to her knees and retched. When the heaving stopped, she wiped her mouth on her sleeve. The hot coals lit Maluk's robe, and it bloomed into a pyre. "Be with the god," she whispered. She didn't like the man but hadn't wished to kill him. He had only been doing his duty.

At her side, Bastian groaned. He tried to prop himself up but flopped back down. He had a black eye, and his nose trickled blood.

"How's your head, hero?"

Bastian grimaced. "Ugh. Still attached. But, the way it aches, I might be better off without it."

"I could remove it for you?" She patted the shamshir.

"Would you? I hardly use it, anyway."

That's the truth, Farah thought. She grinned at the man, and he grinned back.

With the tribe scouring the desert for their missing princess, nobody took note of three more warriors leaving camp. Bastian knew he'd never pass for a nomad, but the darkness hid his features.

As they galloped into the desert, his head throbbed with every bounce. Milo had teased him for his battered face, but he deserved it. He never stood a chance against the giant. He had thought himself a fighter, and not without justice, but Farah shamed him. The woman was amazing.

On the way out of the temple, she had knocked over a sconce, then soaked a rag in the spilled, sticky naphtha. "A contingency," she had told him, but didn't explain what for.

He never asked. They rode through the night in silence.

In the grey before dawn, they stopped in a pass between low, craggy peaks. Wind whistled against stone, kicking up sand and grit. While Bastian and Farah watered the horses, Milo climbed to the crest of a rise. He came back shaking his head. "We're being followed. Maybe a dozen riders, each with a change of mounts, about an hour behind us."

"Can we outrun them?" Bastian asked. Though no one replied, he knew the answer. Their exhausted horses would never outrun fresh mounts.

"Well," Milo said, "I guess it's time for the lady to escape her captors."

Bastian smiled sadly at Farah. They had come so far; he'd almost thought his plan could work. Such a shame. "We may as well hide the sword here. We'll go a little further, to draw them away from this spot, and then rest the horses. I'd like to give good account of myself when they catch us."

Milo nodded his agreement. "We appreciate all you've done for us. Head on back, now, and we'll take it from here."

Farah stared into the distance, where grey clouds grumbled with thunder. She stood there a long while, one hand on the hilt of her sword, the other twined in her horse's mane.

In the end, she let go of the horse. "I changed my mind. I'm not going back."

Somehow, Bastian's heart both leapt and sank. He longed to bring the woman with him, but it would be idiocy. He could offer her nothing but death. "If they see you with us, they'll know you stole the sword. They'll know you killed a tribesman. You have to leave and blame us." He tried to sound more resolute than he felt.

The sun peeked above the horizon, painting the world red. The breeze swept Farah's hair into streamers, and she smiled, grim and radiant. She patted her hilt.

Milo shrugged. "Guess I'll fix breakfast."

Thunder rolled in the distance, drawing nearer. The wind howled in angry gusts.

Naji was first into the pass, just as Farah had hoped. She stepped into the path, blocking him, and raised her hand. Sweat trickled down her brow.

The riders halted, thank the god.

"My wayward sister." Naji spoke loud enough for all to hear. "I hurry to your rescue, only to find you siding with the enemy. Did you set these captives loose?"

"And what if I did? They're mine, to free as I please." She tucked her hands behind her to hide their shaking. And to hide something else.

"They belong to the tribe. And what belongs to the tribe, belongs to *me*." He wheeled his horse to face his men. "Today, I will be emir!" He lifted his sword in the air.

"Naji!" voices cried, as horsemen raised their blades in salute. "Emir Naji!"

Farah waited for the cheering to end. "Oh, I think not," she said coyly. "Not without this." She took the shamshir from behind her back and held it across her palms.

Even sheathed, Naji recognized the blade instantly. His face purpled with rage. "Why," he hissed, "do you have *my sword?*"

"Yours?" Farah took a step toward her brother. Though a dozen men twitched at their hilts, her fear melted away. "This is not the blade of a coward. Of a bully." She took another step, the god's fire coursing through her veins.

"It's the blade of an emir! Hand it over, or I swear I'll cut you down!"

"No!" she shouted back, stalking closer still. Horses shifted beneath uncertain riders. "It's the blade of a queen!"

Standing right before her brother, Farah drew the shamshir. It rasped free of the sheath…

And burst into flame.

Naji's horse reared and threw him to the ground; the others whickered nervously. Wide-eyed men whispered in awe. Whispered a name.

The desert queen.

"No!" Naji groaned. "It's mine! You can't–"

She brandished the flaming blade, and he scurried back. "Haephesto gave me the sword. In his name, swear you will never be emir." Flames licked her hands, and she gritted her teeth to hide the pain.

"You wouldn't dare harm me!" Despite his bold words, Naji's voice was shrill with fear. "It's taboo!"

She thrust the sword an inch from his face, until he flattened on the ground like a worm. "A queen makes her own laws. Now swear it!"

"I swear!" he yelped. "I swear it by the god…"

"You witness this?" she asked the horsemen. They answered with nods and murmurs of assent – shamed as Naji was, he'd never command them again. "Be on your way, then, and report to my father what you've seen."

Naji glared daggers but climbed on his horse and fled. His men followed. The sky went dark, and thunder cracked overhead. The wind raged.

Though it scalded her palm, Farah held the sword until the horsemen were gone from the pass. Not a moment after, she threw it to the ground and stamped it out.

Bastian rushed to her side; astonishment written on his face. He gripped her shoulders. "You… How did you…" He gazed at the sword, slack-jawed, then back at her. "Are you truly the desert queen?"

Farah smiled. With her unburnt hand, she pulled him down to kiss his forehead. Behind his back, already slicing aloe for her burns, Milo grinned and winked.

One day, she'd tell him of the naphtha on the sword, of the flint tucked in her sheath. For today, she would let him believe.

As they turned their mounts toward Harreketh, her

hand bandaged and sword cleaned, Farah felt the first drops of rain

ADVENTURE AWAITS

MALFEASANCE IN PARADISE

JASON RUSSELL

Onoa Island
275 Nautical Miles NorthEast of New Guinea
January 17
3:46pm

Claude Allan sighed in as close to relaxation as he allowed himself once his bare feet arched themselves into the sun-warmed white sand of the beach. Simone allowed the flowey overcoat she had worn down from the hotel to fall away like the press unveiling of some prototype supercar. Admittedly, her sun-kissed skin had no right looking as natural as it did amid the tropical people busily living their daily lives all around.

Two men, wearing what would make a Speedo back home look conservative, walked between them carrying an upside-down narrow fishing boat above their heads. Allan noted the boat was painted scarlet as if to match their loin clothes.

"What do you think?" Simone asked, performing a small pirouette in the sand before him.

"I tend to burn a bit easily on the beach," he began.

"I mean of my suit," she fired back, keeping her frustration in check.

"Oh," he said, hoping the damage hadn't already been done. "It's even more lovely than how you described it."

"You don't think it makes my butt look big?"

"Not at all, dear," he said cheerfully.

"Big is in," she said. "You'd know this if you ever watched The Kardashians with me." He didn't need to see through her sunglasses to know her eyes performed a textbook skyward revolution.

"I mean, it looks enormous, dear. Absolutely enormous."

"What is it?" Simone asked, suddenly realizing her husband's attention was even more distant than usual. She looked over her shoulder at a pair of men much further up the beach. They were clearly not native, dressed in white with safari hats. One had small, round sunglasses and a dark beard. She recognized him immediately. "Don't even tell me!"

"What?" Claude said, palms up and out for added implied innocence.

"Did we fly all the way here to follow Likstine?"

"Don't be ridiculous, dear. You said you thought a tropical getaway would be good for us…"

She was already storming toward the water's edge,

192

right hand open and behind her head indicating his time for rebuttal had expired.

He caught up with her, putting a hand on an already sun-warmed shoulder. "Honey, please. Just listen to me."

She stopped walking. A good sign.

"He's up to something. You know how I can just sense it."

"Did it ever occur to you that maybe *he* needed to get away from you? Some people do just go to the tropics to get some sun and take in the native culture, you know."

"No, Likstine doesn't work that way."

"Apparently neither do we."

"Honey don't be mad. This is your weekend, just like we discussed. Fresh lobster for dinner tonight, the whole thing. Just like in the brochure.

Her shoulders relaxed. She was weakening.

"And the tour?"

"Of course," he said.

"Well we'll see." She dropped her towel and overstuffed bag down into the sand. "If I hear so much as mention of that Likstine's name, I'm flying back home and leaving you to find your own way back."

"Maybe I ought to make friends with those naked guys with the boat, huh?"

"It wouldn't hurt! Now here, rub this sunscreen on my back. Put some on your chest too, you're already looking rosy."

☙❧

"How was your lobster?" Claude Allan asked his wife in their hotel room without taking his eyes away from the binoculars he had directed out the window.

"You already asked me that four times. It was mushy. Nothing like that cold-water shellfish you get in New England."

"That's right," he said, only half listening. He made a mental note not to ask again. He could see Likstine on the beach but, even with the binoculars, he was too far away to be able to read his nemesis's lips. The man he was talking with looked somehow familiar too, but the tropical setting of a thousand brilliant colors working in perfect harmony was throwing off his ability to place him.

"What are you looking at?" Simone asked, yanking his attention back into the room.

"Just the ocean."

She approached the window, squinting out toward the beach. "What about it?"

"The swells." He hoped Lickstein was a bit too far out of range for her to see with the naked eye.

"It looks calm from here."

"Well it is. Now. But I want to be ready for when the swells begin."

Simone stood beside him a moment longer. "Alright, well, I'm going to take a shower. Wash all this sand out from between my toes. When I get out, maybe we can get that coconut scented massage oil I picked up at the gift shop downstairs out and work away some tension." She turned and walked away from the window.

"That sounds wonderful," he said, picking up the

binoculars once more. "How was your…" He caught himself.

"What did you say?" she called over her shoulder on route to the bathroom.

"Nothing. I'm going to grab some ice."

Martin Likstine, once an esteemed colleague at the university back in France, had managed to get himself into a heap of trouble with the deans of both administration and academia when it came to light that he had been using university resources for unapproved (and unethical) experimentation.

While Allan didn't know the extent of what Likstine had been doing in their shared department to warrant eventual termination after a lengthy and costly investigation, he was able to piece together some ideas. From what Allan could recall, he'd been linked to various terrorist organizations that were providing funding for germ warfare development. What became of those allegations, Allan couldn't say, as Likstine wasn't arrested. However, his activities in the years to follow were no less suspicious.

He had formed two privately held corporations in as many years, one of which was dedicated to cutting edge robotics and quickly went under after investigations of fraud and money laundering. The second, and most recent as far as Allan could tell, of Likstein's companies was trying to secure military subsidizing for artificial intelligence weaponizing potential.

He was about as close to mad scientist classification as Allan dared fathom and, after getting a tip from another colleague that Likstine was planning something big, Allan had no choice but to beat him to the South Pacific. The fact that Simone had been pressuring for a getaway at the same time simply made the opportunity all the more irresistible.

By the time Allan had reached the back entrance of the hotel, Likstein and his familiar faced friend were gone.

Dejected, he returned to the room to find Simone was already in bed. "Where's the ice?" she asked.

"The South Pole?"

She shook her head. "You're acting awfully strange. You sure you're alright?"

"Of course, dear," he said, faking a smile. "Just tired. And excited about the tour tomorrow."

January 18
8:47am

The next morning, about fifteen tourists gathered in the front of the hotel awaiting the bus's arrival. The Onoa Islands were home to the native Pai Pai Peoples, a proud and fiercely territorial tribe who had earned a bit of a reputation for slaughtering enterprising Europeans of the 16th century.

While the island was a peaceful community now with an economy built around tourism, the tour promised an intimate look into the culture's more uncivilized past.

"I'm glad you agreed to come with me," Simone said as the bus appeared around the corner, its spotty white paint and dark rust patches apparent before it cleared the cluster of palms in front of the parking lot.

"I do hope we're up on our tetanus boosters."

They shared a seat fairly close to the front of the bus, Claude sitting on the aisle side once it was clear the windows didn't open. "Did they mention if this thing's air conditioned?"

A thin dark-skinned man wearing a Walking Dead t-shirt stood from the driver's seat. "There is no air conditioning on the bus," he announced. "Some windows will open. Some will not."

"Well, now you know," Simone mumbled quietly.

"I don't suppose Yelp is a thing out here?"

The tour consisted mostly of a series of right hand turns that would have been difficult to negotiate for a golf cart. The bus, wheel bearings squealing in protest all the while, cut hard turns that still managed to smack palm fronds and scrape the underside of low hanging electric lines. The driver grimaced incessantly, filling in the endless succession of turns with quips and facts that could mostly be gathered from picking up a pamphlet in the hotel lobby. "This is the spot of a massacre," he said on the approach to nearly every new block.

"I wonder if it would be more practical to just start telling us where there wasn't one," Claude muttered. "And how about letting us know who was winning these massacres and who was losing?"

"The tour concludes with a tour of the site of Mak-kiehadru. That is here, now," the tour guide/ bus driver said. He swung the bidirectional doors before the bus had fully stopped. "Enjoy the shrine. Fifteen minutes."

Passengers began funneling off the bus.

Claude yawned, debating whether or not getting up would have been worth the energy required. "What is Makkiehadru?"

"Who," Simone corrected. "He was the greatest warrior of the Pai Pai Nation. Aren't you even listening?"

Just then, he spotted Likstine entering the shrine. He was on his feet in an instant. "Well, come on, then," he said, taking Simone by the hand. "I must have missed that part. It's time we learn a little something."

The shrine was constructed of traditional Pai Pai building materials, reminiscent of the aboriginal gunyah - trees and bark seemingly forming the outermost walls while the neatly thatched roof framed the structure with overhanging corners. . Inside was no less humid, though the shade was welcome.

"It smells funny in here," Simone observed as they crammed inside the small structure.

"A lot like the bus," Claude agreed. "Just without the diesel fumes."

Likstine turned away from the framed hand-drawn map he had been carefully studying on one of the walls. "Claude Allan," he said, taking off his round sunglasses. "Can it be?"

"It can," Claude said, forcing a smile.

198

"I haven't seen you since that whole debacle with the university," Likstine said. He came over to shake the other's hand.

"Right. Right," Claude said, pretending to be surprised it had been so long.

"Aren't you going to introduce me to your better half?"

"Oh?" He paused, forcing Simone to let go of his hand to shake Likstine's.

"Simone Allan," she said.

"Martin Likstine," he replied, kissing the back of her hand. "And this is my associate Adrian Komakov."

The other man turned and nodded at them both, clearly far less interested in making acquaintances than he was on the map he and another man had been studying.

The name, like the man's face, was immediately familiar to Claude. He was something in the scientific community. "So what brings you to Onoa?"

Likstine put his sunglasses back on. "Oh, you know, a little culture."

"Of course," Allan agreed.

"One can't help but admire the Pai Pai's resilience. Led by Makkiehadru, their warriors were able to best our ships and vastly superior technology for nearly two hundred years. It boggles the mind to imagine what today's armed forces would be capable of with such a tactician at their disposal. I am of the opinion we still have much to gain from his example," Likstine said earnestly. "Now if you'll excuse me."

"Of course," Allan said again, cussing silently at

his own redundancy.

"Look at this," Sione said, tugging her husband back into the thick of the crowd.

"What is it?"

Amid a display housing a myriad of beads, head-dresses and brightly painted pottery, a single weapon was mounted to a plaque on the wall.

"It's the actual spear that pierced the heart of Makkiehadru. He was, according to ancient documents, betrayed and murdered by his own trusted general in the end."

Claude studied the nasty looking barb at the dull metal tip. It was pitted and corroded. "Did they have generals back then?"

That night, despite the air conditioning working to maximum capacity, Claude Allan tossed restlessly, his shallow dreams refusing to clue him in on the name and face of the man with Likstine. "Komakov," he muttered, not quite awake. A few moments later, he moaned, "Makkiehadru." He pulled the covers off of Simone. "Bus driver."

"Alright," she said, sitting up and putting on the light. "I'm freezing and you're fidgeting every minute. Either go downstairs and get yourself something to help you sleep or I'm taking the blankets into the bathtub with me."

Partially dressed and shuffling, Claude Allan approached the downstairs hotel bar with an extended yawn. He pulled himself onto the barstool next to the only other patron in the place. It was a young woman, conservatively dressed, with a black briefcase on the floor beside her. She didn't look native.

"What can I get you?" the bartender asked, wiping down the bar with a white towel in the process.

"Something to help me sleep."

"Ah, a nightcap," he said with a sly grin.

"Yes. One of those."

"I'll make you up my own special blend. But don't be far from a bed because when it kicks in, you're liable to wake up on the floor."

"Wouldn't be the first time," Claude mused.

The woman beside him didn't laugh. At this proximity, he could see the papers she had strewn about before her. "You shouldn't bring your homework to a tropical island," he said. "Too many distractions."

"And interruptions," she added.

"My apologies, I didn't mean to distract."

After a pause, she flipped the folder before her shut and sighed. "No, you're fine," she said, picking up her drink. It was a tropical looking concoction with a slice of pineapple impaled upon the side of the glass. "I'm here on business. And not making any progress."

"I suppose that's better than my situation. I came here on a hunch that someone was about to do something horrific and I've yet to see proof of any suspicious behaviour." He thought for a moment. "Aside from my own."

He could tell from the corner of her eye something in his words gave her pause. "I don't mean to pry," she began, "but would it surprise you to discover I am here for the very same reason?"

The bartender set his drink down on the glossy. "Nurse it," he warned.

"I don't think that would surprise me much," he admitted. "Especially if that's your job."

"Well, I'm a private eye from the United States," she said, slightly lower.

"And I'm pretending to be one," he replied. "France."

After a chuckle, she extended a manicured hand. "Jennifer."

He shook it, wondering if he should kiss the back of it like Likstine did with Simone. "Claude."

"Claude, I can't say much about my client, but what do you think about a master thief on an impromptu trip to the tropics to meet with some characters of questionable background?"

"Well, naturally, I like him already. The question I have for you is what do you think of a convicted mad scientist and a mysterious Russian man also taking an impromptu trip to the tropics to take in some culture?"

Her smile dissipated. "Who are you, really?" she asked without making eye contact.

"I told you already."

"Would this scientist happen to be named Martin Likstine perchance?"

This time, it was Claude's smile that faded. "As a matter of fact, it would…"

"Bartender," she announced, "If it's okay with you, we'd like to move to a table."

"Huh," Claude said, sipping his drink. It was the odd combination of fruity and fiery, with a lingering numbness reminiscent of cough syrup. "So this thief you followed here from Texas. I think I saw him earlier. He was with Likstine and another scientist. Komakov. Adrian Komakov. Does that name mean anything to you?"

She flipped through her briefs. "Oh yes. Disputatious Russian bioengineer."

That was it! He'd been in the news periodically for unethical experimentation in cloning human body parts. The trouble he'd been facing, it seemed, was that the nations with economies healthy enough to support the pricey technology required to perform such work happened to be the ones with enough ethics to ban such research in the first place. Naturally, he'd connect with Likstine. "But why?" Allan wondered aloud.

"Let's look at the three common denominators here," Jennifer said without looking up from the papers scattered about the table. "We have a shady businessman, a master thief and bioengineer known for cloning. All on a small tropical island with little to no warning."

"With a pair of geniuses hot on their trail, let's not forget," Claude added, the effects of the liquor overtaking him.

"Where did you say you saw them again?"

"A shrine." He thought for a moment. "Something

with an M. Mihundra."

She pursed her lips.

"Mikandre. No, that's not it. Makkando. Makkie-hadru!"

"What could they possibly want to steal from such a site?"

A thought, one so disjointed as to likely have escaped him altogether in sobriety, made Claude's eyes widen. "They want to clone Makkiehadru," he blurted out.

Jennifer looked up at him. "Is that even possible?"

"Of course. With the right equipment and a complete lack of scruples."

"I mean, wouldn't they need DNA or something?"

He nodded. "It would have to be tissue. Maybe blood."

"And where could they possibly obtain some?"

He froze, all the events of the day prior locking into place like a puzzle. "I know just the spear. Let's just hope we're not too late."

January 19
12:17am

It was shortly past midnight when they arrived at the Shrine of Makkiehadru. The scene was lit by a pair of authentic-looking native torches that cast dancing shadows onto the wall opposite the entrance to the small hut.

"Are you sure it's a forgery?" Jennifer asked.

"I'm positive," Claude said, squinting at the spear

upon the wall. He was slightly dizzy; a sensation made no easier by the flickering light. Still, he had no doubt. "The original looked aged. The tip was patinated."

Jennifer moved in closer. Indeed, the spear tip here was suspiciously clean, silvery, and reflective.

"The swap has already taken place," Claude added. "Just as I feared. We're too late."

She opened her handbag, revealing a Kahr CM9 9mm pistol.

"But you know where to find them?" he asked.

She nodded. "We'll have to try to grab a cab, though."

"I'd advise skipping the bus."

They arrived at a darkened but modern lab building that butted up to the water's edge. It was dark inside and the front door locked.

"If this were a movie," Claude observed, "there would have been a crackle of thunder when we got out of the car."

"Around back," Jennifer shouted.

Claude was running to keep up with her though the dark, swatting away foliage and trying not to twist an ankle on the uneven terrain. "How did you do that in heels?" he said, trying to catch his breath.

"We can still catch them." She was untying a small motor-equipped raft from its mooring on the dock.

"But they're in a speed boat," Claud noted. "Shouldn't we call the Navy or something?"

"They've got to cross the channel. Speed isn't as important there as is maneuverability."

Thankfully, the raft's small 2-cycle outboard fired up on the second pull and Claude could steer using the till. He spun the raft in a tight arc away from the dock and twisted the throttle to its stop. The little engine revved hard, churning the water in a wide valley behind them. There were no lights on the raft itself, but there were on Lichstine's boat - at this point a tiny star in the black sky of ocean all around.

"Can't this thing go any faster?" Jennifer demanded; her voice barely audible above the high revving motor at Claude's side.

"Wide open," he yelled back.

"What?"

He shook his head. That would be the first of many such exchanges as they crossed the bay. As she had predicted, though, the speed boat had to come to a near stop where the stony walls of the harbor narrowed before dumping out into the Pacific. The raft, bobbing and hopping as it rode the boat's wake, was able to make up significant time here.

To Claude's surprise, Jennifer had her 9mm in hand by the time the boat was in clear visual range. On her knees, with one hand on the front rocker of the raft, she steadied the pistol within her right and squeezed off three rounds into the boat's stern.

Claude, eyes wide, clicked the throttle down to keep them from rear- ending the craft ahead. Now barely above idle, the motor was quiet enough for them to hear several shots of return fire. These were softer sounding, and the report echoed off the buildings far behind them. Rifle, most likely, he concluded. Thankfully, the dark colored rubber of the raft coupled to a complete lack of lighting worked to their benefit, as not a single shot seemed to have found them.

"Get in closer," Jennifer said, nearly losing her balance. She kicked her heels off onto the raft's floor.

Claude brought the raft in close enough to where it bumped the boat. "Do we even have a plan?"

"Yes. Don't die." She tried to pull herself up onto the hull of the boat but couldn't lift herself. "I need a boost."

Claude clumsily walked over the raft's three thwarts and leaned forward to wrap his arms around her legs. The kick must have come from above, catching her shoulder and causing her to topple over the side. Warm salt water splashed his face.

Claude saw the silhouette of one of the three men aboard the small boat raise the rifle at him. He instinctively reached out and found the bottom rung of a small metal half-ladder that was apparently hard mounted to the boat's hull. With adrenaline-induced speed, he was up and over the rail and wrestling for control of the gun in a flash.

Somehow, his opponent was able to lever the rifle's stock around and catch Claude with it under the chin. The surprising blow took him off his feet and sent him smashing onto the floor of the boat.

The other two men, one of whom was surely Likstine, turned away from the boat's steering wheel. The unmistakable sound of a bullet being chambered filled his ears. Panicked, Claude reached for something to aid him back to his feet when he felt it. It was undoubtedly the spear, wrapped in several layers of heavy nylon and strapped in place by a pair of Velcro fasteners.

Just then, Jennifer, soaking wet and waving around her handgun, appeared on the top of the ladder. "Which one of you sons of bitches kicked me," she demanded.

Their attention momentarily turned away from him, Claude undid the straps and, with all his might, threw the spear over the side of the boat. He heard the splash before he began running toward the stern. There was shouting behind him, a gunshot, and then another. The boat was in motion. He could feel that before he jumped.

The fall played out in slow motion, a small eternity of weightlessness before the warm, dark water swallowed him whole.

He surfaced to the sound of the boat thumming away toward the open ocean and a secondary splash as Jennifer hit the water. "You okay?" he called out into the darkness.

"Fine," she replied, only slightly annoyed. "But I think I'm going to need a new gun."

"Perhaps I can interest you in a spear instead?"

"I'll take you up on that. If we can find it."

"Or the raft, for that matter," he added.

"I can hear the raft," she said after a moment. "It's bobbing over here against the breaker."

He began to swim in the direction of her voice. "The real question now is whether or not spears float."

"Wooden handle," she said, grabbing a hold of the

raft's rope.

It was shortly after dawn by the time they found and retrieved the spear. Indeed, it floated along like a piece of driftwood, caught in a swirling current where the water of two temperatures merged. Much to their relief, Likstine and his ilk made certain to protect it meticulously. Within the nylon wrapping was a tightly sealed waterproof bag lined with blocks of Styrofoam.

"They wanted to make sure this beauty was perfectly preserved by the time they got back to Russia," Claude observed as they walked back to the shrine.

"I still don't know how you put all the pieces of the puzzle together so quickly," Jennifer said.

"Is there such a thing as scientific intuition?"

"I've never heard of it if there is."

He laughed. "I knew it was a long shot."

"Why would anyone want to clone a five hundred-year-old tribal warrior?"

"I bumped into Likstine at the shrine earlier. He spelled it out for me, only I didn't realize it at the time. He'd have one of the world's greatest military tacticians available to the highest bidder. It turns out the governments of the world are willing to pay pretty big bucks to have the edge over their opponents these days."

She smirked. "You almost have to admire the guy. That is pretty crafty."

"Well, he very nearly pulled it off. What he wasn't counting on when putting together his team was a private eye tracking his star burglar."

"Or a resourceful former co-worker," she added.

"And the worst part is our heroic efforts will never be made public. Just a couple of world-saving nobodies once we get this spear back to where it belongs."

"I don't know," she said through a smirk. "Anonymity has its benefits too."

"True. I don't think I could handle being mobbed for autographs."

"To the authorities, then?" She nodded in the direction of the nylon bag containing the spear he was carrying.

"Yes, with our superhero recommendation that they increase the shrine's security."

"A shame a few bad apples have to ruin it for the rest of us."

"Better safe than sorry, I suppose," Claude said. "We can't have clones of Makkiehadru or Rasputin or Hitler leading our armies, now can we?"

She fought a chill. "What a terrifying prospect. You will continue to keep an eye on this Likstine character then, won't you?"

He sighed. "Whether I want to or not. Much to the disappointment of my wife."

January 19
8:20am

The bartender apologized for having dumped the remainder of their drinks when they returned to the hotel bar. "I did not think you would return," he said in

210

strained English.

"We nearly didn't," Claude said jokingly. "Ever."

The man laughed, though it was clear he knew not what was funny about the response.

"I don't have any hard evidence to connect my guy to the heist," Jennifer admitted. "One of these days I'm going to catch him slipping just enough to put him away once and for all."

"Do you think the Onoa government would extradite even if we had him dead to rights on this one, though?"

She pursed her thin lips. "You do bring up a valid point," she said. "The thing about guys like him is they are fueled by their own ego. We may have put a stop to this one, but the next one will happen. It will be bigger, possibly better planned, but undoubtedly higher stakes. It's the thrill of the hunt, I suppose."

"I get that very same feeling about Likstine."

"Well, if you ever need me," she reached into her bag and revealed a business card.

"Business card, huh? Do people still use these in the digital age? I'm holding out for the day when we all get those QR code symbols tattooed on the back of our hands. People just scan them with their phone and we're in their address book."

She laughed. "That's actually pretty clever. You just come up with that now?"

"I've been harboring that one. Trying to come up with a way to make money off it. Apple isn't returning my calls."

"Well, until then, use that card if the world should

ever need saving again, okay?"

He extended a bruised hand. "I hope we never meet again."

"I couldn't have said it better myself."

He got back to the room to find Simone still sleeping peacefully in bed. He quietly got undressed and slipped into the covers beside her, thankful that the firmness of the hotel's mattress made the process easier than it would have been at home.

The pillow felt incredible to him this time, accommodating the sides of his aching head with the perfect angle and resistance. It was entirely possible he was beginning to slide into the syrupy fuzziness between awake and asleep before the foam inside the pillow had finished compressing due to the weight of his skull upon it.

Just then, Simone's alarm began to go off, making him jump.

"Rise and shine, sleepy head," she said.

He could only moan in reply.

"No sleeping in today," she continued. "I have a busy day planned for us. First, we're going to be doing couples yoga on the beach this morning with Jean Pierre. Then we're going to take another bus tour. This time to the far side of the island to watch the natives weave bracelets. Then, I was thinking we could take a boat ride out across the harbor."

He groaned, flipping the pillow atop his head.

"Don't ignore me, Claude Allan. You promised me

this was my vacation."

"No, you're right," he said, sitting up. "I'll just need a couple coffees to get underway."

She looked over at him. "Look at you, you'd think you were up all night saving the world or something the way you act when it's something I'd like to do."

He just smiled.

ADVENTURE AWAITS

EUGENE ANGOVE AND THE DASTARDLY DEFAMATION

TIM MENDEES

April 19th, 1938. Mayfair, London:

Bang! Bang! Bang!

The sound of the ornate brass door knocker slamming against the stout black door echoed down Mount Row.

"Algernon Stephenson!" An irate chap in rumpled tweeds bellowed through the letterbox. "Open the door this blasted instant, you unmitigated bounder!"

"Sir..." The man's valet purred as he placed a white-gloved hand on his shoulder. "May I advise caution. Do you really want to attract attention... under the circumstances?"

Eugene Angove straightened his back, puffed out his bewhiskered cheeks, and counted to ten. "Blast it,

Hampton, I keep forgetting that I'm a damned fugitive. Maybe we should try around the back?"

Hampton looked up and down the street, it was in the grip of a thick *London particular* making visibility poor. Blurred splotches of light from the gas lamps lent the street a spectral aspect as they peeked through the pea soup. They could have been inches away from being apprehended by the local constabulary and been none the wiser. "I think that might be a good idea, sir. I think there is an entry down near the gentleman's tailor on the corner."

"Fine. Let's have a look." Eugene stamped down the three steps to street level and retrieved his hipflask from his inside pocket. "I have to warn you, Hampton. I might not be able to restrain myself when I get hold of the blackguard."

Hampton couldn't help but agree with the sentiment. He was well accustomed to his employer's bluster, but this time he felt no need to defuse his explosive temper. "Indeed, sir. Follow me."

As the duo scuttled down Mount Street, Eugene drained the last drops of less-than-fine brandy from his hip flask and ruminated over recent events. The duo had returned from Peru to a less-than-heroes-welcome at Ye Olde Mitre public house in Holborn. The stuffy landlord had taken one look at their dishevelled attire and had them pegged as undesirable vagrants before you could say, *Fagin.* It was only when Mr McKinnon's valet Thompson spotted them on his return from the WC that they were finally recognised and ushered into the private back room.

"By God, Angove, what do you look like?" Stephenson guffawed. Tossing a tatty copy of Crowley's *The Book Of The Law* onto the table next to his brandy, he shot out of his wingback chair and ushered Eugene and Hampton to a secluded corner table. "Did you get the black stone?"

"We are fine, thank you for asking." Eugene sneered then pulled an object wrapped in an oily rag out of his pocket and dropped it onto the table with a *clatter*. "There, take the blasted thing. I never wish to see or hear of it ever again... understood?"

"Oh dear, had a spot of bother, did you?"

"Bother? *Bother?* You could say that Stephenson..." Eugene Angove proceeded to rant and rave about their adventure from shadowy New England streets to that hellish temple deep in the Peruvian Rainforest. He made a point to relate in great detail every time they were shot at, insulted, run off the road, or bitten by mosquitoes. By the time he was finished, Eugene was exhausted, so the snifter he was handed by Hampton was very welcome indeed.

Stephenson, who had examined the stone by this time, offered a couple of half-hearted apologies then called for his valet, Wilkins. The furtive-looking fellow promptly appeared with a cheque book in one hand and a fountain pen in the other. The sizable number he scribbled followed by his florid signature went a lot further in placating Eugene than his hollow words had.

"Well, I'd like to say that it's been a pleasure seeing you again, Stephenson... but you know that I'm a terrible liar." Eugene drained his brandy in one gulp and smiled.

"I take it that this means we are finally even?"

"Indeed." Stephenson nodded, puffing cigar smoke out of his pursed lips.

"And you will *forget* all the things that could cause me grief?"

"Consider them forgotten, Eugene... and I am grateful, you know? It's just that business has to come first, but I hope we can be friends again... one day."

Eugene stood and shook Stephenson's hand. "We'll see."

"Oh," Stephenson called out as Eugene started to walk away. "Did the lighter I gave you come in handy?"

"Eh?" This caught Eugene off-guard, he was still labouring under the misapprehension that he'd pinched it. "What do you mean, gave?"

"I thought it might be useful in sealing in anything *unpleasant*." Stephenson grinned like a particularly smug Cheshire cat.

"Wait... you knew?" Eugene was both shocked and furious. It appeared that Stephenson had possessed some inkling of the horrors they were to face and neglected to tell them. To rub salt in the wounds, he'd thought that the elder sign on the lighter sealing the ruined temple had been a happy accident and had been slapping himself on the back for discovering it.

"Take care, Eugene!" Stephenson stood and waved cheerily as Hampton dragged his fuming employer out of the room.

The following evening, Eugene and Hampton had finally arrived back at Eugene's estate in Cornwall. The journey had been far more arduous than it should have

218

been due to leaves on the track somewhere on the Great Western line. The circuitous route they'd been forced to endure had left Eugene in something of a prickly mood. As a result, he had swiftly drunk himself into a stupor and stayed there for the best part of a week.

Finally rousing himself from the bottom of myriad bottles the following Saturday, He and Hampton had taken a leisurely drive down to Penzance to see his beloved Truro take on the home side in the Cornwall Cricket League's opening match. The first day had seen plenty of googly's bowled and glasses of gin drained. At the end of the day, Eugene had fallen into the backseat of his Rolls Royce Phantom as drunk as a newt and in fine spirits. Looking forward to the second day, Hampton had steered them back towards Bodmin Moor.

Those high spirits quickly evaporated, however, when Hampton pulled up to the driveway and noticed that the gate was open. Parking on the verge, he stepped out and peered over the hedge. "What the deuce?" He muttered to himself as he took in the scene. The place was simply swarming with police. He'd not seen so many Peelers in one place since he'd last attended a parade. Deciding not to rouse Eugene until he knew what was going on, he slowly crept through the gate, making sure that he stayed in shadow and out of sight. His plan was to get close and hear what the rank-and-file were talking about. As luck would have it, he didn't need to.

"Oi, Hampton... Over 'ere" A rough voice hissed from behind a privet hedge. It belonged to Graves, the gardener.

"What the Devil is going on, Graves?" Hampton

whispered as he joined the gardener behind the bush.

"'Aven't ye 'eard?" Graves thrust a copy of the evening edition of the Betyls Cove Echo into Hampton's hand. "They 'ave warrants for Master Angove's arrest. They're searchin' the 'ouse for *artefacts*."

"Artifacts?" Hampton unfolded the newspaper and stared aghast at the front page. "Oh, Hell's teeth!" Under the one-word headline that simply read, *Thief*, was a picture of a grinning Eugene Angove.

Without another word, Hampton raced back down the driveway like his backside was ablaze. Jumping into the car, he backed quietly out of the driveway, pulled a sharp U-turn and drove back out into the wilds. Eugene snored loudly as Hampton avoided civilization and took them out to the darkest parts of the moor. Once he felt they were far enough out of sight, he pulled over and roused his master.

As you would imagine, Eugene Angove took one look at the newspaper and exploded. Everything detailed in the article was precisely what Stephenson had promised to forget. Only one person knew about his less savoury dealings other than Hampton, so there was only one person to blame. The force of the betrayal soon had them speeding towards London with revenge on their minds. This is how they ended up in a dank alley behind a row of plush townhouses in Mayfair.

"Here we are," Eugene growled as he pushed open the back gate to Stephenson's residence. Marching down the short weed-choked path, Eugene raised his fist and prepared to give the back door a good walloping.

"Wait, sir!" Hampton breathed as he grabbed Eugene's arm. "Look." He raised a gloved hand and pointed to a smashed kitchen window.

Eugene reached out his hand to the back door and was surprised to find that it creaked open without much force being applied. Cursing the fact that he didn't have his trusty revolver with him, he stooped down and picked a half-brick out of a pile of debris. Placing a finger to his lips and nodding at Hampton, Eugene pushed the door open all the way and stepped inside. Reaching along the wall, Eugene located the familiar hump of a bakelite dolly switch and flicked the lights on.

"What in God's name has happened here." Hampton gasped as he poked his head into the kitchen. Stephenson's cook, Martha was lying face down on the chequered tiles with one of her kitchen knives sticking out of her back. Hampton scuttled over and felt her neck for a pulse. "Poor woman's as dead as a stone, Sir... She's cold, I think she's been dead for a couple of days at least."

Crash!

The sound of breaking glass coming from Stephenson's study alerted both men to the fact that they weren't alone. Hampton grabbed a knife out of the block next to the large Belfast sink and followed Eugene down the corridor. His shoulder was still healing from where he took a bullet in Peru, the last thing he wanted was another fight. The study door was ajar, and the room appeared to have been ransacked. Furniture had been overturned and a pile of books and papers were strewn across the floor. Eugene peered around the door and spotted a slender figure dressed from head-to-toe in black hunched over the desk.

Clenching his half-brick in his right hand and raising it above his head, Eugene bellowed like a buffalo and lunged for the intruder. Alerted by Eugene's ruckus, the figure spun, lunged, and walloped Eugene in the nose with a savage jab. His foot hit a couple of pieces of paper sending his legs one way and his body the other. Eugene flopped to the floor in an undignified heap.

Hampton brandished the knife and stepped towards the intruder but stopped sharply when she pulled out a gun and lifted her black veil. "Oh, do put that thing away, Hampton." She purred. "I'm on your side."

"Sorry, Ma'am." Hampton babbled as he dropped the knife and rushed to help Eugene to his feet.

"Edith? … What the ruddy Hell are you doing here!" Eugene exploded and he clenched a tatty handkerchief to his bleeding snout.

"What do you think I'm doing here, you oaf?" Edith Stephenson smirked. "The same as you, I'd wager. I came to give my adoptive sibling a damn good thrashing." Edith Stephenson was in her late fifties but her athletic body and elfin features made her appear much younger. Her eyes blazed with a mixture of rage and concern. Eugene didn't know her very well, but he knew well enough that she was a very dangerous individual.

"I want to know what the bounder thought he was playing at, defaming my honour and branding me a thief!" Eugene pulled out the crinkled newspaper and waved it under Edith's nose.

"That's what a lot of people would like to know, Mr Angove…"

"Eh?"

"I take it," Edith sighed and fluttered her eyes. "That you have only seen the one paper in the last day or so? It seems that my brother hasn't only defamed you, Eugene. He's defamed the entirety of the Brotherhood of Tamesis! Even Mr McKinnon has been forced to go into hiding until he can square things away with Mr Chaimberlain."

"The Prime Minister's involved?" Eugene gasped.

"I'm afraid so, and as you would imagine, he's not exactly got a lot of free time at the moment, what with everything that's going on with Germany... Algernon's smears have reached the highest echelons of British society. Mr McKinnon is in the process of convincing the PM that everything my brother is reported to have said to the press is nothing more than fabrication. I know that there is no truth in any of the reports, but you know what the press is like. We will be able to vouch for your innocence soon enough and absolve you from prosecution."

Eugene shuffled his feet nervously.

Edith cocked an eyebrow. "It *is* all lies... isn't it, Eugene?"

"Erm... yes, all lies! ... not an ounce of truth in any of it." Eugene's cheeks started to turn as red as his nose.

Now it was Hampton's turn to shuffle his feet nervously.

"Oh, good God." Edith's palm met her forehead. "Oh well, I don't suppose it matters. What matters is that we find my brother. I came here ready to give him a slap, and now I find myself concerned for his safety. I don't think he had anything to do with the string of defamations. I assume you saw the body in the kitchen? Both of his maids have been killed also. Their throats slit while they were bound and gagged. A lot of his files are missing, and look..." She held out her hand to Eugene and Hampton.

"Fish scales?" Hampton guessed.

"Indeed. They were under one of the maid's fingernails... it seems that she tried to fight off her attacker."

"Those are some big fish scales." Hampton mused. "Sir! You don't think it's our friends from Innsmouth again, do you?"

"I fear you are right," Edith cut in. "A fish-like eye has been daubed on the master bedroom wall in the maid's blood... a bit of a giveaway."

"The black stone!" Eugene exclaimed. "I bet they were after the blasted black stone! ... where is Algernon's safe?"

Edith sighed and pointed to the painting of her deceased guardian, Robert D'Onston Stephenson, that hung over the fireplace. It was swinging free on two concealed hinges. Eugene pulled it aside and looked at a previously concealed safe. It was gaping open and completely empty.

"Bugger." Eugene spat.

"My thoughts exactly." Edith turned back to her brother's desk. "I think they have taken him with them. They must think he knows how to use it."

"Does he?" Hampton asked.

"It's possible. My brother has an obsession with the occult that borders on mania... he got it from Uncle Bobby."

"But what can those fishy devils do with it now the

224

temple is sealed?" Eugene asked.

"You don't think that's the only such place, do you? There are dozens of sites in Europe alone... One such place in Binger, Oklahoma has recently come to our attention. Outside the village is what was believed to be a Native American burial mound. A small group of archaeologists vanished under mysterious circumstances while trying to uncover its secrets. A couple of weeks later, one of the men reappeared, visibly malnourished, and babbling about a place called K'n-yan."

Eugene held his hand up to stop Edith mid-flow. "The place those goons were trying to open a door to was called N'kai, not K'n-yan."

Edith rolled her eyes. "If you'd let me finish, I was about to say that the two plains are believed to intersect and that the doomed inhabitants of K'n-yan worshipped a being known as Tsathoggua... ring any bells."

All the colour drained from Eugene's cheeks. "Hampton, see if you can find any brandy, will you..." Hampton nodded primly and opened the drinks cabinet, Eugene continued. "What makes you think this has anything to do with Algernon?"

"His notes, and this map." She swept a hand over the desk. "He had been obsessed with it since it was reported to us by the American authorities. When you brought him the stone, he became worried and sent a team over there to secure the site... we last heard from them on the morning that the defamations hit the paper."

"And you think the two things are connected?"

"Well," Edith smiled. "It would be a dashed coincidence otherwise, wouldn't it?"

"Pardon me, Miss Stephenson," Hampton interjected as he filled a glass almost to the brim. "What I don't understand, is why the order of Dagon want to raise this Tsathoggua chap... won't Dagon be a tad miffed?"

"From what we can gather," Edith replied. "These guys are a kind of splinter group. They call themselves the Brotherhood of the Toad. I guess it's like the fact that not everyone in England is C of E... Some Innsmouthers follow a different ancient abomination. Plus, the two aren't historically opposed. They are both devotees of Great Cthulhu."

All those glutinous syllables were hurting Hampton's head. He was tempted to drain the glass himself but thought better of it. He nodded and smiled as though it all made perfect sense and passed the brandy to Eugene before pouring himself a small Scotch.

"So, what do you intend to do?" Eugene took the overflowing glass of brandy from Hampton and swept it down in one mighty gulp.

"Well, before you interrupted me, I was about to use the telephone to contact one of our contacts in America and get him to send a local Sheriff to see if there is any sign of my brother in Binger... then, we shall see."

April 24th, 1938. Oklahoma City, Oklahoma:

"How do we keep getting roped into these things, Hampton?" Eugene grumbled as he stepped onto the runway at Oklahoma City Municipal Airfield.

"I really couldn't say, Sir." Hampton peered up at the sun and instantly regretted being dressed in black. "I don't think we had any choice... again."

That much was true. After Edith had spoken to her various contacts and waited patiently for a response while Eugene emptied Stephenson's drinks cabinet. A strange group had been seen in the area around Binger. They had come equipped for digging and had threatened the locals with violence on the few occasions anyone got close. Meanwhile, a man answering Algernon Stephenson's description had changed aircraft in Botwood, Newfoundland in the company of two men described as having the *Innsmouth look*. He didn't appear to be a willing guest.

Edith had then left the duo at Stephenson's home with a trio of corpses while she went to an undisclosed location to confer with Mr McKinnon. The following morning, she had reappeared in the company of a towering chap with a luxuriant moustache and a military bearing and McKinnon's driver. The man was introduced as Captain Thomas Danvers from the RAF and he was to be their escort on a mission to the mound in Oklahoma.

Eugene had ranted, raved, and stamped his feet. He had told Edith Stephenson under no uncertain terms that he was not going on any damn fool rescue mission. Edith had listened to him calmly as he bellowed and blustered. In the end, none of his arguments mattered. All Edith had to do was remind him that all she needed to do was call for a copper and he would be popped in the chokey for quite some considerable time. The fact that he knew only too well what would happen if they opened the way for

Tsathoggua and his formless spawn was the icing on the cake. Eugene may have been a rogue but when it came to matters of national security, he could be counted upon to do the right thing.

Less than two hours later, Eugene, Hampton, and Danvers were boarding an Avro Ansen at RAF Northolt to begin the first leg of their journey. After switching to commercial flights in Newfoundland, they had made a point of changing aircraft at every stop to ensure that they weren't followed. Things had gone relatively smoothly... despite Eugene's foul mood. He and Danvers had taken an instant dislike to each other. As a former Captain in the British Army, Eugene was not going to be taking orders from a *Crabfat*. It seemed that the rivalry between services also carried over into retirement.

Eugene couldn't understand why he needed a *babysitter* in the first place. Edith had explained that, as a member of the Brotherhood of Tamesis, Danvers was authorised to liaise with the United States government and law enforcement. While Eugene, a dealer in antiques and avowed drunkard, was authorised to do precisely bugger all. They needed the help of the Caddo County Sheriff's Department, so they needed someone with authority along for the ride. Hampton didn't see what the problem was, surely three heads were better than two?

"What now?" Eugene asked Danvers as he picked his rucksack off the asphalt.

"We are scheduled to be met by a Deputy Williams. He is going to drive us down to Binger and drop us at the guest house we are to be billeted in." Sweeping back his Brylcreem-slick hair, Danvers peered through the heat shimmer at the airport buildings. "I think the car park is over that way... follow me."

Eugene flipped him a mock salute followed by a disrespectful V-sign once his back was turned. "Come along, Hampton... he'll probably have us court marshalled if we don't." Falling into step behind the dashing airman, Eugene cocked his head and whispered to Hampton. "I don't know about you, but I'm getting a nasty case of Deja Vu about this. If we see a suspicious-looking Ford on the road, just yell."

Hampton smiled. His employer was of course referring to when they had touched down in Massachusetts recently and a Ford being driven by some Innsmouth goons had tried to run them off the road. He knew that Eugene was being flippant, but he could tell from the tone that he was only half-joking.

"Look, I think that's our guy!" Danvers called out as he rounded a corner and saw a man that looked like a baked potato with arms and legs in a ten-gallon hat and a pair of wire-rimmed sunglasses sitting on the bonnet of a banged-up police vehicle. "Tally-ho! Deputy Williams, I presume?"

Eugene rolled his eyes. Clearly, Danvers didn't mind drawing attention to himself. The sharp suit he was wearing was further evidence of this fact. He looked more like he was about to go dancing than tackle a hostile force.

Deputy Williams spat tobacco juice onto the ground then grabbed the brim of his hat in greeting. "Howdy, welcome to the great state of Oklahoma." He held out a flabby paw in greeting which Danvers took and gave a vigorous shake.

Eugene and Hampton performed the same ritual. Williams' leather-gloved palms were hot to the touch. Eugene looked at the rotund gentleman's uniform. It looked to be three sizes too small and his shirt was buttoned up all the way to his chin. In that heat, it was a wonder the man hadn't boiled himself to death. Clearly, his boss was a stickler for the rules. Nothing else could explain why he was dressed like he was on a recruitment poster. Eugene chuckled to himself, he'd been erroneously led to be believed that the US Sherrif's department was a slovenly bunch.

Williams waddled over to the trunk of the black and white Ford Model 48 and opened it so the trio of Brits abroad could deposit their luggage. "If you'd like to step aboard, I'll have you in Binger in no time." He held the passenger seat forward so that Eugene and Hampton could climb in the back then clicked it back into place and gestured for Danvers to climb inside.

"I assume we are going to have more backup than just this doughy fellow?" Eugene hissed in Danvers' ear as the Deputy walked around the wedge-shaped front of the car.

"Yes, we have a bunch of men waiting for us, now... be polite." Danvers glared at Eugene in the rear-view mirror.

Suitably cowed, Eugene tried to arrange his legs in the cramped space and muttered to himself about needing a stiff drink. Hampton smirked to himself. Danvers had made Eugene promise to lay off the booze until they got to their digs. This was the longest his employer had gone without a drink since he was in short trousers. Even when stuck alone together in the middle of the rainforest, he'd somehow managed to find a way to refill his hip-flask on a semi-regular basis by looting the Innsmouth goons' camp.

The suspension groaned as Deputy Williams flopped into his seat and slammed the door. The car wheezed into life, and he hit the accelerator. After navigating the exit of the airport, Williams steered them west onto State Highway 152, through Mustang and out towards Union City. Hampton gazed out of the window at the vast expanse of agricultural land. Swirling clouds of red dust hovered over the nearby creeks and rivers like spectres. Once they hit Union City, Williams steered them south towards Minco.

After they had crossed the Canadian River, Hampton knew that they would be hanging a right at some point before they reached Minco. After all of their recent trials and tribulations, he had made a point of memorizing as much of the route as humanly possible. So, when they sped past the turning, and he could clearly see a sign for Binger, he knew something was wrong. Digging his elbow into Eugene's ribs to get his attention, he called out in a very clear voice, "Deputy Williams, I think we just our turning back there."

Williams waved his hand and gurgled, "I'm taking us the back way to avoid pryin' eyes."

Danvers smiled and returned to gazing out of the window.

Eugene looked at Hampton, knowing that he would know if there was indeed a back way. Hampton shook his head almost imperceptibly and started to slide his hand into his jacket. Hampton never carried a gun but that didn't mean he was unarmed. His fingers closed around a particularly savage butterfly knife. Before he could use it, however, Eugene had drawn his revolver.

"Turn the car around, Williams," Eugene said in a firm voice as he held the revolver in full view of the car's inhabitants.

"What in the name of sanity do you think you are doing, Angove?" Danvers yelped in outrage.

Williams said nothing but started to accelerate.

Eugene poked the barrel of the gun against Williams' neck and used it to pull down his shirt collar. Hampton gasped. "Gills! He's one of them!"

Revealing his shark-like teeth, Williams snarled and jerked the wheel. Eugene was tossed to the left, and his finger hit the trigger. The bullet missed Williams and shattered the windshield. Williams' sunglasses fell into his lap revealing two bulbous unblinking eyes.

Danvers leapt into action and tried to wrestle Williams' hands off the wheel. The bulky Innsmouther lashed out and punched him in the jaw with so much force that it was a miracle his head didn't spin around. Blood and teeth sprayed the dashboard, and Danvers slumped over, out cold.

Eugene raised his gun to the back of Williams' head, but the big man saw the glint of metal in the mirror and swerved the car once again. "Bollocks!" Eugene cried as he fumbled the gun, and it went skittering down the side of the driver's seat.

"Iä! Tsathoggua!" Williams croaked in triumph.

232

"Here!" Hampton cried as he pulled out his knife and opened it with a well-practised flick of the wrist. Eugene took it and jabbed it into Williams' neck. The Innsmouther bellowed in pain and reached instinctively for the blade. The car hit the side of the road and careered down a short slope and into a fence. The velocity of the impact against a stout post flipped the Ford onto its roof. Eugene and Hampton both howled in alarm as they skidded along a ploughed field upside down before coming to a stop as it crashed into a metal outbuilding.

The red dust stirred up by the car hung in the air like a miasma as Hampton crawled out through the shattered rear window. "Give me your hand, Sir."

Eugene did as instructed, and with Hampton's aid managed to wiggle free of the car. They hadn't been able to get a response from Danvers, so they had been forced to find another way out of the wreck. "Well, that's just chuffing marvellous." Eugene grumped as he dusted himself down and looked at the wreckage. "Where the bloody hell are we?"

"Never mind that for now, Sir... can you help me with Mr Danvers?" Hampton yanked on the passenger-side door until it opened. Danvers flopped out onto the soil.

"I don't think Mr Danvers will be any more use, do you, Hampton?" Eugene winced and crossed himself. "Poor sod."

Danvers' neck was clearly broken, and he wasn't

breathing. Whether the fatality was caused by Williams' punch or by the crash was anyone's guess. Eugene and Hampton took him by the arms and dragged his body away from the wreckage and into the metal shack. Laying him down next to some bags of feed, they covered him with a sack, and Hampton said the Lord's Prayer. Neither of them were believers, but in absence of a reverend, it would have to do.

"Here," Eugene said as they stepped outside, closing the door behind them. "I'm sure he'd want it to go to good use." He thrust a Webly service revolver into Hampton's hand."

"But... Sir! You know I hate these wretched things. You said it yourself, I can't hit a barn door."

"You did alright in Peru."

"I was firing blind!" Hampton turned the gun over in his hands. After the last war, he had vowed to never again fire a gun in anger. Not that he did much shooting in the war. Hampton had been one of *The Moles*, the Royal Engineers that spent most of the conflict digging trenches.

"Then, I'll make you a blasted blindfold!" Eugene snapped. "We are going to be facing Lord knows how many of these bounders, and I'm not going into this as the only armed man... got it?"

Hampton gritted his teeth and raised the gun... pointing it right at Eugene's face.

"What the hell are you doing, Hampton?"

"Down, Sir!"

Crack!

As Eugene dived out of the way, Hampton pulled the

234

trigger. The bullet sped from the muzzle and slammed into Deputy Williams' forehead. Both men had been too engrossed in their bickering to notice him waddling up behind Eugene with one hand trying to stem the flow of black ichor from his neck and the other holding Hampton's knife. If he'd hesitated for a single second, Eugene would have been slaughtered.

Catching his balance on the shack, Eugene spun around just in time to see Deputy Williams drop like a sack of wet laundry. "Jolly good show!" He whooped and rushed over to pat Hampton on the back. "See, I told you it would come in handy."

"Point taken," Hampton muttered as he flicked the safety on and tucked it into his waistband.

Walking over to the trashed Ford, Eugene opened the trunk and dragged out their luggage. "Just take the bare essentials, Hampton. Ammunition, first aid..." he grinned and slipped a half-bottle of brandy into his inside pocket. "That sort of thing. Oh, and money... we might need money. I assume there will be a tavern in Binger."

"Very good, Sir." Hampton rolled his eyes. "What's the plan, then?"

"Well, I suggest we go to that farm over yonder." He pointed towards a cluster of buildings to the south. "Then, I suggest we see if he has a telephone. If not, we ask him politely to drive us to Binger where I fully intend on going to this damned mound and kicking some arse. I don't know about you, Hampton, but I'm right cheesed off with this Innsmouth lot." He stuffed his pockets with bullets and fished his gun out from under the seat.

Once they were suitably prepared, Eugene and Hampton joined a dusty track and started to walk towards civilisation.

The sun was starting to sink by the time Eugene and Hampton reached the farm. Skirting a couple of rusty grain silos, they were about to turn the corner past an old apex barn when Eugene heard something that chilled his blood. It was almost like the croaking of an enormous toad. Holding his finger to his lips, he held Hampton back and peeked around the barn.

Outside the farmhouse, was another police vehicle. Standing around it, were three other men the size and shape of the alleged Deputy Williams. One of them, wearing a sheriff's star, was looking at his wristwatch pensively

Muttering oaths to himself, Eugene scanned the yard. There was another goon off to the right dragging the body of someone dressed like a farmer into another outbuilding.

"Dammit," Eugene whispered. "I think I've figured out where *Williams* was taking us... I don't think the local law enforcement is going to be much help."

"You mean?"

"I'm afraid so, Hampton. I think the foul smell coming from inside the barn is our backup."

"Hell's tits."

"Quite." Eugene carried on looking around. "Aha." He announced as he looked back towards the road and saw a stable complete with some fine-looking horses. "Are you okay to ride, Hampton?"

"It's been a while, Sir, and I'm hardly dressed for it." He was right, neither man was. It wasn't just the practical aspect that was the issue, they hardly looked like native Oklahomans. With Hampton in his suit and Eugene in his tweeds, they couldn't have looked any more British had they been draped in the Union Flag. "Sir, over there... the washing line."

"Well spotted, Hampton. Let's go..."

Ten minutes and lots of expletives later, the two British gentlemen looked like Billy The Kid's over-the-hill uncles. The farmer's clothes were too tight on Eugene and too baggy on Hampton. Still, at least they would blend in better. As luck would have it, three of the horses were saddled and ready to go. Eugene postulated that the farmer and a couple of hands must have been getting ready to go out when the Innsmouth Boys turned up.

"Blimey, Hampton." Eugene winced as he cocked his leg over a stout-looking Buckskin mare. "These Levi's are a tad snug around the old gentleman's veg-etables. I don't know how these cowboy chaps manage to wear them all the time without doing themselves a mischief."

"Agreed!" Hampton yelped as he too saddled up.

"Right, Hampton. Follow me. If we are lucky, we can get back to the road without being seen..."

"There they are!" The Innsmouther that had been dragging the body of the farmer rounded the corner just as they were leaving the stables.

"Balls!" Eugene spat. "Hampton... ride!"

Both men held tightly onto the reins and urged the horses into a gallop. The two magnificent animals sprung into action. Their hooves thundered on the dirt track back to the road. The roar of an engine announced that they had company. The police Ford was quickly gaining on them despite being full to bursting with Innsmouth meat. Soon, the horses reached the junction with the road.

"Which way, Hampton?"

"Right. Then the turning is on the left about a mile down!"

Eugene scanned the horizon. Across the fields directly ahead, he could see a road snaking into the distance. It was the road to Binger. "Sod it, go straight across the field!"

Hampton looked at the heavily planted and ploughed fields on the other side of the road. "You can't be ser..."

"Just follow me, Hampton!"

Hooves thundered the asphalt of Route 81 as Eugene led them across the road and straight down the bank on the other side. The horses whinnied as they vaulted a low fence and raced across a furrowed field. The horses slowed to navigate the rows of vegetables but didn't stop.

"Over there, a farm trail!" Eugene pointed and steered his horse in the right direction.

The police car flew down the bank and slammed through the fence, splintering it into matchwood. The Innsmouth boys weren't giving up despite their car behaving like a demented kangaroo over the vegetable beds. It was no use... if they made it onto the trail, they would catch up in no time. Eugene knew that it was now or never.

Pulling hard on his horse's reins, he drew his revolver. "Keep going, Hampton!" As the horse reared back, he turned and loosed off three shots at the vehicle. "Bingo!" A loud bang announced that he had hit one of the front tires. The next time the car bounced, it went sideways, taking out a scarecrow and rolling onto its roof.

"Oh, well done, Sir!" Hampton bellowed as he brought his horse to a stop.

Eugene brought his horse around and took careful aim at the tank of the car. Slowly, he squeezed on the trigger.

Boom!

The Ford erupted, sending a cloud of soil, vegetables, and body parts into the air. Eugene whispered gently into his horse's ear to calm her down before leaving the burning car behind him and trotting after Hampton.

"Come along, dear boy," Eugene said with a wide grin, pointing towards the road. "Next stop Binger."

The mound loomed against the night sky as Hampton and Eugene approached it from the cover of a cluster of black walnut trees and thick scrub. The area stood out from the rest of the well-farmed and maintained area as being wild and overgrown. This was definitely a plus in their favour, as was the fact that they had managed to see off at least three of the Innsmouth boys and left the rest stranded outside of Minco.

Once they had reached Binger, they had hastened to the guest house that was run by an old family native to the area, the Comptons. The patriarch had dutifully called the authorities and informed the state police of what had happened to the local Sherrif and his men. The area would soon be swarming with armed troopers. Eugene had had a celebratory brandy then bid the man farewell. When questioned why he didn't leave it to the troopers, Eugene had shrugged and said that he was under orders. Hampton knew the truth, however, he knew that they would be out of their depth... and then there was Stephenson to consider.

"Can you see him?" Eugene whispered as Hampton peered through a pair of binoculars that Eugene had lifted from Danvers' bag when Hampton wasn't looking."

"There are two big guys with guns standing around by a tent. I assume he's in there."

"What about the rest of the camp?" The Innsmouth group had set up a sizable camp around the mound, though most of the equipment probably belonged to the members of the Brotherhood of Tamesis that Stephenson had unwittingly sent to their doom.

"It looks clear... I can only assume that they are *inside* the mound."

"Now's our chance then, Hampton. Let's take them unawares." He pulled out a bowie knife and nodded at Hampton who took out his butterfly knife and returned the gesture.

The two hulking figures were sitting with their backs to the tent passing a bottle of hard spirits between themselves. They were both moaning about not getting to see

K'n-yan. It was only as they approached the tent and saw the size of them that Eugene held his hand up and hastily rethought his plan. There was no way they would take them out with a knife without some difficulty. Looking around, he spotted a couple of picks that had evidently been used to get into the ancient mound. He nodded to Hampton, who nodded back.

Thunk! ... Thunk!

Algernon Stephenson had been starting to despair when he heard the unmistakable sound of lumpen skulls being cracked with mining equipment. When Eugene Angove poked his head into the tent, he could have kissed the old devil. "Eugene! … Thank God!"

"There you are you old bugger." Eugene grinned. "I've got a ruddy bone to pick with you... I thought you were going to *forget* about my business deals?"

"My dear fellow, I'm so sorry. I didn't get around to burning the files, and these Innsmouth ruffians made me hand over everything to do with the Brotherhood. God alone knows who told them that I had all the dirt or who leaked it all to the press ad the police, but that's a mystery for another day... Now, hurry up and untie me, will you? We don't have much time."

Eugene moved around to the rear of the barrel he was tied to and cut his bonds. "I take it the stone is *inside* the mound?"

"Indeed."

Eugene moved to his Stephenson's feet and cut the ropes binding them together. "And... if we don't stop them, the world will be neck-deep in manure?"

"That's about the size of it," Stephenson grunted as

Eugene helped him to his feet.

"Well, what are we waiting for, then?" Eugene held the tent-flap for Stephenson who stepped outside and commenced stretching and shaking his extremities.

"Sir, over here," Hampton called out. He was rummaging in an equipment tent and came out holding an electric cap lamp in one hand and a mining helmet in the other. "It looks like the archaeologist chaps had some of those new-fangled Edison model K cap lamps."

"Ah, yes." Stephenson puffed out his chest proudly. "Our boys have only the finest equipment."

"Didn't do them much good though, did it?" Eugene muttered as he peered into one of the other tents and saw a pile of bodies wrapped in sacks and piled like cordwood.

"Alas, no," Stephenson said somberly. "I'm afraid that I underestimated these brutes. I thought that you had finished them off in Peru. I had no idea that the Brotherhood of the Toad was such a large group. I thought it was just a couple of disgruntled ex-Dagonites trying to one-up the EOD."

"Here." Eugene passed Stephenson his hipflask while he drank straight from the half-bottle. "You look like you could use a stiff drink."

Stephenson took a sip and handed it back. "Thanks... Right, shall we put an end to these devils, then?" He hurried over to the fallen Innsmouthers and riffled their pockets, eventually coming away with a Colt six-shooter and a handful of bullets.

Clipping the heavy wet cell battery to his belt and putting on his helmet, Eugene used the light to scout the

242

mound. Makeshift steps and a path had been gouged out of the earth on the western side. He called out to Hampton and Stephenson, instructing them to follow his ascent. Once at the top, Eugene gazed at the perfectly square opening that had been created.

Stephenson panted as he joined Eugene at the summit. "There are steps winding down, but they are bloody treacherous. One of their thugs dropped like a stone, so keep your back's flat to the wall and edge your way down. It will take longer, but at least you won't end up as meat paste. I have no idea what to expect when we get down there. *The Book of Eibon* calls it the 'blue-litten land' and the lost civilization of a highly advanced race that formerly worshipped the Great Old One, Yig. When they discovered the fissures to N'kai and explored its secrets, some of the people chose to embrace Tsathoggua instead and strived to bring him to K'n-yan... their civilization fell soon afterwards."

"Having met one of Tsathoggua's spawn in Peru, I can hazard a guess as to why," Hampton added as he lay on his belly peering down into the stygian abyss.

"Indeed," Stephenson said pensively. "That being said, I advise extreme caution."

"Right!" Eugene said chipperly. "When we have all stopped stating the bloody obvious, can we get on with going to our certain doom? I want to make it back to Binger before the bar closes."

Hampton was the first to swing his legs over the hole and place them onto the top step. They had been hewn out of solid rock and were slick with moisture. Taking a few steps down, they became less damp and therefore less deadly. He turned and steadied Eugene who came next followed by Stephenson. Once they had all found their feet and their lamps were adjusted correctly, they started their descent.

After around fifteen minutes of shuffling crab-like down the winding steps, they began to widen, and the mound started to open out. Clusters of alien-looking luminescent blue fungi started to appear in larger and larger clumps. After a while, they didn't need their lamps.

"Hey, look at these wall carvings!" Hampton called out in wonder as he gazed at an enormous depiction of some kind of hybrid of man and snake.

"Hmm." Stevenson stroked his moustache thoughtfully. "I believe that is Father Yig..." He scanned the walls. "And this fish-looking fellow is Dagon. Yes! This is a depiction of the K'nyanians pantheon of gods."

"Who's this one?" Hampton pointed to a depiction of something that looked like a giant shrimp with wings and tentacles.

"I'm not sure... I think it might be Ger'igguthy.

"And this squid-headed chap with wings?" Eugene chipped in.

"Ahh... That, my dear fellow, is Great Cthulhu."

Hampton pointed to another. "And we all know who this toad-looking devil is..."

"Tsathoggua!" Eugene gasped and took his hip flask out for a quick nip of restorative fire.

Hampton continued the rest of the descent in silence, as did Eugene. Stephenson, however, proceeded to rattle off a list of names that no human mouth was intended to speak. "... Shub-Niggurath, Yog-Sothoth, Azathoth,

Nyarlathotep, Cthugha, Ithaqua, Gla'aki... This must be the most complete depiction of the Great Old Ones anywhere hitherto discovered. Damn, I wish I had a camera! There are several missing, but this is staggering!"

Hampton didn't share Stephenson's enthusiasm. The hideous carvings made him nothing but nauseated. It was a blessing when the carvings ended, and the steps reached the floor. Each man needed to pause at the bottom and catch their breath. They had gone so deep that their ears had popped rendering them disorientated. It was almost like they had passed through some kind of veil between one world and another... Hampton wasn't convinced that wasn't the case.

Stepping around the pulverised remains of an Innsmouther, Eugene walked towards a corridor carved into the sandstone wall. "I'm assuming we go this way?"

As Hampton opened his mouth to speak, the ground beneath their feet started to rumble.

"Oh, Hell!" Stephenson barked, pushing past Hampton and elbowing Eugene out of the way. "They've started the ritual... come on, we don't have much time!"

The perfectly smooth walls glittered with lines of quartz as the light from their helmets bobbed and bounced as they ran. Under any other circumstances, the effect would have been beautiful. Under the present circumstances, however, all it did was add to the surreal and dreamlike quality of their surroundings. The passage snaked for roughly a quarter of a mile before abruptly ending...

"Well, bugger me sideways! ... Just look at this place. I feel like I'm in a surrealist artist's head." Eugene gasped as he came to a sudden stop at the tunnel exit. Before them, was a sprawling landscape bathed in blue light from the abundance of fungi. A strange kind of wispy blue grass blanketed the rolling hills and valleys. In the distance, they could make out the ruins of a once-grand city composed of non-euclidean geometry that hurt the eyes even from such a way off.

"Cripes, it's more beautiful than I'd ever imagined." Stephenson marvelled. "Look... over to the west, that black monolith... that is one of the Tsathoggua shrines, his foothold in K'n-yan. That must be where they are."

Hampton was the first to move. What he was seeing was so alien that he had decided to focus on the task at hand, lest he lose his grasp on reality entirely. The roof of the cavern world was invisible. All there was above was a lambent blue glow. The fungi must have completely engulfed the rock and acted as a pseudo sky. A few seconds later, the other two followed.

The small hillock that led to the tunnel sloped down to a sluggish river. Cloudy water trickled over lumps of quartz and onyx like a kind of milky slime. Hampton had no desire to touch it and took a running leap over to the other bank. Stephenson did the same. Eugene, on the other hand, was too fagged out to pull off any athletics and instead used some of the larger chunks of rock as stepping-stones. Pausing halfway, he stooped down and selected a couple of choice lumps of Quartz. His magpie mind functioned even when he was in a weird land and in mortal peril.

Hampton was the first to scramble up the hill on the opposite side. The increasing tremours made keeping upright difficult. Upon reaching the top, he motioned for them to keep low. Crawling on his belly like a child of Yig, he slithered into position and peered down at the scene below. The onyx monolith was around sixteen feet tall, a foot and a half thick and octagonal in shape. At its base was a toad-like sculpture similar to the one in Peru. It was clearly a shrine to Tsathoggua.

Standing in front of the monolith with his arms aloft was a slim figure in a black robe. He was flanked by two Innsmouth thugs toting Thompson sub-machine guns. The robed figure was holding the black stone above his head. He was chanting and muttering in Aklo, the language of the Great Old Ones. A small tear in reality was starting to open up in front of the Tsathoggua statue. Fingers of red light started to push their way into the blue realm as his chanting rose in pitch.

"What do we do?" Hampton hissed over the rumbling of tectonic plates.

Stephenson's brow creased. "I'll try a counter chant... then we will sneak up behi..."

"Bollocks to this!" Eugene cut him off, getting up on his knees and pointing his revolver at the insidious trio. His gun barked as he emptied all six chambers at their foes. One of the Innsmouther's was hit three times in his barrel chest and dropped to the ground, killed instantly... the other bullets went wide.

"Cobblers! Cover me while I reload!"

Stephenson and Hampton drew their guns, but before they could open fire, a large shadow fell over them, and Eugene got the barrel of a Tommy gun shoved in his ear.

"Drop 'em." The Innsmouther sneered. It was the one from the farm outside of Minco. The one that had been dragging the bodies into the barn. He had somehow escaped the State Troopers. Stephenson and Hampton reluctantly tossed their revolvers away. Eugene, however, stubbornly held onto his. "I won't ask you again, smooth skin."

"Sir..." Hampton pleaded.

"Arse!" Eugene finally exploded and lobbed his revolver back down towards the river.

"On yer feet." The bulky hybrid in a Deputy's uniform snarled. "You'll be a good gift for Tsathoggua."

Herding them like sheep, the enraged hybrid led the trio down to the monolith. The other surviving thug grabbed Hampton off to one side and stood next to him with his gun trained on his chest. Stephenson was led off to the other side while Eugene was placed level with the priest and dropped to his knees with a heavy chop across the shoulders.

"Stop, you fool..." Stephenson pleaded. "The formless spawn will kill us all!"

"Not so, Sir..." The priest chuckled turning around and shrugging back his hood. "Your notes on the control incantation have proved dashed useful."

Stephenson cried in outrage. "Wilkins? ... What's the meaning of this?"

"Your bloody valet?" Eugene said incredulously. "You really should vet your staff with more care, my good man."

Wilkins tipped his head back and cackled. "Just because I don't have the Innsmouth look, doesn't mean

248

that I'm not family... extended family, that is. My sister married into the Marsh family. That makes these fine fellows my brothers."

"You utter bounder!" Stephenson raged. "You've been in my service for decades."

Grinning from ear to ear, Wilkinson guffawed. "Indeed I have... Now, if you will excuse me, I have a god to wake." Turning his back on them, Wilkinson raised the stone in the air and resumed his chant.

The fissure in reality started to stretch wider and wider. Through the shimmering portal, Hampton could see amorphous black blobs and strange humanoids covered in umber fur lined up like an army on the other side. The end was nigh. If they invaded K'n-yan, they would then flood through into *his* world. Despair gripped his heart, then something happened... A mighty tremor sent his guard wobbling. Without thinking, he dived into him and drove him to the floor. As they wrestled around on the blue grass, he slipped his butterfly knife from his boot and proceeded to stab his foe, over and over again.

As Stephenson's guard turned and raised his gun to shoot Hampton, he used the brief distraction to rear back and kick the Innsmouther between the legs as hard as humanly possible. It doesn't matter how big you are, being punted like a rugby ball in *that* tender region is enough to drop you. The man's bulbous eyes crossed, and he fell to his knees, splitting his stolen uniform down the back. Stephenson followed it up with a knee to the jaw, then wrestled the gun from his hands and commenced battering him to oblivion.

"It's too late!" Wilkins gloated at the rift reached the

floor, and the abominable horde started to advance. The black stone was glowing with power.

Eugene reached in his pocket and took out an almost perfectly round lump of quartz. Rubbing it on his chequered shirt, he took a run and bowled a perfect googly. The quartz hit the black stone with a *crack* and sent it spinning through the void. The ground lurched as with a colossal *bang*, the rift started to flicker in and out of reality.

"Nooo!" Wilkins bellowed as he jumped after the stone. As his body hit the ground, the rift slammed shut, bisecting the deceitful manservant leaving only his body from the waist down twitching on the grass.

The land of K'n-yan was rocked by colossal earthquakes as clumps of blue fungi fell from the roof. The land around them was crumbling. Hampton and Stephenson joined Eugene as the monolith toppled.

"Now what?" Hampton panted.

Eugene smiled. "Now, dear fellow... we run!"

Landing in a heap at the base of the mound, Eugene reached into his pocket and took out his hip flask. Hampton had already flopped onto the ground like a beached starfish. Stephenson soon slid down the grass and landed beside him. Their flight to the steps had been bad enough, but their climb had been worse. Almost as they started their ascent, the tunnel to K'n-yan collapsed. It was almost like someone closed a door on that strange realm as the shaking stopped the instant the doorway was sealed.

K'n-yan had been destroyed.

Passing the flask between them, the trio looked up at the sky. It was a balmy and peaceful night. There was no indication of anything being awry... except for the corpses littering the campsite, that is.

Eugene finally got to his feet and checked his pocket watch. "Come along, you chaps. There's still a couple of hours until closing time."

Hampton stood and smiled before helping Stephenson up.

"It's you're round, by the way." Eugene continued, looking at Stephenson.

Stephenson shrugged. "Fair enough, I suppose."

"... And, when we get home, I'm standing over you while you burn those blasted documents that nosy PI gave you... understood?"

Again, Stephenson shrugged. "Fine."

"... And you can buy me a new tweed suit... and a new revolver..."

Hampton chuckled to himself as Eugene Angove reeled off a list of expenses for Stephenson. It was good to know that after everything he'd seen that night, some things never changed...

ADVENTURE AWAITS

A WING AND A PRAYER

JONATHAN INBODY

Of all the hangars on all the airfields in South America, why'd she have to walk into mine? I wasn't particularly approachable, or even particularly cheap, but my reputation for reliability seemed to send a constant stream of desperate souls straight to my door. Her soul, however, seemed a lot cleaner than that of my usual clientele.

The black habit she was wearing mostly failed to cover up her natural curves, and the pale, green-eyed face peering out from under her cap was unmistakably striking. She was attractive, for a nun, and as she set her suitcase down at my door, I wondered where it was someone like her could be heading.

"Are you Beatriz Serrano?" she asked, squinting to look at me in the bright sunlight streaming into my dingy hangar from outside.

"It's either Captain Serrano or Triz," I replied. "Only my mother calls me Beatriz."

"But you are a pilot?" she asked.

I nodded, gesturing over one shoulder at my plane. I slipped my feet down off of my desk and straightened up, then brushed dust off of my shirt and stood. As I walked over to her, she seemed to bristle, avoiding my eyes as I took her in.

"Where are you going?" I asked, lightly kicking at her suitcase with one boot.

"The San Miguel Mission, outside of Porto Velho."

"That'll take you into the Amazon."

"Yes, I know," she replied. "The priests at the mission have been trying to convert one of the local tribes; I've been sent to aid them in that end."

My eyes narrowed, and I looked past her at the mostly empty airfield. "There are plenty of other pilots who would take you there. Why me?"

"Because you're a woman," she replied. "Mother Superior told me I shouldn't travel alone with a man."

I clicked my tongue. "Well, she's not wrong. Alright, Sister… What did you say your name was?"

"Isabella," she answered. "And I *didn't* say."

"Well, Sister Isabella," I continued, quickly leaning down to tighten the laces on my boots. "We can haggle on the price while I do the pre-flight checks, add in half an hour for fueling and we can be ready to go just after lunch."

She smiled. "Splendid."

She looked past me at my plane, then back over at me as I got back to my feet. "Is this it?"

"That's the *Sapphire*," I replied, almost beaming. "Two-seater biplane from Avro, out in the UK. I originally intended it for use as a training vehicle for rookie pilots, but I managed to pick one up cheap and take out the second stick. It's a bit simple, but it handles just fine."

"Why *Sapphire*?"

I gave her a sidelong glance and smirked. "What? You don't think blue's my color?"

She looked away, almost blushing. Maybe today would be interesting after all.

Later, as we circled the end of the runway to get ready for takeoff, I turned back to give her a pair of goggles. She took them and our fingers brushed past each other, and for a long moment we looked into each other's eyes. She cleared her throat and put the goggles on, shifting her suitcase between her legs underneath her as she fastened her seat belt.

"I hope you've got a strong stomach," I said, turning back to face the runway. "The skies can get pretty choppy over the jungle."

"I'll be fine, Captain," she replied tersely.

I nodded. "If you start to get sick, just lean over the side of the plane - that way you can feed the animals rather than stain my seat."

"That's vile."

"Just practical," I shot back.

I started moving us forward, letting my short hair blow back in the wind as we picked up speed. By the time I started pulling back on the stick and we lifted off of the runway, I could hear her quietly praying in the seat behind me.

"You don't need to bother with that," I called back to her over the wind. "In the air, your life isn't in God's hands anymore; it's in mine."

"Well, consider me reassured," she called back.

We leveled off in a minute or so, coasting through the air at a comfortable height as we started for the jungle, and by the time we reached it the air was still enough to try to talk again.

"So what's it like being a nun?" I asked, my voice thick with wry amusement. "I imagine you don't get out much."

"No, I don't seem to," she replied. "But I wouldn't anyway, I've always been bookish."

"What do you read?"

"Oh, all sorts of things; the Bible, historical texts, poetry…"

"Poetry?" I repeated. "Any poets in particular? I'm a fan of a lot of the Greeks - Sappho for instance."

She didn't respond.

"Don't know that one?"

She chuckled. "Perhaps I know it too well."

I turned my head to get a better look at her and raised an eyebrow. "Well now you've got me downright curious, Sister."

"Then I'm sorry, but- *look out!*"

With a wet thunk, a small shape slammed into the propeller, then burst into shreds of bloody flesh as the blades reduced it to a pulp. A splash of red mist covered the lenses of my goggles and I reached up to wipe them with the back of my sleeve, then tried to straighten out the *Sapphire* as we lost altitude.

"What was that?" I called back to Sister Isabella.

"I don't know," she replied. "But it looked like-well, it didn't seem to have feathers!"

"No feathers? Then how-"

The words caught in my throat as I looked at the side of the propeller, where a half-shredded limb flapped limply in the wind. It was a wing of a sort, with a batlike membranous sail stretching down from a thin, long-fingered hand, but the skin covering it was a sickly, reptilian red.

"What is it?" Isabella asked from behind me.

"I'm not sure," I replied. "It's nothing I've ever-"

A loud, warbling shriek rose from underneath us, first alone and then echoed by others just like it. I leaned over the side of the plane and looked down, and when I saw what was soaring on the wind beneath us, I could hardly believe my own eyes.

A flock of huge, featherless birds moved below us in a rainbow of colors, gliding on massive, batlike wings just above the thick fog surrounding the jungle treetops. Their heads were long and sharp, with curved crests that rose like the rounded petal of a flower from behind their heads, and knife-like beaks that stretched out in front of them like spades. They flew in a staggered crescent, with the largest members of the flock at the front and the smallest at the back, moving in near synchronicity as a wave of avian life.

I had seen them before, or things close enough to them, but only in dime novels or as skeletons hanging in museums. Still, to my eyes, they were pterodactyls.

One of the larger things near the back of the soaring flock peeled off from the others, shrieking angrily as it shot up towards the *Sapphire* in a purple blur. At its movement, the flock seemed to break apart into two equally sized wings, each one making a wide arc as they fanned their wings out and rose on the choppy air currents to our altitude.

I straightened out the plane, wiping the last flecks of blood off of my goggles as I wracked my mind for a plan of action, then turned back at the sound of Isabella's voice.

"What are they?"

"They're dinosaurs, Sister," I replied. "Or something close enough. I think one of their little ones just flew into our propeller."

"Dinosaurs?" she asked incredulously.

"Seem to be," I shot back. "What's the matter; don't they teach prehistory in confirmation classes anymore?"

Brightly colored shapes rose all around us, each one more brilliantly vibrant than the last in the afternoon sunlight. They were circling now, looping around us in wide rings as the one moving on its own rose underneath us. It pulled its wings in and plunged downward, then flared them out and shot up, riding the wind as it soared like a bullet at the *Sapphire*'s left wing.

"Hold on!" I yelled, jerking the stick to one side.

The plane lurched to the right as the pterosaur shot past us, then turned into a spiral as I desperately tried to stop it. I tugged the stick back and our nose turned upward, sending us soaring up into the circling cloud of rainbow creatures as the propeller roared.

The cloud scattered as we blasted through it, and

258

wings of every size and color seemed to move past us as I leveled us off, surrounding me with an array of rainbow light as I fought with the stick.

I turned to look over my shoulder and caught Isabella's eye. She looked terrified, queasy, just like I did, but there was something else in her look that held my attention. Was it trust?

The purple creature pursuing us flapped its huge wings and rose on our tailwind, then twirled in a furious barrel roll and slammed into our back. The *Sapphire* lurched forward and dove as I desperately pulled back on the stick, and I felt Isabella's hand dig into my shoulder.

I pulled our nose up and climbed again, feeling my stomach drop as sweat beaded on my brow. The thing was still coming, gaining on us quickly as it darted downward, and Isabella's scream was the only thing that warned me before it struck.

It hit the wing and sent us spinning, tearing at the canvas with taloned feet as its knife-like beak plunged down for me. I slid down in my seat and the beak swung over me. Then it turned back and opened to reveal a gigantic, toothless mouth. The smell of rot hit my nose as I pressed myself back into the seat, my hands still struggling against the shaking stick.

Finally, we hit a favorable air pocket and our wing swung back out to the side, jarring Isabella and I in our seats as the creature lost its grip on us. The canvas flapped, tearing off in long strips as I heard more shrieks from all around us, and I gritted my teeth. It wasn't over yet.

"We have to get out of here!" Isabella yelled from

behind me.

"What exactly do you think I'm *trying* to do?!"

Three or four of the smaller shapes dove towards us, smashing through the canvas of the wing and battering into the side of the engine. They dropped like rocks, plunging down towards the trees, and I saw one of the larger creatures dive after them.

"They're killing themselves!" Isabella yelled from behind me.

"They're trying to kill *us*!" I shot back. "They just don't know how!"

I swung us to one side as another group of the small ones attacked, then overcorrected and slammed into the last one in the line. Its wing crumpled as we sideswiped it, and it cried out in fear as it dropped out of the air.

One of the larger pterodactyls, this one bright green, swept down underneath it, catching it on a sail-like wing. The smaller one rolled back and skidded to a stop, then grabbed the larger one's body with the two-fingered hand at the top of its uninjured wing and held on for dear life.

I pulled back on the stick, but we didn't tilt up. I pulled harder, but no matter how much force I used, our nose only drifted down. I looked at the back of the plane, where our rudder sat jarred out of place at the edge of the canvas, then over at Isabella.

"I can't get any height!" I yelled, pointing back at the jammed rudder. "You'll have to reach back, see if you can dislodge it from whatever it's stuck on!"

"What?" she yelled back incredulously.

"I have to steer!" I said, giving the stick another furious tug. "You've got to clear it, or we're going to drop

260

right out of the sky!"

She looked down, watching as the densely packed trees whooshed by underneath us, then looked back up at me. "Are you sure?"

I nodded. "I'll keep us as steady as I can, but if more of those things come after us, I'll have to move fast!"

She turned to look back at the rudder, the color draining out of her face.

I reached back with one hand and took hers, then squeezed it tightly. "I won't let anything happen to you; I promise! But you have to trust me!"

She nodded nervously. "Do you really think you can get us out of this?"

I smirked. "Why don't we find out together?"

Isabella reached down and unbuckled her seat belt, nervously whispering what I assumed was a prayer as she stood up in her seat. Then she turned and bent over the back of the plane, stretching her arms out towards the rudder. I glanced back, trying to not spend more than a second staring at her ass, then looked below us as we kept sailing down towards the trees.

"Can you get it?"

She stretched an arm out and fanned open her hand, the tips of her fingers just brushing against the rudder. "Almost! Let me-"

She leaned out further, balancing precariously over the edge of her seat as the wind flapped through her habit. She swayed, almost fell, then lowered a hand to catch herself and froze. She was shaking, and not from the cold, and even from behind I could tell by the look on her face.

"Don't freak out on me now, Sister!" I yelled back, quickly glancing at the surrounding sky to make sure more of the creatures weren't diving. "We don't have time; we're almost-"

I looked down at the trees rushing up just underneath us, then turned back to look at her. She turned her head to look at me, her face pale and eyes wide, and as I raised my eyebrows, she shook her head.

"I can't do it!" she called up to me. "I can't; I could fall!"

"If you don't, then we'll both fall!" I yelled back.

She swallowed hard, then turned back to look at the rudder. She pulled herself further out of her seat, inching her knees along the top of the plane, then reached out again. This time, her fingers wrapped around the rudder.

"It's stuck!" she yelled back, yanking on it furiously.

"I know it's stuck, just pull it!"

She raised her other hand from underneath her and grabbed the rudder, then slid her legs underneath her body and sprang back. This time, the rudder bent back into place, and the plane swept suddenly upward. Isabella fell forward and hit the rudder, holding on for dear life as she almost slid off of the back of the plane.

"Hold on!" I called back. "I'll level us out!"

"Triz, you're- *Aaaiieee!*"

I turned my head to look at the back of the plane, but she was gone. I looked up, following her echoing scream to where she was thrashing wildly in the sky, hanging in the clenched-shut talons of a huge blue pterodactyl.

Shit. I pulled back on the stick and swung the plane

262

up, making a wide turn to the right as I scanned the open air for where the thing had taken her. There were so many of them weaving around each other in an angry flock, but all I had to do was find a tiny splash of black. If I could spot the habit, then- *there!*

I soared up towards the circling flock, staring through the spinning propeller as I watched her fight against the titanic flyer's iron grip. It had her by the shoulders, each talon digging into her flesh, and she was furiously grabbing at its legs as though she expected to pull herself free. Below her, some of the smaller creatures began to circle, expectant drool dribbling down from their open mouths expecting a meal. They shot up one by one, biting at her ankles as she kicked at them.

I quickly ran through the options in my head. The propeller would mulch the little ones, wouldn't it? Hadn't it done that to the first one? What about the big one?

I reached up with one hand and straightened my goggles. This was going to get bloody.

I pulled back on the stick and the plane shot up, then blasted into the circling flock of smaller creatures. One smacked into the wing and rolled off as another creature dove to avoid me, but I managed to get the one nipping at Isabella's heels.

With a sickening whirr, the creature splattered through the fan, spraying bits of tangled flesh and reptilian skin out in a red cloud around the front of the plane. I wiped off my goggles and kept turning upward, making a wide arc to get a better angle on the big one.

Isabella turned her head to watch me as I circled, her eyes pleading to me as she struggled against the creature's grip, and when I aimed the propeller in her direction, I saw them widen. I only had one shot at this; I had to make it count.

I swept downward to pick up speed, then shot back up on pure momentum and collided with the back of the gigantic creature's head. The propeller sawed through the back of its long crest with a series of thunks, and as the nose of the plane smashed into its skull, I saw its talons suddenly open.

Isabella dropped, screaming and flailing in all directions as she plummeted down towards the jungle below. Some of the smaller creatures dove after her and I pushed the stick forward, tilting the nose of the plane down into a steep dive. Could I even get there in time? Hopefully, with how baggy her habit was, it would create enough drag to slow her down. Otherwise, I - Well, I didn't want to think about otherwise.

She flipped end over end, arms outstretched and her mouth open with a barely audible scream. I overtook the creatures, diving after her, then spun the plane to avoid hitting her with a wing. With one hand white-knuckle clutched on the stick, I reached out with the other, fanning my fingers open to grab the edge of her habit as I swung underneath her. If I got the angle right, I could just…

The plane swung underneath her, and my fingers brushed through her habit. I closed my fist and pulled, changing her angle of descent and pulling her into the side of the plane with a loud smack. She grabbed the edge of her open seat with both hands, still screaming even though no sound was leaving her mouth.

264

"I'm going to tilt us so you can slide back into your seat!" I yelled back, both hands already back on the stick.

The plane swung to the side, and she slid forward, then fell back into her seat in a terrified heap. I could hear her raggedly heaving as she straightened herself, and when she raised her head behind me her chin and neck streaked with vomit.

"Are you alright?" I asked.

"Do I *look* alright?!" she yelled back. "You could have killed me!"

"You're welcome," I replied dryly.

A loud shriek sounded from above us and I turned my head to look. The massive pterodactyl, the one whose crest I had chopped to pieces and whose skull was half-smashed, was diving after us, its taloned feet extended like knives out in front of it.

"Better strap yourself in, Sister; your friend's coming back!"

I glanced down at the trees rushing past underneath us, then back up at the gigantic creature bearing down on us. If it got a hold of us, it could tear the plane to pieces before I even had a chance to react. There was, as far as I could figure it, only one way out. I'd have to find a clearing somewhere.

I scanned the top of the jungle in front of us, then my eye caught a long stretch of open air between lines of thick, tangled trees - a river!

"Are you ready?"

"Ready for what?" Isabella asked back.

"Just hold on!"

I shoved the stick forward and the plane's nose

turned down, plunging us down just as the trees disappeared from underneath us. With a sharp turn to straighten out our path, we flew a few hundred yards above the rushing river, and as I lowered us further and the rushing trees rose up on both sides of the plane, I gritted my teeth.

I heard trees crack and smash behind us and looked back to see the massive pterodactyl bursting through the edge of the jungle in a cloud of splintered wood. It spread its huge wings and fanned them down, darting up and away from the patch of destroyed trees as it soared out after us over the river clearing.

The huge blue shape was gaining on us, opening its jagged beak in anticipation as it neared the back of the plane.

"What do we do?" Isabella yelled from behind me.

"I don't know!" I called back. "I didn't think it would follow us down here!"

I looked back to see Isabella heave her suitcase off of the back of the plane, then watched it spring open as it smashed against the side of the gigantic pterodactyl's face. Clothes burst out and covered one of the creature's eyes, sending it into a confused spiral as it tried to clear its vision.

It swung wide and clipped a tree, snapping the tip of one of its huge, leathery wings. The wing folded and tore, and the creature plunged down into the water. It landed with a splash, rolling end over end like a skipped stone for a few yards before disappearing beneath the water's surface.

"Quick thinking, Sister!" I called back, and I felt

Isabella's hand squeeze my shoulder in reply.

"Nice flying!"

I smiled, reaching a hand up from the stick and placing it on hers. Maybe today wasn't such a disaster after all.

The back of the plane lurched down suddenly, and I heard Isabella scream. One pterodactyl had landed just in front of the back rudder, clacking its toothless jaws as its talons tore at the metal.

I caught movement out of the corner of my eye and saw a flash of color, then jerked the stick to the left as another pterodactyl slammed itself down onto our right wing. The plane wobbled and almost flipped as the creature bit apart the canvas covering the wing, and no matter how much I seemed to move the stick, it wouldn't shake off.

I looked at the rushing river below, stretching out in front of us like a winding snake. I knew we couldn't stay airborne, not with so many of them still after us, but could we risk a water landing? Did we have a choice?

The question was answered for me as I heard the crumpling rip of metal from behind. The creature on the back of the plane tore the rudder off and tossed it aside, sending it flipping down into the water as the plane descended.

The pterodactyl on the wing lunged for me and I punched its spade-like beak, then grabbed for its neck with one hand while I held onto the stick for dear life with the other. If I lost control, even for a second, we'd both be dead as soon as we hit the water.

Isabella shrieked, and I heard a fleshy rip as I turned

my head to look. She was standing up in her seat behind me, half-inside the pterosaur's open mouth. She had her hand clutched on the underside of the creature's upper jaw, and a foot stomped on the bottom, and her free hand wrapped around the monster's wriggling tongue. She tightened her grip and pulled, and I heard another squelch of tearing flesh as the tongue ripped in half.

The creature fanned its wings out and lifted off of the falling plane, then turned and disappeared into the trees, trailing spatters of dribbling blood behind it from its tongueless mouth.

Isabella tossed the squirming tongue off the side of the plane, then turned and gave me a look. "They didn't teach me *that* in confirmation classes, either."

A smile crept across my face. "Yeah, I kind of figu-"

I felt a stabbing pain as the other pterosaur's beak bit down on my shoulder, its hooked end digging in just above my collar bone. I screamed, then turned and slammed my elbow against it, but it only closed its jaws even tighter.

The creature pulled its neck back and lifted me out of my seat, tearing my hand away from the stick as I kicked my boots out for something to use as leverage. It was impossibly strong, and I could feel numbness spreading down my right side as my arm dangled limply in the rushing wind.

Isabella dove forward, grabbing my legs with one arm and the stick with the other. She pulled back, trying desperately to level us out as the pterodactyl tried to pull me out onto the wing, jarring us both with each angry tug.

268

I grabbed the creature's thick neck, punching uselessly at it as I looked up into its furious eye, and I watched its eye narrow as it bit down harder into my shoulder. I felt something snap and my arm went slack, sending bolts of pain radiating down my side as I screamed again. It was tearing me apart.

I turned my head to look at Isabella, her arms fully extended between the stick and my legs, and when our eyes met, I saw hers widen.

"Let me go, Sister," I said weakly, kicking my feet slightly to make sure she caught my meaning. "I'm not worth dying for."

For a second, I saw the thought move across her face, and then her eyes darted down to the stick. Come on, Isabella, do the smart thing. Save yourself.

Suddenly, she let go of my legs, and I flew backwards into the creature's chest with a dull smack. She shot down to the stick with both hands and shoved it to the left. The wing pushed up underneath us, jarring the pterodactyl out of where it had dug its talons in, and as it turned to try to catch itself, its jaws opened on my shoulder.

For a second, I was in free fall, then with a firm hand on my leg Isabella pulled me back into my seat, holding me snugly as the plane spun down towards the water. She pressed herself up against my body, wrapping her arms around my back to shield me, and just before we hit bottom, her lips found mine.

The plane smashed into the rushing water and flipped end over end, pulverizing the wings and obliterating the propeller as water rushed into the seats. We plunged down beneath the surface and smashed into the sand at the water's bottom, then bounced to a stop against a rock and started slowly float back up.

We splashed up from the water and grabbed a hold of one of the *Sapphire*'s broken wings, then held onto it for dear life as it floated down the quickly moving river. I spat up a mouthful of water and looked over at Sister Isabella, whose torn habit was dangling in shreds behind her as she adjusted the soggy clothes underneath.

Our eyes met, and she smiled, then leaned in and gave me another long kiss. As she pulled away, I let out a chuckle of disbelief.

"I didn't think they let nuns do that."

"They don't," she replied. "But I think maybe it's alright if we almost died."

"Is that why you did it?" I replied, deflating slightly. "Because we're not dead?"

She shook her head, blushing slightly as her smile widened. "I wanted to before."

I laughed and looked down the river, where clouds of froth rose up around the sides of a steep waterfall that seemed to drop off into nothing.

"Well," I said, sidling closer to her on the broken wing, "I think we could both stand to do a little more of it, given that we might be almost dying again in a minute or two."

She leaned in. "There's no one else around to hear my last confession anyway…"

With a tremendous splash, a gigantic shape burst up from the water's surface behind us, shoving aside the crumpled plane as it lunged forward. It was the blue pterodactyl again, the big one, its head half-smashed and broken, wing flapping limply at its side, and it shrieked with wordless fury as it raised its taloned feet up and out of the water.

A talon tore through the wing beside us and broke it in two, sending Isabella and I scrambling for another piece of wreckage to hold on to. The current seemed to quicken as it swept us along, and I struggled to keep my head above water as I heard the huge pterodactyl shriek. It shot its head down into the water, missing my legs by inches, then opened its mouth and pushed it forward to scoop me up like a pelican.

I rolled and grabbed onto its broken wing, hanging limply at its side as it thrashed back and forth. Where was Isabella?

The creature shot its head down towards me, biting at its own wing as I swung my legs up to avoid its snapping beak. I pushed off of its smashed crest and leapt back into the water, then dove under the surface and began frantically swimming. We must have been getting close to the waterfall - the roiling current was almost tearing me apart.

I felt a hand grab mine, and I shot to the surface, where Isabella clung to me, gasping for breath. We bobbed in the rushing water, being thrown back and forth as we held each other close, and as we reached the edge of the waterfall, I gave her one last kiss.

The bottom of a huge beak swept underneath us and scooped us up from the water, then threw itself back to try to swallow us. We grabbed at the slick inside of the mouth, kicking at the pterodactyl's wriggling tongue, and as I pulled myself up and partially out of the huge gullet, my eyes went wide - we were still moving.

The immense creature swayed and toppled over the edge of the waterfall, squawking angrily as it plunged down the steep drop, with us dangling from its mouth. I reached out for Isabella's hand, but it slipped out of my grip, and she tumbled end over end out the side of the mouth. I heard a fleshy rip, then felt her hand grab mine, and in a moment I was being pulled up and out of the creature's open beak.

We soared up on the humid breeze, then floated down in a wide spiral as the gigantic creature underneath us kept plummeting. Its broken wing was now just a bloody stump, and as I looked up past Isabella's smiling face, I finally understood. The crumpled wing fanned out above us like a parachute, clutched with white-knuckled hands as it flapped in the whipping wind.

I heard a loud squelching crunch as the huge pterodactyl slammed into the jagged rocks at the bottom of the waterfall, barely audible above the thundering water itself. The body sagged off of the rocks, leaving bits of torn-up flesh behind, then bobbed down into the water and began to float down-river, the dead creature's shattered jaw hanging limply open out to its side.

Our makeshift parachute rippled and tear, and Isabella's eyes met mine just as it gave out. We dropped thirty feet and plunged into the water, narrowly avoiding the massive knife-like rocks. Underneath me, Isabella wasn't moving, but as far as I could tell, she had only fainted. Lucky girl.

I pulled Isabella up towards the water's surface with

my good arm, dragging her underneath the thundering water towards a flat-looking rock behind the falls, then bobbed above the water's surface and looked around. We seemed to be at the mouth of a cave, now, opening hidden by the waterfall, and a dark one at that.

I pulled myself up onto the long, flat rock and dragged Isabella after me, then waited as she caught her breath. I ran a hand through her wet hair, then down the side of her face, and when her eyes fluttered open and met mine, we both smiled.

"Still with me?" I asked softly.

"No," she replied with a grin. "I think I've died and gone to Heaven."

She sat up and I got to my feet, then walked further down the rocky outcropping towards the back of the cave. A vast, yawning darkness stretched out in front of me, and from how far the echo traveled when I spoke, there was no end anywhere in sight.

I looked behind me at the rippling water, then followed the crooked shoreline to the opposite wall of the cave. A skeletal body in the golden armor of a Spanish conquistador laid crumpled at the edge of the water, leaning against the distant wall, his armor punctured and bent outward in enough places to make him look like a human pincushion. Clutched in his bony hand was a long, curved sword, stretched out in front of him as if warding away some unseen attacker.

I slowly walked over, then reached down and pried his skeletal fingers off of the sword one by one, but when I moved to pick it up, I heard a soft growl from the darkness beside me. A small, huddled shape stepped forward into the light and lowered its head, showing off two long teeth that curved downward from a snarling feline mouth.

I had seen it before, or something close enough to it, but only in dime novels or museums. Still, to my eyes, it was a sabre-tooth tiger.

The small creature shook its head, showing off a thin red mane, then turned and ran back into the darkness as Isabella and I shared a look. She walked over to me quietly, eyeing the sword.

A larger tiger, no doubt the mother given its maneless head, stepped around the smaller creature as it fled and emerged from the shadows, her long teeth gleaming in the light dancing off of the rushing waterfall behind us. She snarled, and my hand wrapped around the conquistador's sword.

Isabella pressed herself up against me as I raised it, tensing up as the sabre-tooth stared daggers at us from the dark, and at the moment it got ready to pounce, I couldn't help but chuckle.

Of all the caves in all the jungles in South America, why did we have to wash up in hers?

LIVING GHOST

T.R. EARNHART

"You could help you know", Emilia Mickens looked up from her cleaning task to glare at her new roommate. Celeste Puddu seemed utterly content to nestle among the built-up grime of their room.

"I'll get to it. Watch this." The darker-haired girl lifted both her hands up to slam them down on the bed. A cloud of dust and dirt erupted, causing both girls to choke. Thankfully, Emilia had the foresight to open the window to help air out as she cleaned.

"That was dumb." Celeste said when she managed to breathe a little more normally.

"Yes, you are," Emilia commented before another round of hacking coughing stole her breath. Grumbling, Emilia tucked a blond curl that escaped her headscarf.

Seven years. It had been seven years since the first time the two of them became sisters of the coven. True

Emilia didn't have any blood siblings, but she was certain that wasn't how they were supposed to act. According to her mother, Sisters of the Coven were supposed to be your new family. Courtship rights were transferred from the father to the Coven. If witches outlived their husbands, they moved into each other's cottages until they died.

Worst-case scenario, Emilia and Celeste could be stuck with each other for decades.

If seven years of training didn't fix that devil-may-care attitude, nothing would.

So Emilia assumed that Celeste would be just as committed to their new life as she was. Especially considering Celeste was from an impoverished background.

Damn rich people. Celeste shook her head as she gathered the smelly bedding to haul downstairs.

Celeste always felt a pang of annoyance when the other girl began to lecture. What did the blond know of hard work? Seven generations of witches and magi had cultivated the Mickens' name into one associated with wealth. Marrying into the family guaranteed an easy life.

Unlike Celeste's upbringing. Watching what happened to her mother had left a deep scar on her heart. Her father had been injured while herding the pigs, so her mother went back to picking up work from their local guild outpost. Crap jobs no one wanted, but since she was desperate, she took what she could. One night she came home, sat by the fire, and never woke up.

Magic depletion.

A fancy way to say 'worked to death'. Celeste was the one to discover her in the morning.

There was no point in cleaning. Sure, she'd take care of the bed, but that would be it. No point in wasting energy when she had plans. She gave a passing glance at Emilia, who was halfway under the bed trying to sweep up as much as she could.

Careful. Don't want to over-exert yourself. Celeste thought as she left the room.

After she had a little internal laugh, she caught herself. No. She needed to focus now. They had finally made it. Now it was time to focus on what was important. Making the right sort of friends.

While Emilia would be content to be shoved into the back room of a guild somewhere being paid pittance, Celeste had bigger plans. Larger guilds meant more money coming through. If she played her Tarot cards right, she could be put into the field where she could make even more money. A few hours on the line should be enough to air out any bad smells for now.

Lunch was being served when Celeste came back inside. Emilia kept glaring over her soup and hard bread. Sensing the tension in the room, the woman they were renting from began to question their plans.

"Is there a specific guild you want to contract with?"

"I'm torn between runes or working in a pharmacy." Said Emilia quickly. Surprised she didn't injure herself with the sudden change in her mood, Celeste ignored the girl's babbling. While the two witches were discussing the pros and cons of either focus. Over their sponsor's head, a large light grey tabby hopped onto the open windowsill. As Celeste stared, she noticed the cat only had one eye to squint at her with. For some reason, the cat made the girl smile back in response.

"You know what, I think I have I can show you." Announced their sponsor getting up from the table suddenly. The second the older woman left the room; Celeste dropped her spoon to get up. She made her way to the scrap bucket filled with leftovers from the past few days. The red of the fish head seemed out of place as she laid it in front of the one-eyed cat. As if she had done it before, Celeste began to scratch under the cat's chin.

"So, if you use this line in your work-Celeste, what are you doing?" Their sponsor had returned with a keepsake box in hand. Looking around, Celeste realized both the cat and the fish head were gone.

"Nothing." She replied weakly.

Emilia finished her lunch before excusing herself to get ready. She changed out of her cleaning clothes into something more presentable. As she was lacing up her bodice, Celeste had joined her. She didn't bother to change, just fix her hair a little bit. Redoing her long dark braid, she then grabbed her wand off her bed to shove into her bodice. Winching at how sloppy the girl looked.

"I can fix it if you want." Emilia found herself saying. Seeing the other girl's expression, she elaborated. "Your hair."

"What about it?" Celeste asked, glaring at the back of Emilia's head. Using the mirror, Emilia straightened herself to address her fellow witch. Mirroring the look her mother used when she wanted to command respect.

"You know today is the most important day of our lives, right?"

Celeste scoffed.

"We're about to meet with a group of old, judgmental, elitists with you looking like you just fell off the pig cart." That last jab causing Celeste to smooth down the front of her outfit a little bit. She pursed her lips like she always did when she was deep in thought.

"Fine." Emilia gave a smile of approval as she motioned the reluctant witch to take a seat. When Celeste sat down, she pulled her wand from her bodice. Makes sense she didn't want the glass-like instrument poking her in the rib. Emilia liked to see what colours and shapes other magi wands looked like.

Made from pure white beach sand and the magi's blood that manifests into a glass spun pen. Rather than calling the tool 'blood pens' guilds insisted on calling them *wands*.

Celeste's wand reflected her perfectly, Emilia thought. Slighter shorter than Celeste's own it was clear, allowing the colours streaking throughout to appear as if he had captured a sunset. Beautiful, yes, but she preferred her ice blue with tiny snowflakes inside more. Once she was finished with the braid, she checked over her work. No matter how neat her hair looked, she still had the air of a pig farmer.

"Hold on. I have an idea."

***

Celeste tried not to fuss too much with her much tighter braid as they made their way to the main guild-hall. There, they were separated for individual testing. The room they were placed in had a table standing in the middle, laden with all sorts of magic-related items. She was alone, with no idea what she was supposed to be doing. She chose to hover close to the table, looking over everything.

"Eager to start, I see. The sooner we get this over with, the better." True to Emilia's warning, the man was old, judgmental sounding. By the way, he eyed her shoes peeking out from under the borrowed cloak, as elitist as they came. Not trusting her voice, she pulled out her wand.

She wasn't ready for what the elderly man was throwing at her. Sure, she knew that her knowledge was going to be tested in a practical setting. Yet, she wasn't expecting to use runes to extract the cooling properties of mint to then refract sunlight through a crystal to light the fire for the potion. All that would've been bearable, if it wasn't for the invasive nonstop questions.

Who else in her family had magic? How far back does magic go in her bloodlines?

By the time she was able to think again, Celeste found herself slipping into bed for the night. Staring up at the ceiling, she tried to remember if she ate dinner.

"Mew?"

Oh yeah. Emilia had forgotten to close the window.

"Kitty. Kitty," said Celeste weakly. As the cat nestled down for the night, she reached down to stroke the dusty yet soft fur.

"I cannot believe you let that stray into our room." sniffed Emilia, upturning her nose. Emilia had the decency to delay giving Celeste a tongue lashing. The girl took a deep breath, making a self-calming motion with her hands. "It's fine. Not like you named it or anything. Naming it means you're making it you're familiar."

Celeste kept silent to have the rant end that much quicker. When they rounded the corner and the guild came into view. Inside, they were ushered away to separate areas. Too focused on following the woman dressed for apothecary work, she failed to say goodbye to Celeste.

The man was dressed for rune work. Celeste followed him deeper into the guild. Past several witches and magi, busy with their tasks. To appear eager, she pulled out her wand to fiddle with as they walked. They kept going. Right up until the hustle and bustle from everyone was just echoes in the distance. The man then opened a door to usher her inside.

A storeroom? Am I going to clean out dust? She thought, looking around for any sign of what she was going to be doing. When the door closed behind her, she turned to address her new mentor. There was a rustle of paper, a hard pressure on her forehead.

Next thing she knew, she was staring up at the dusty ceiling.

"What happened?" Celeste asked, looking around.

Her whole body felt numb as she was barely able to move her head. She managed to see her mentor bent over an object on the floor. As she stared, the door opened again to reveal a much larger younger man entered.

"This her?" He asked, bending over to examine the object.

"Yeah. I will send a letter for her things. Make sure not to bruise her. The client won't want damaged goods." said the runemaster. The larger man grunted as he turned the object over to face Celeste better.

She screamed when she saw her face facing towards her.

Emilia wanted to wait for Celeste so that they could walk home together. She waited until she was ushered out of the building. So she walked home, alone with her ever-increasing panicky thoughts.

"Mew?" She knew that voice. Finally paying attention to her surroundings, she saw the one-eyed stray Celeste had been messing with. It was sitting on the barrels stored outside the home, its long tail flicking in the dimming daylight. Seeing that dirty cat stare at her with its single piercing eye made her insides twist. Just beyond the two of them, the door to her home opened. Coming out was a young man carrying Celeste's trunk.

"Hey what are you doing?" Emilia rushed to stand in front of the man.

"I was sent to collect the belongings of the witch Celeste Puddu."

"I find that hard to believe." Shot back Emilia not backing down.

"She was giving a new mission as per the order of the higher-ups. If you are jealous, that is your business." the man then stepped around the stunned Emilia.

No matter how many days had passed, the same twisted feeling never left her stomach. She was living her best life. Her dream. So why did everything feel wrong?

"Madame Mickens. Retrieve some of the fermenting jars from the storeroom."

"Yes, master."

Eager to please, she made her way to the storerooms as quickly as possible. Realizing in her rush she didn't have the forethought to bring a torch or lamp of sorts. She left the door open as far as possible to allow as much light in as she could. Even in the dim light, she managed to find the small clay pots tucked away in the back. Yucca root needs complete darkness to unlock the stomach-soothing properties for the medicine they were making. She was grabbing the third pot when her hand touched something cold and smooth. Recoiling out of instinct for a second, her curiosity prevailed as she reached back down to see what it was. She let out a small gasp when she realized it felt just like a wand. Pocketing it for later inspection, she collected the third pot to take back.

She forgot all about her finding right up until she was shedding her cloak for the day. Pulling it out, she inspected it in the light. Hands trembling, she almost dropped the wand when she recognized the sunset colours.

Breath coming up short, she sunk to her knees while holding the wand to her chest.

"Celeste, what happened to you?" she asked aloud.

'Wish I knew.'

Emilia gave a screech, dropping the wand on the ground. Breathing hard, she looked around for the source of the whisper. Not seeing anyone, she glanced back down at the wand lying innocently on the floor. Kneeling, she picked up the wand gingerly as if it was about to explode any second. She looked around again, waiting for something to happen again.

"Hello?"

Emilia? the whisper in her ears sounded louder.

"Yeah?"

Oh my god. You can hear me. You can actually hear me. It was Celeste's voice. There was no doubt. She sounded like she was crying. Instinctually Emilia clutched the wand closer to her chest. Looking around, she noticed a cloud of coloured mist near Celeste's empty bed.

"What's going on?" She squinted as the mist began to solidify in front of her eyes.

I wish I knew. I mean, I do know what happened, but I don't know exactly how it happened.

"Did you see who killed you?"

I didn't die! I'm just, she gestured as if trying to find the words from thin air. *Not attached to my body anymore.*

"So...you're not a ghost then?"

"I know my body is still alive. Look." She pulled on the front of the outfit she was wearing. Instead of the worn dress, borrowed cloak outfit she wore the last time she saw her. Getting on off her own bed, Emilia managed to make out a crest on the shackles on Celeste's ghostly form.

"Is that a dragon? A bird? Maybe a griffon?" She muttered, squinting to see the shape clearer.

That narrows it down. Celeste snapped back, shaking her sleeve back down. She got up to look out the window. Knowing not to press the issue, Emilia went back to her side of the room. She pulled out the box her mother gave her to protect her wand. She nestled Celeste's wand next to her own. The only sound interrupting the quiet was the hushed whisper of her getting into bed. She snuffed out the light as Celeste continued to stare blankly out the window.

Morality had never been a murky issue for her. Good and bad. Right and wrong. Black and white. Easy.

Ghosts. Ghosts were bad. But Celeste was her sister, and she never hurt a fly. Hell, she almost became familiars with half the animals back home.

"Emilia, eyes up." Barked out, the apothecary master snapped her out of her thoughts. Once their eyes met, the master laid into her. "You need to leave personal issues out of my ward. You took an oath, not a week ago, Ms. Mickens. Uphold that oath or else."

You'll sell me off too?

"Yes, master." Emilia nodded. Uphold her oath she shall. Satisfied, they went back to their picking and pruning. "Master, do you know who has a winged crest?"

⤐⤏

The view from her room was infinitely better than the limbo of the storeroom. As she watched the world go by, the one-eyed cat made an appearance. Stretching in the morning light, the cat made her way up towards the window.

When she arrived, she gave a loud meow as if demanding Celeste's attention.

So you can see me? Or at least feel me. She attempted to stroke the cat. Even though she passed through, the cat still acted like she was enjoying the attention. All the while, a light blue swirling dust began to float off the cat. It responded to her touch as if she were solid.

For the first time since waking up, she felt anything. Desperate for the warmth, she used both hands to stroke the cat.

"I know you like that. Huh? Big Mama."

The light blue colour turned into a soft orange. Her favourite colour.

Guess you're my familiar now. The cat only purred as it curled up to take a nap. All Celeste could do was chuckle to herself at the obscurity of it all.

"House of Detritus," Emilia announced the second she got into the shared room. Celeste turned away from counting the smoke tendrils as the night settled in.

Have a good day I take it?

"I asked around and Duke Erik of the House of Detritus frequents the guild to buy the best ingredients for their elixirs."

Ok. So we have a name. Now what?

"I'm not sure. Look, we at least have an idea who we're up again." At Celeste's dejected look, she added on the idea that had been running through her head on the way home. "Maybe a staff member might be a little more loose-lipped." She made a drinking motion.

"Maybon is two weeks away. Lots of people will be in town just for fertility elixirs. Between the festival and all the auctions going on, no one would notice us."

Us?

"Of course. If nothing else, you would make a great lookout."

I can see this all going to hell real quick.

"Well, the other option is for you to just sit here for the rest of your life." Celeste offered, pulling on her nightshirt.

Do you even have a plan?

"We have two weeks. I'm sure we can come up with something by then."

Celeste did not need sleep, so she thought she could've come up with a smart well thought out plan. She thought wrong.

Emilia had taken to using Celeste's wand as a hairpin so she could keep the girl close. In preparation for the festival, everyone was working around the clock picking and packaging ingredients. The night before Maybon, the girls had no solid idea to act on. Hanging back after everyone else departed to rest up for the holiday, they were allowed to talk freely.

When are the auctions again? Celeste asked, looking at the bunches of ingredients. *Elixirs take time to simmer. I know these hyacinths need to steep for an hour in rainwater before use.*

"I'm sure they have servants working on it throughout the night." Shrugged Emilia as she placed her now clean shears back in the communal basket.

"Emilia, I knew I could find you here burning the midnight oil." Emilia froze as her master approached. How much did she hear?

"Since you are here, I have a special errand I need you to run." She didn't allow Emilia to protest. "These flowers need to go to Diritous workshop as soon as possible." She then left Emilia with her mouth agape.

I don't know what just happened, but I'll take it. Emilia gathered the bunches in one of the many baskets as quickly as possible.

It took some asking around, but they managed to find the workshop. When Emilia imagined a workshop, she was thinking of the tiny stable-like situation as they have at the guild. What loomed in front of them was a mansion.

"Is this the right place?" Emilia thought aloud.

It's here. Announced Celeste, freezing up.

"What is? Wait, are you saying your body is here?" She asked, looking around as if to see a clue or something obvious.

Yes. In there. Emilia pointed towards the mansion-like warehouse.

"Of course it is." Taking a steadying breath, she

rolled her shoulders before saying. "No time like the present."

There was a light pouring out of an add-on on the side of the building. Peaking inside, she saw several people shuffling bottles of lilac-colored fertility elixirs at different worktables. Everyone was wearing masks to prevent accidental inhalation of fumes. To increase the chances of pregnancy, an aphrodisiac was added to ensure multiple copulations. Made sense you didn't want a room full of people trying to have sex when they should be working.

Once Emilia entered the workshop, she used her sleeve to cover her nose. Noticing her, the overseer came over to snatch the basket from he hands. He handed it to the closest worker to get them to start soaking the flowers.

"Finish what you're doing, then go eat. Can't have you passing out me." He yelled to the rest of the shop. Worried about the fumes, Emilia began to leave when she noticed a spare mask hanging on the wall. Looking at her outfit, she noticed the other workers were also wearing the same coloured work cloaks. Plain black except for the dried mud clinging to her own. Weighting the risks, she slipped, grabbed the mask as if belonged to her she walked out of the workshop.

"This should buy us some time." Even though no one could hear her, Celeste nodded. Giving a nod of her own Emilia re-entered the workshop to join the scatter of people making their way further inside the mansion. In the hallway, Celeste began to drift right while everyone was heading left. A stack of crates blocked the view of the two doors that hid further down the hall. Celeste phased through the door to give an excited scream.

Fiddling with the knob, she discovered the door was locked.

"Can you reach yourself?" Saying it out loud was just weird.

"No. I'm too far." she then proceeds to call out to her body to try to call it to her closer. "DAMMIT!"

Looking around, Emilia tried to the other door. It opened, revealing an office. Cupboards filled with documents, no doubt. An extravagant desk sat in front of a large window. Desks mean paperwork and paperwork means-

"Ink." Sure enough, pewter topped resealable ink well sat half full on the desk. More than enough to write the rune to open the simple lock.

Someone is coming. Celeste phased into the room. Panicking, she realized there was nowhere to hide. She threw open the window to jump out. Despite her best effort, she could only close the window so much. Ducking down, she was still able to hear the conversation between the two people.

"You said she'd still be able to do magic. You said she would be ready by Maybon. The auction is in a few hours and an infant can do more magic than her! At this rate, we'd be lucky if a brothel takes her."

Those bastards. Growled Celeste.

"There are ways around it, sir. At the very least, she would be an ideal vessel to make a magically gifted child. That has to be worth something." Emilia felt like her eyes were going to fall out of her head. Her breath was coming in bursts.

"Let's just take her to the auction house. I don't need worthless inventory cluttering up more storerooms anymore."

The voices left the office, yet Emilia couldn't bring herself to move. There was no way they could sneak her out now. If they don't do something, there would be no way of getting Celeste's body back. Staggering to her feet, she tried to follow after them. By the time Celeste had picked up on the trail, they managed to spot the carriage trot down the street.

"We'll never catch up to them." Bemoaned Emilia as the carriage turned the corner.

"Muur?" Looking up at her was the stray Celeste fed.

Big Mama. Is this where you go?

"Of course you named it. We don't have time for this."

Why would my familiar be hanging out here though?

"She followed you, of course." Both girls paused for a second as the weight of those words sunk in.

You knew my body was here, didn't you? Celeste glanced down the street where the carriage had disappeared. *Can you find me again?* The cat took off down the street with the two witches in tow.

Big Mama lead them down several winding streets. She hopped up the stairs of a building connected to the docks. While Celeste was cooing at her familiar Emilia was surveying the building. It was well kept, with fresh paint and glistening windows.

A woman's high-pitched giggle caught her attention. Creeping around the building, she noticed the side door leading to the outside was thrown open, allowing groups of well-dressed people in. While the working class was sleeping, resting as much as they could before the dawn, the rich were partying. In the light, Emilia was aware that even if she slipped inside her outfit would alert everyone she didn't belong there.

Sighing, she slumped against the building she was starting to feel her exhaustion creep into her bones. A large lump in her pocket caused her to plunge her hand into her pocket to investigate. In her hand she held the stolen mask and inkwell she forgot she pocketed.

I can work with this. Celeste said, placing a hand on Emilia's hand. *Black and white are always in fashion.*

She was wrong, but Emilia wasn't in the mood to argue. Kneeling in the stolen light from the party, Celeste guided her friend through the rune pattern. That transformed the simple mask into something more intricate. Fancy enough for a party, but not enough to garner attention. With a corner of the poster tacked to the side of the building.

Now clean and wearing a navy-coloured cloak, she dawned the mask before stepping into the light. Heart pounding in her ears, she was expecting large figures to materialize out of the crowd to haul her out. It was hard to follow Celeste through the sea of bodies before they made it to the back, where there was an auction going on.

On a raised platform, a man was talking about a young man staring blankly across the crowd. Around his wrists were the same shackles that Celeste's ghostly form was wearing.

"We have a thirty-five-year-old man. No wife or children. Has to experience with flowers and vegetables. Good for those who want to keep a healthy garden." He gave a wink towards the audience before snapping back to a more professional tone. "His incurred debt is-"

How are we going to get back there? Emilia could only shake her head since there was only a small set of stairs that was in plain view for the whole room to see. The man on stage was shuffled off towards those stairs. The man who purchased the debt ushered his new servant out a side door. Possibly towards the carriage he had waiting.

Emilia wandered around as more indentured servants were sold. She managed to eat some bread as her eyes began to burn. People were leaving in a steady trickle. When only a quarter of the party remained, the doors to the warehouse closed. A hushed, excited murmur fell over the crowd.

"And now for the jewel of our auction tonight." He motioned for the crowd to look at the side where the servants were being led out. Emilia's heart dropped as Celeste's body was being led out onto the stage.

She had a vacant stare, as if she was looking thousands of yards away.

"A rare find indeed. Nineteen and-" He paused "A witch." Murmurs grew to a dull roar. "And before any of you ask, yes, she can still do magic." He motioned for the assistant to bring out some supplies.

Of course, it would be that bastard. said Celeste.

"You know him?" Emilia whispered back.

That is master LaMonte. He was supposed to be my Rune Master, but he decided to do this to me. She jabbed her finger towards the stage where Master LaMonte was performing magic, pretending it was Celeste.

He had her perform very flashy colour changes on her clothes. He handed her a chicken feather for her to transform into a vibrant peacock feather.

"We will now start the bidding at two hundred gold."

"Two-fifty."

"Three hundred."

The price kept raising as all she could do was stand here. If she had more than a little bread in her stomach, she would've vomited. Remembering an event from her own childhood, Emilia made her way towards the exit. While everyone was shouting out their bid, she was able to slip out the door unnoticed.

What are you doing? I'm still inside.

"Exactly." Looking at the well-worn tracks in the packed dirt, she walked a little further down to carve a rune in the bottom of a severe hole in the ground. "If they like runes so much then they'll love this one."

A water rune?

"All the driver will see in this light is a small puddle. Hitting it at full speed. Nothing slows down a fancy carriage like a broken wheel."

That's brilliant.

"Don't praise me yet. Here they come. Hiding just outside of the poor light, they waited. True to form, the driver hit the pothole hard enough to crack the wheel. When a man poked his head out to bark at the driver, Emilia struck. She approached the carriage, delighted she found it unlocked. Inside, the wife was focused on the fighting to realize Emilia had entered the carriage. Grabbing Celeste, she began to pull her when the wife noticed the movement.

She let out a screech. Emilia pulled the barely responsive Celeste after her. The husband caught up to them quickly. She squeaked in pain as she was slammed into a wall. Falling to the ground, she scrambled to face her attacker.

"Release my property at once."

"Let go of my sister." Emilia managed to scream back. Standing over her, she had never felt more helpless. Reaching into his coat, he pulled out a flintlock to point at Emilia.

"Now. You're going to do as I say. No one needs to get hurt."

While Emilia was trying to drag her body to safety Celeste was trying everything to re-enter her body. If she could only take back control, she could go with the man to escape later. There was no need for Emilia to be a part of this any further. It was dark, and she was still wearing her mask. As Emilia was slammed into the side of the building Celeste's wand came loose from her hair. Their connection was now severed. If Emilia were to run now or be dragged away, she would be left alone.

Reaching out she tried to touch her chest to see if that would work. It was an uncomfortable blood red with several runes intersecting to create the monstrosity branded on her chest. When her hand got too close a sharp shock wave rippled through her causing her to recoil.

Why won't you do anything? She choked out looking into her own eyes seeing if there was any sign of recognition. Looking into her own dark eyes she saw the tears she wanted to shed. Through the fuzzy connection, the spiritual Celeste was able to move her hand towards her wand.

Grasping her wand, she caught the attention of the man attacking them. He was demanding to know what she was doing. Celeste meant it when she stated she would rather die than allow her body to be used as a broodmare or whatever else he had planned for her.

Do it.

With as much energy she could muster Celeste drove the pointed end of her wand into her heart.

Emilia screamed. The man was shouting. Celeste felt her heartbeat under her hand as the world turned black.

Sobbing Emilia held her limp sister to her chest. After everything they had been through, she never once thought Celeste would do something so extreme. She was broken out of her grief by a loud bang coupled with a shattering of glass. Jerking her head up Emilia saw the now crazed rich man being wrestled by his driver.

"Sir, we need to leave. Their bot worth it." He protested pulling his master backward by his armpits. The gun must've gone off when his driver tried to pull him away from the scene. Some shouting from the building the bullet went into caused the men to tense up. In a flash, they retreat to their carriage leaving Emilia cradling her bleeding sister.

"Why are you crying? I'm the one that's hurt."

All Emilia could do was stare as Celeste smiled weakly up at her.

"I'm back."

"Welcome home." Giggled back Emilia hugging her sister a little tighter.

THE
ADVENTURERS

GREGG CUNNINGHAM

GREGG CUNNINGHAM, 50, is a short story writer from Western Australia who has contributed to various genre anthology books since 2014. He hopes to one day clean off the dust bunnies and find a home for his current Space opera manuscript hidden in a shoebox under his bed since 2017.

Full Metal Horror Zombie Pirate Publishing 2017 Relationship Add Vice Zombie Pirate Publishing 2017 Phuket Tattoo Zombie Pirate Publishing 2018 World War 4 Zombie Pirate Publishing 2018 Grievous Bodily Harm Zombie Pirate Publishing 2019 Angels, Black Hare Press, 2019 Beyond, Black Hare Press, 2019 Deep Space, Black Hare Press, 2019 Monsters, Black Hare Press, 2019 Apocalypse, Black Hare Press 2019 Storming Area 51, Black Hare Press, 2019 Worlds, Black Hare Press, 2019 Bad Romance, Black Hare Press 2020 Raygun Retro Zombie Pirate Publishing 2020 Banned, Black Hare Press,2020 Passenger 13, Black Hare Press, 2020 School's in, Black Hare Press,2020 2113, Black Hare Press, 2020 Wardenclyffe Black Hare Press 2020

Connect Website: cortlandsdogs.wordpress.com

JASON RUSSELL

Jason Russell is a novelist from NY and cofounder of the new science fiction publishing house Starry Eyed

Press. He has recently edited the space opera anthology Strange Orbits for Black Ink Fiction (available now).

You can learn more about him at:

https://www.goodreads.com/author/show/6564149.Jason_Russell

CHRIS CORNETTO

Chris Cornetto is a physics teacher by day and writer by night. In addition to physics, he has degrees in chemistry, philosophy, and psychology. He likes exploring ethical questions through fantasy settings and enjoys long walks with small dogs. His stories have appeared in Metaphorosis, Hypnos, Silver Blade, and DreamForge Magazines.

EMMA K. LEADLEY

Emma K. Leadley (she/they) is a UK-based writer, creative geek, and devourer of words, images and ideas. She's had over 30 pieces of speculative flash fiction and short stories published by independent presses, including Fox Spirit Books. She was a Grindstone Literary 2019 Microfiction Winner with her 144-word story, "Nothing to Lose" and Publishers Weekly described one of her stories as 'standout'. She lives in Nottingham with her husband and a pampered rescue greyhound. Visit Emma online at

https://www.autoerraticism.com/publications

or on Twitter at https://twitter.com/autoerraticism

DAVID BOWMORE

David was born in gypsy caravan, on a wintery night with the sound of thunder and the flash of lightning welcoming him into the world. Forty-five years later, he started writing fiction.

True to his coming into the world, he has lived here, there and everywhere, but now lives in Yorkshire with his wonderful wife and a small white poodle.

In his time, he has worn many hats; head chef, teacher and landscape gardener.

His award-winning book of connected short stories 'The Magic of Deben Market' was enacted by Book-Streamz in December 2020.

Discover more about David's writing at
www.davidbowmore.co.uk

BRANDI HICKS

Brandi Hicks hails from West Virginia, USA, and despite her best efforts, still lives there. She writes in multiple genres, but hates writing bios. Brandi is an expert procrastinator, an avid crafter (much to the dismay of those around her), and the kindest person you'll ever meet (and humble). She is a co-founder of Paramour Ink and Black Ink Fiction.

http://www.brandihicks.com
www.blackinkfiction.com

TIM MENDEES

Tim Mendees is a horror writer from Macclesfield in the North-West of England that specialises in cosmic horror and weird fiction. A lifelong fan of classic weird tales, Tim set out to bring the pulp horror of yesteryear into the 21st Century and give it a distinctly British flavour. His work has been described as the lovechild of H.P. Lovecraft and P.G. Wodehouse and is often peppered with a wry sense of humour that acts as a counterpoint to the unnerving, and often disturbing, narratives.

Tim has had over seventy published stories in anthologies and magazines with publishers all over the world. His novellas, Burning Reflection, Spiffing, and The Creeping Void are out now.

When he is not arguing with the spellchecker, Tim is a goth DJ, crustacean and cephalopod enthusiast, and the presenter of a popular web series of live video readings of his material and interviews with fellow authors. He currently lives in Brighton & Hove with his pet crab, Gerald, and an army of stuffed octopods.

https://timmendeeswriter.wordpress.com/
https://tinyurl.com/timmendeesyoutube

VOLUME 2

T.R. EARNHART

T. R. Earnhart is a former military brat with strong ties to her backwoods Tennessean roots. From video games to classical literature she one day hopes to spread her stories wide. For now, she lives in Utah as a veterinarian technician with her little family.

https://trparnell87.wixsite.com/website

S.O. GREEN

Simone Oldman Green (they/them) is a genre-fluid writer and editor living in the Kingdom of Fife with husband, John. Author of over 70 published works with imprints including Dragon Soul Press, Black Hare Press and Eerie River Publishing. They also won 3rd Place in the British Fantasy Society's Short Story Contest 2018. Writer, vegan, martial artist, gamer, occasionally a terrible person (but only to fictional people). They thrive on the unusual, which might explain why there are so many cats.

https://thebasementoflove.blogspot.com/

Facebook: https://www.facebook.com/thebasementoflove

Twitter: https://twitter.com/SOGreenWriter

JONATHAN INBODY

Jonathan Inbody is an author, filmmaker, and podcaster from Buffalo, New York. He specializes in writing horror and science fiction, but also writes any other genre that can have a monster in it. He is an avid reader of early 20th century Weird Fiction and an aficionado of B-movie genre cinema, and his acid horror anthology podcast Gray Matter, which combines his love of both, is coming soon.

Twitter: https://twitter.com/InbodyWriter

MORE FROM
BREAKING RULES PUBLISHING EUROPE

ADVENTURE AWAITS

Face of Fear by C. Marry Hultman
e-book:books2read.com/u/49lVg0

Dawson Junior G3 by Brian Wagstaff
e-book:books2read.com/u/4EP99E

Boy in the Wardrobe by Esther Jacoby
e-book: mybook.to/Boy-Wardrobe

New Life Cottage by Esther Jacoby
e-book:books2read.com/u/m0wAzW

The Wait by Esther Jacoby
e-book:https://books2read.com/u/4Dgz8Q

Liebe ist Warten by Esther Jacoby
e-book:https://books2read.com/u/mZaVD2

Musing on Death & Dying by Esther Jacoby
e-book:books2read.com/u/49lVg0

Earth Door by Cye Thomas
e-book:books2read.com/u/mKyXKv

Graffiti Stories by Nick Gerrard
e-book:books2read.com/u/m2MQOR

Punk Novelette by Nick Gerrard
e-book:books2read.com/u/4jLpqv

VOLUME 2

Struggle and Strife by Nick Gerrard
e-book:books2read.com/u/4DRyqr

Fake Escape by Natalie Hughes
e-book:https://books2read.com/u/bMXL5X

Murder Planet by Adam Carpenter
e-book:books2read.com/u/bMXllV

Generation Ship by Adam Carpenter
e-book:books2read.com/u/49Nk8M

Cold as Hell by Neen Cohen
e-book:https://books2read.com/u/bxennv

Six Days to Hell by E.L. Giles
e-book:https://books2read.com/u/bWrLyq

Just 13 anthology
e-book: https://books2read.com/u/mKy1B9

Lost Lore & Legends Anthology
e-book: books2read.com/u/m2RrwG

Adventure Awaits volume 1 Anthology
e-book: https://books2read.com/u/3Gw8o8

Death House
e-book: https://books2rcad.com/u/bWrODW

Find us at:
http://www.breakingrulespublishingeuro.com

VOLUME 2